The Killing Figure

by A.J. McNair

For my sister,
the other half of my dark heart.

About the Author

Over the last ten years A.J. McNair has led a compelling, yet somewhat dangerous, life working with a wide range of wild animals. In the summer of 2014, whilst volunteering at an exotic mammal rescue centre in Europe, they struck upon an idea for a crime based murder mystery story. Since then this simple idea quickly grew into something more. What started out as a standalone story soon evolved into a series of books, the first of which you hold in your hands now. With a deep love for the natural world, horror, film and a fascination for the best & worst in human nature, A.J. McNair continues to create a literary universe filled with captivating heroes and fascinating villains.

Other works available:
Wrath

Facebook Page:
A.J. McNair

Chapter One

The Artist

She looked beautiful, even in death.

As the detective walked over the oak floorboards they creaked under his feet, the empty walls of the art studio echoing every footstep back at him. The room was old and poorly insulated. Single windowpanes with draughty wooden frames allowed in the morning light, dew still clinging to the outside edges. Summer had arrived and the earlier mornings had come with it.

Located in Northern Hallow, the college had been built back in the forties but had undergone multiple refurbishments since then. The art studio remained one of the least touched sections of the whole building, making it a favourite haunt for those wishing to escape to a more nostalgic period, away from the chaotic and noisy current times.

Despite being an art studio the room was noticeably lacking most of its artwork, all except four individual paintings, one for each wall. She was laying in the centre of the room, with each painting facing towards her. The detective stepped cautiously closer to her, his eyes dancing from one painting to another. Each painting appeared to depict one of the four seasons, with a young woman the central focus in each.

The Winter painting showed a young woman frozen to death in an icy wilderness. She was curled up in an almost foetal position, her arms wrapped around her legs in a feeble attempt to keep warm. Partially covered by fallen snow, she was naked, her bare skin exposed to the bitterly cold and biting winds of winter.

The Spring painting depicted another young woman laying dead in a lush green meadow, surrounded by all kinds of colourful flowers. Some of these flowers in turn provided her with some modesty, deliberately positioned in order to conceal her more private female regions. To the detective's eye the young woman resembled Eve from the Garden of Eden, minus Adam her male counterpart. A couple of young animals including a lamb, a leveret and a duckling stood either side of her, frolicking with youth.

The Summer painting showed another young woman dead at a beach, again her naked body partially covered by dusty yellow sand and washed up debris from the ocean. A few seagulls and several crabs scavenged around her body, feeding off her lifeless form. Washed up seaweed, discarded fish nets and plastic waste also surrounded her final resting place.

The final painting of Autumn depicted yet another young woman, dead and hidden amongst the leaf litter of an ancient dying woodland. The most prominent colours in the painting were red, brown and orange. A nearby squirrel foraged for acorns around her body, whilst a lone and prominent stag stood idly by, watching her from the background. Several toadstools peeked out from amongst the leaf litter near to her.

His attention shifted from the woman in the paintings back to her. The curious detective squatted down by her side, reaching into his inner jacket pocket for a notebook and pen. As he flicked through the pages he occasionally glanced back at her face. Her large dark eyes stared up at the ceiling, cold and lifeless. Finally arriving on a blank page in his book he began to detail the scene that lay before him.

"What have we got then Jerry?" a gruff older voice asked from behind him.

Detective Inspector Jerry Wilder turned around to see the stern figure of his partner Detective Lieutenant Vincent Harrington, the bright flash from a nearby camera catching him by surprise in the process. The glare slowly cleared from his squinting eyes and Jerry could once again see his partner's imposing frame. A man of African heritage, Vincent wore the years of hard detective work on his face, within every miserable wrinkle at least one story to tell. With a prominent brow only overshadowed by his dark grey fedora, Vincent had broad burdened shoulders covered by a heavy trench coat. Jerry paled in comparison to his partner, in age and experience, being barely out of his twenties. Another flash from a forensic's camera clicked off to the side of him.

"Where to start really?" Jerry replied.

He swiftly ran a hand through his short spiky blonde hair, laced with styling product, in quick contemplation.

"Her head has been decapitated, with the majority of the neck still attached. The torso has been severed just above the waistline along the belly button, in what appears to have been one clean cut. The waist and legs remain intact. Her arms have been severed just above the elbows, leaving the entire body divided into five neat sections." Jerry summarised.

The dead woman's long wavy black hair was neatly brushed under the back of her head and away from her face, leaving the majority of its length covered behind her shoulders and upper back. This only further highlighted the distinctive six to seven inch gap between her head and upper torso, a similar distance between her lower torso and waist. What was most interesting about her body though was that all the large severing wounds had been sealed with melted brown plastic of some kind.

Even more curiously her feminine region had also been sealed over with the same melted plastic in a somewhat vague attempt to cover her modesty. This eerily mirrored the fate of all the women in the surrounding paintings. The curves of her ample bosom were all that remained, her nipples having been cut away and replaced by the same brown plastic sealant. Beside her left hand was a painting pallet, with five individual dollops of red, yellow, blue, green and white paint arranged neatly on it. To her right hand lay an artist's paint brush, clean and unspoiled by paint.

"Do we have an ID on her yet?" Vincent questioned.

"Roberta Woods. She's a final year student here." Murphy answered from one corner of the room.

Detective Inspector Patrick Murphy was the middle man between Jerry and Vincent, in age and years of service. Being a man of medium stature in his late thirties, Jerry found Murphy far easier to get along with than Vincent. The old man was still stubbornly stuck in his old ways. Murphy had a thick head of brownish red hair and a large broad nose, paralleled with round yet emotive eyes. Murphy always tried to see the funny side in most things, having a darkly dry sense of humour was a key component to remaining sane in his grim line of work.

"Did anybody see anything?" Vincent asked.

"Nothing, no security cameras here either." Murphy answered.

"Who found her?" Jerry asked.

"The janitor, doing his morning rounds. Poor bastard is really shaken up by this." Murphy replied.

"Can you blame him?" Jerry rhetorically asked.

"Does he have an alibi?" Vincent followed up.

"Yeah his wife, he was home all evening. The killer must have crept in during the night to arrange all this." Murphy guessed.

He gazed longingly at Roberta again, sighing loudly to himself.

"Why is it nearly always the young hot ones?" he complained.

"Because they're young, and hot as you put it. The wicked tend to punish the innocent." Vincent monologued.

"We don't know whether or not Roberta here is innocent yet. We'll need to do a background check on her, but I suspect it will come up with nothing incriminating." Jerry said.

"Only twenty one years old and already an absolute stunner." Murphy rather inappropriately remarked.

Jerry had to agree with his leering colleague. Roberta really was remarkably beautiful, even divided into five pieces. Between her exotic look, pale skin and sensual physique he had to remind himself once again she was dead. She was almost

8

frozen in time like some perfectly preserved Inca woman from the High Andes.

"She must have some South American in her somewhere. Perhaps Brazilian?" Murphy conveniently theorised given Jerry's earlier thought.

He stooped over her body and motioned to reach between her legs.

"Patrick!" Vincent remarked.

Jerry had to silently admit to himself that he secretly wished to look upon her womanly temple as well.

"They have taken care and more importantly time to display her in such a way. It is almost like she is a piece of artwork in herself now. All the cuts are clean, no bruising, very little blood." Vincent noticed.

Roberta was indeed pale, her body appearing to have been partially drained. Not a single red droplet of blood was to be seen in the entire studio. Beforehand her skin would have been almost golden mocha in colour, her sun kissed tropical tone now gone forever. After taking a third, more detailed, look at the surrounding paintings, Jerry came to a realisation.

"She's the woman in the paintings!" he declared.

Sure enough the deceased woman in each painting had exactly the same long black wavy hair, large dark eyes, slightly curved down nose and skin tone as that of Roberta.

"Are they her paintings?" Murphy wondered.

Jerry stepped away from Roberta's body to look at each painting closer. In each bottom right hand corner was the distinctive signature 'R.Woods'.

"Experience is telling me this is just the beginning of something. There is meaning to this somewhere," Vincent ominously wondered. "the only question is what?"

Amidst the comings and goings of the forensics team through the single doorway, a uniformed officer approached Vincent, instructing him that the college's principal and Roberta's close friend were waiting outside.

"Tell them I will be there shortly." Vincent informed him.

Vincent got up and accompanied by Jerry left the art studio to begin their questioning. As they both stooped under the yellow crime scene tape, spun across the narrow doorway, they made their way through a steadily growing crowd of student spectators. Some of whom were close to tears upon hearing the news of Roberta's tragic fate. Out in the populated hallway the college's principal comforted a much younger woman than herself.

"I am DL Harrington and this is DI Wilder." Vincent introduced to the two women.

"I'm Mrs Waller the principal and this is Roberta's close friend Gemma." Mrs Waller answered, Gemma softly weeping in her embrace.

Mrs Waller was a woman in her early fifties, medium build with curly blonde hair, her rather ample chest highlighted further by a very tight fitting cardigan. Small patches of which were now dampened from Gemma's crying. Gemma herself was around Roberta's age, slim figured with long wavy ginger hair, a lightly freckled faced and bright blue eyes. Jerry was immediately attracted to this young vulnerable thing.

"You both knew Roberta well?" Jerry followed up, his eyes transfixed on Gemma.

"Yes she was a very talented painter, on her way to much bigger and brighter things. She had just secured a prestigious job offer at a large gallery in the city. She was going to move there after she graduated." Mrs Waller answered.

"Do you know anyone who possibly had a grudge against Roberta, was jealous of her talent or wanted to harm her in any way?" Jerry asked.

"No no she was a very sweet girl with a kind nature, well liked by many of her peers." Mrs Waller replied, gently smiling at the thought of seeing Roberta alive once again.

"Is there anyone we can contact, friends or family?" Vincent questioned.

"I believe her parents are still away on an extended vacation. I'm sure we have their emergency contact details on file here." Mrs Waller detailed.

"Her boyfriend didn't come in today." Gemma suddenly added into the conversation, before retreating into her sobbing state again.

"And his name is?" Jerry enquired.

As he took out his notebook and pen to write this new information down, Jerry could feel a small wave of jealousy begin to stir inside him upon hearing the news that Roberta had a boyfriend.

"David Stephens, he's a student here also." Mrs Waller added, her closeness with Roberta evident.

"Any chance we can get his phone number or address as well Mrs Waller?" asked Vincent politely.

"Well yes, I'll have to go to my office to check. I'll be back in a few minutes." said Mrs Waller.

She released herself from Gemma's hold, leaving her alone with the detectives.

After a few moments of awkward silence as Jerry looked this girl up and down Vincent spoke.

"Gemma, would you be able to answer some questions for us?" Vincent carefully asked the clearly distraught young woman.

Gemma simply nodded, not even looking up as she nervously held her arms against her nubile frame.

"Did Roberta collaborate with anyone on her artwork?" he asked.

"No, she did it all herself," she replied, not looking up. "it was her final year project."

"Can you tell us anything more about Roberta's choice of art?" Jerry added.

"She only needed to paint two pieces, but she did four instead." Gemma admitted.

"Any idea as to why she would give herself so much extra work pressure?" Jerry continued.

"Roberta just liked to paint ok!" Gemma cried, sounding irritated by the barrage of questions.

She was soon rejoined by Mrs Waller.

"Here you are detectives." she announced, handing over David's contact details to Vincent.

"Did Roberta say anything to you about her artwork Mrs Waller?" Jerry asked.

"I'm afraid she had a rather strange fascination with death, sometimes even her own. It was a common theme throughout her work here. Roberta said death was cyclical, never ending and all year round. That's why she focused on the seasons of the year for her final project." Mrs Waller detailed.

"Why would someone do this?" Gemma asked aloud.

"That's what we're here to find out." Jerry answered sympathetically.

With this he placed a comforting hand on her boney shoulder, tightening his grip ever so slightly. Jerry's fingers soon discovered a bra strap under her flimsy t-shirt, causing his pulse to race faster and his pupils to dilate. What with a heat wave now gripping Hallow City and Grace withholding physical relations between them, Jerry's libido was becoming too strong to control. Jerry couldn't help but admire this pretty young redhead before him, in need of so much comfort right now.

Not knowing of Jerry's true intensions Gemma began sobbing again before running off to join her classmates, in turn running away from the real horror that lay only a few hundred yards away from her.

"Thank you for your help Mrs Waller. If we have any further questions we'll be in touch." Vincent kindly said, handing Mrs Waller his card.

"Thank you detectives." Mrs Waller replied before turning to head back to her office.

Vincent turned to face Jerry again with purpose.

"What was that about?" Vincent hastily asked.

"What?" Jerry answered slightly confused.

"I saw the way you were looking at that poor girl, and then touching her like that! You do not get involved kid or else you will start making promises you cannot keep." Vincent cautioned the young naive detective.

"Sorry but I couldn't help but reach out." Jerry confessed.

"Keep your distance. I know you are new around here but remember that." Vincent cautioned further.

Jerry looked to his feet to sheepishly shrug off Vincent's words of warning.

"But honestly, have you ever seen anything like this before?" Jerry questioned, trying to change the subject and draw the attention away from him.

"No, nothing like this," Vincent admitted. "this is something new and new is never good in Hallow."

"Why cut her body into five parts? Why not more or less?" Jerry pondered.

"I am sure Edward will fill us in on his findings when she is back at the precinct later." Vincent thought.

"And why cut her nipples off?" Jerry continued to ask.

"I need a strong cup of tea before we really get into this." said Vincent, removing his hat to mop at his brow with a handkerchief.

Vincent moved to leave the stuffy building in a quest to satisfy his caffeine craving. It was early morning on a Monday and the humidity in the college was steadily rising further with the increasing outside summer temperature. True summer had finally come to Hallow but there was certainly nothing joyous about this day. Gemma's perfume still lingered in the air around him so Jerry breathed it in deeply before he too left the building, savouring every bit of its fruity sweetness.

A few hours later, after the crime scene had been cleared, Vincent, Jerry and Murphy ventured down to the morgue that lay beneath the Police Precinct. All three men were curious as to what the artist's body would reveal to them. They once again found Roberta's body laying in front of them, only this time the setting was very much different.

Bright flickering halogen lights harshly illuminated her form from above instead of gentle morning sunlight. The dusty old floorboards of the art studio were now replaced by a long sterile metal autopsy table, with Roberta laying on top of it. With the plastic sealants having been removed her modesty was now fully unveiled.

"That's some extreme waxing right there! A Brazilian after all." Murphy leered.

"Pipe down Patrick." Vincent cautioned.

Above her head stood a tall pair of taps complete with a short extendable metal hose. At the base of the table just below her feet lay a circular grated drain. Paired together the hose and the drain were there to wash away the death after each gruelling autopsy. Running down between her chest, Roberta's torso now wore the fresh Y scar of an autopsy procedure, now loosely held together by surgical stitching.

It seemed fruitless to piece Roberta back together again. At the base of the torso and at the top of her waist, Roberta's innards had begun to ooze and spill out of the gaping cavities left behind from the removal of the plastic seals. She now looked like any other mutilated corpse from any number of other homicides, rather than the remarkable beauty frozen in time she briefly once was. Jerry's macabre interest in this girl was definitely fading now.

By her side stood Head of Forensics and resident precinct mortician Edward O'Hara, already dressed for the occasion in his blue overalls, apron, gloves and mouth mask. A tall man of gangly propositions with medium length wispy brown hair, Edward seemed noticeably excited by their arrival, quickly finishing his notes on a clipboard.

"What more can you tell us Edward?" Vincent questioned.

14

After pulling down his mouth mask and taking off his black rimmed glasses Edward replied, whilst mopping away his sweaty brow.

"Well she was severed into five pieces, that part is quite clear," he began. "and I found very little blood in her body. Roberta appears to have been drained of virtually all her blood possibly beforehand, as you guessed. You may be able to see there on the right side of her neck, slightly obscured by the main cut across the base of the neck, a small area of bruising."

Using the end of his pen, Edward pointed out the area on her neck that had been stabbed.

"There are some minor abrasive markings around her ankles also, suggesting she was tied up at some point. My guess is the killer hung her upside down by her ankles and with a single blow of a knife severed her carotid artery, causing her to bleed out in seconds. I found minute particles of blood in her hair and on her face. The killer must have cleaned the body afterwards." Edward detailed.

"How generous of them!" Murphy snorted sarcastically.

"Was she alive at this point you think?" Jerry asked Vincent.

"Most likely. Our killer would have wanted her to know exactly what was going to happen to her. It's what most of these sick bastards get off on. They want to see the pain and fear they inflict in the eyes of their victims." Vincent hastened to answer. His years as a homicide detective carried weighty experience.

"What else did you find?" Vincent questioned Edward further.

"Despite the large cut between her torso and waist, nothing has been removed. All her organs are accounted for, although slightly lacerated by the main severing." Edward informed.

"So no black market organ harvesting then?" Murphy guessed.

"Any idea for time of death?" Jerry asked.

"It's difficult to say. She could have been killed a few days ago, maybe even a week." Edward guessed.

"She wasn't reported missing. Her parents are away on vacation and her boyfriend says they were taking a break from each other. The killer had all weekend to do this." Murphy said.

"So she was knocked out, hung up to be bled and then finally cut into five pieces with all the wounds sealed with melted plastic." Vincent summarised.

He hoped to understand the situation far better when heard aloud in his own words.

"Any idea of how the killer could have cut her so neatly like this?" Jerry asked.

"Well the cutting was done post mortem and after she was drained. Possibly an electric handsaw, maybe even a large band saw perhaps? The areas that have been cut are slightly serrated." Edward pointed out.

"So we start looking at industrial sites, in machine factories, chop shops, anywhere that has large cutting implements." Vincent instructed.

"Also not a single print on her. We dusted her body and the entire crime scene but came up with nothing." Edward said.

"Our killer isn't stupid then!" Jerry remarked.

Edward moved to stand closer to what remained of Roberta's midriff.

"I took the liberty of inspecting all her nooks and crannies, you know just incase the killer left anything behind for us." Edward remarked with a wry smile, exposing his irregular teeth.

Edward's crude smile unnerved Jerry even more than his words. His disjointed teeth resembled a vandalised graveyard, abandoned and eroded by the unstoppable march of time.

"Nothing has been inserted into her body cavity, vagina or anus. She wasn't sexually assaulted, no sign of forced entry or foreign secretions anywhere on her. Her hymen was still intact so she appears to have been untouched, so to speak." Edward concluded.

16

"Was intact? Until you fingered her, right Ed? We don't need to arrest you for necrophilia now do we?" Murphy quipped.

"No and shut up Murphy! Don't be so vile!" Edward snapped.

Murphy's level of dark humour was hit or miss on some people. His working relationship with Edward was tenuous at best.

"Alright settle down, the pair of you." Jerry cautioned.

"So this was not sexual then." Vincent concluded, hoping to get the investigation back on track.

"If she was a virgin then maybe we have a potential motive there." Jerry added.

"Anyway as I was saying before I was so rudely interrupted," Edward continued. "I did however find something very strange in her mouth."

Edward produced a small transparent evidence bag from a nearby work surface. Within it there was a man, a small plastic man to be exact, only a few inches in height. Jerry took the bag from Edward's slender fingers for a closer look. Upon further inspection the man appeared to be a tiny butcher.

He was mainly white in colour, with a long green and white checkered apron covering the length of his front. The butcher's head was topped by a wide brimmed woven reed hat, his pink face a dry little smile framed by grey printed mutton chops. Also within the contents of the bag were a tiny meat cleaver and link of sausages.

"What the hell is this?" Jerry spoke aloud.

"A toy of some kind?" Edward guessed.

Vincent stepped closer to have a look also.

"The sausages and cleaver were in the hands of the figure, the meat cleaver in the right, the sausages in the left. No fingerprints on them either, just traces of her saliva." Edward added.

"Why a butcher?" Jerry questioned.

"Maybe it's their calling card. A butcher by name or nature perhaps?" Murphy theorised.

"I am getting too old for these games." Vincent sighed, rubbing his tired old eyes.

"Hey wait! Somewhere with large cutting implements. What about a slaughter house? It could also explain the butcher figure." Jerry guessed aloud.

"That is a good thought kid." Vincent agreed with his young partner.

"Fingerprint analysis shows that the paint brush and paint pallet found with the body belonged to the victim, as well as the paintings at the crime scene." Edward added.

"Seems like she had an odd fascination with death after all, even her own." Jerry said.

"I can understand that, except the whole part about your own, I mean my own, I mean what I said before." Edward stuttered.

Both detectives looked at Edward as if not surprised by his comment. Edward cleared his throat and innocently looked to his clipboard of notes as if to draw attention away from him.

"I'll just pop her back then." Edward anxiously announced after a few seconds.

He carefully took hold of Roberta's body parts and replaced them back into a large black body bag before wheeling her over into storage.

"He is a rather strange fellow." Vincent whispered.

"He's a little peculiar yes but I'm sure you'll miss him though" joked Murphy.

"Yes I will, Edward always means well. He is just a little socially awkward." Vincent replied.

"So when do you actually retire?" Jerry asked Vincent

"Couple more months to go." Vincent replied, sounding like he was counting every single second.

"Any plans about what you're going to do?" Murphy enquired further.

18

"I am moving over to the Coral Isles to go and live with my brother at his house. He retired a few years ago, being a man of business he could afford to retire much earlier than I." Vincent chuckled.

"I didn't know you had a brother." Jerry dropped into the conversation.

"No point in us getting close is there? Soon I will be gone and you will be my replacement." Vincent bluntly put.

"Yeah, but until then you can at least share a little right?" Jerry thought.

"What more do you want to know then? My brother and I are essentially the same as one another, only differing in our career choices. He never really liked people, only their money. He wanted to make lots of money doing very little work and I wanted to spend my years catching murderers, rapists and pedophiles for littler pay. We lost touch for some years but at least now we will get that time back when I move over there." Vincent replied.

"Sounds good. Drinks on the beach and the like?" Jerry guessed.

"Indeed, plenty of drinks and all the hours of the day to perfect my swing." Vincent fantasised, picturing all his hours of golf to come.

"And you? Big day drawing ever nearer! How are you feeling?" Murphy asked Jerry.

"Excited, nervous. It's been a long time coming but I'm looking forward to married life. Looking more forward to our honeymoon getaway though." Jerry replied with a small smile.

"Where will that be then?" Vincent asked.

"Funnily enough, the Coral Isles" Jerry answered.

"Sun, sand, sweat, sex..." Murphy began to list.

"I guess Grace is still holding off on things between you then?" Vincent interrupted.

Jerry's insufferable yammering about his fiancee's plan to postpone physical relations between them until their wedding

19

night had unintentionally become a daily point of conversation for Vincent. He anticipated this, asking the question before Jerry inevitably brought it up again haphazardly.

"She says it will make it more 'romantic' on our honeymoon." Jerry huffed, quoting his fiancee.

"Listen to me kid. The key to any successful marriage is that the husband does whatever his wife wants him to. If she is happy then you will be happy. I always did what I wanted when my wife and I were together and so she must have got tired of trying to change me, causing our marriage to end the way it did." Vincent recounted.

"Grace and I understand what we want from each other, and besides I'm the boss in the relationship!" Jerry firmly put, feeling his masculinity being challenged.

"And yet she's the one calling the shots on your time together in the sack!" Murphy laughed.

"Get use to that feeling kid. That is married life for you." a smug Vincent warned.

Chapter Two

The Butcher

The urban sprawl of Hallow City was divided almost completely in half by the River Mana, which flowed down from the Northern lands. Mana's source could be found even further North, beyond the densely forested and rarely explored mountains that paralleled Garden Ridge City. The river itself cut directly through Hallow and flowed West, out towards the ocean. North of the River Mana, around one third of the entire city, were the more affluent districts of Hallow. The majority of business, education and government was conducted in these wealthier areas. Hallow's crucial and central transport links were also found here. The intricate subway system branched out under the entire city and the river like an unstoppable slime mould.

Located South of the River Mana resided the remaining two thirds of the city and its older, more industrialised districts. Both the middle and working class lived out their lives in these less affable, more confined areas of Hallow. Tradesmen, doctors, teachers, veterinarians and even prostitutes could all be found scratching out a living here. Having been ravaged by a huge fire less than a century ago, the Southern slums of Hallow were quickly rebuilt on a sea of ash by cheap foreign labour. Little regard was given to the thousands of lives lost in the fire, which was later referred to as the Great Blaze of Hallow. Crime and civil unrest were common place in the South, especially after the influx of migrant workers brought about by the fire's destruction.

Nestled safely amongst the protective and slow moving waters of the River Mana stood two islands. The Hallow City Police Precinct and its adjacent courthouse could be found on the largest of the two, connected to the mainland either side by only two bridges. Legal firms, luxury apartments, a handful of bars and several small eateries were also scattered along the island's edge.

The precinct had been built many decades ago but since then the island, and all its buildings, had undergone multiple refurbishments to bring it further into the modern age. Due to its long narrow shape and five fingerlike projections on the East end, the island resembled a human limb. As such it was nicknamed the Arm by Hallow's criminal underworld.

The smaller island to the East was home to Hallow's old prison house, closed long ago due to inhumane treatment and living conditions. One wing of the prison housed the most violent, dangerous and criminally insane of all inmates. Just outside the island's fortress-like walls, right by the river's edge, was the prison gallows which stretched out over the water. Back when the death penalty was allowed, public hangings were a common sight from Southern Hallow.

The prison island was nicknamed the Frying Pan, due to its predominantly round shape and broad handle like spit which stretched out towards the Arm's webbed hand. A single wooden bridge, named the Narrow, was constructed to connect the two islands together. As a convicted criminal of the HCPD, if you were sent across the Narrow it was highly likely you would not be coming back. A very dark and desolate new life awaited you within the Frying Pan's walls.

Sixty years ago the prison was finally condemned and the inmates were moved outside of Hallow to a new safer prison house. The Frying Pan was soon abandoned and left to fall into disrepair. But then in the seventies Hallow City Government reopened the island. The old prison house was restored and turned into a museum. It quickly became a popular tourist attraction for those who wanted to take a guided trip back into Hallow's dark past. One might even be able to see where the noose rope had worn away the gallows wooden beam, from the thousands of hangings conducted there.

It was Wednesday morning. Jerry awoke to the harsh sound of his alarm clock and the familiar sight of Grace, his bride to be, laying next to him. The couple's new minimal apartment was located near to the city centre of Hallow, South of the river. High rise office complexes and other apartment blocks surrounded their building on all sides, greatly reducing the level of natural sunlight reaching them. Their bedroom was modest, with some decoration dotted around here and there. Grace's diploma hung beside a framed photo of Jerry dressed in his finest at his own graduation from the police academy.

Hallow City was dank and depressing, constantly riddled with crime and ongoing socio economic troubles. And yet despite all this Grace had come with Jerry regardless. She could have just left him for someone else and have avoided coming to such a desolated city altogether, but she hadn't. Her love for Jerry was that strong.

Grace quietly stirred further as Jerry moved to wrap his arms around her body, pulling her closer to him. The intoxicating smell of her jasmine scented conditioner still clung to her long black hair. Jerry had always had a particular weakness for Oriental women. Grace's Vietnamese heritage had struck him like a bolt of lightning the minute he first saw her all those years ago. Jerry began to caress her chest and softly kiss her neck, to which result she awoke.

"You can cut that out Wilder" Grace softly giggled to herself.

Ignoring this remark, Jerry continued his playful groping, his mind set on only one thing.

"Jerry!" Grace startled loudly, halting his advances.

"Oh come on Grace! It has been weeks since we did anything together! How are you coping with this?" Jerry complained.

"Because I'm not as much of a horn dog as you are. Besides we already decided to wait until our wedding night, making it that much more special." Grace justified.

"No you decided that. I just went along with it because I'm starting to not get a say in anything now!" Jerry snapped, frustration starting to rear its ugly head.

"Then go for a jog or maybe a cold shower!" Grace teased.

"A jog? In this city?!" Jerry exclaimed, as if Grace were crazy.

Grace turned over to comfort him but Jerry moved away from her advances, leaving their bedroom to take a shower. Weeks of pent up frustration were starting to take their toll on the young detective as he had started to waver for other women and not Grace. Roberta's friend Gemma had been one of many. But more worryingly even Roberta the artist herself had looked good to him.

As Jerry climbed into the shower and turned the water on, he could begin to feel the tension flow out of his body with the cascading warm water. He thought of Roberta once again, alive and frolicking in her paintings, bare chested and beckoning him to join her. He thought about how lucky her boyfriend must have been to lay with that beautiful creature in his bed, her purity ironically holding things off between them as well. Jerry moved to grab himself but stopped immediately upon realising what he was doing.

"Snap out of it!" he spoke aloud to himself.

Jerry slapped himself hard in the face to awaken from his macabre fantasy. But the overpowering feeling quickly returned again in Jerry's uneven mind, an unavoidable desire as strong as ever. His expelled seed soon drained away down the plug hole with the rest of the water. This temporary release however didn't aid Jerry in the slightest, only making him feel more ashamed and empty inside. Jerry exited the shower cubicle and began to dry himself off.

Wrapping a long towel around his waist he ran the sink half full of warm water to shave. After soaking his tired face with a warm flannel for a minute or two he lathered up some shaving foam and spread it all over the necessary areas. Going against his

24

usual routine, he moved to start at the base of his neck but cut himself badly with the very first stroke of his new razor, rather close to his jugular artery.

"Ow, dammit" Jerry exclaimed to himself.

As his blood mixed with the white shaving foam it began to draw a red line down his neck. Jerry could suddenly think of nothing else but Roberta's decapitated head, her lifeless dark eyes staring back at him as blood leaked out from underneath. Jerry washed off all the foam and put a plaster over the fresh cut. He could feel his sanity starting to slip for some peculiar reason and decided to shave later, hoping his head would be clearer then. As he stepped out of the bathroom Grace was already waiting outside for him.

"There was a call for you from Vincent. They've found another body." she informed him, sounding downbeat.

"Did he say where?" Jerry simply asked.

"He said to go to a family butcher shop on the edge of the city called Green's Meats." Grace instructed.

Jerry hurried to their bedroom to get dressed as Grace closely followed behind him.

"Jerry, we need to talk more later regarding some of the wedding arrangements." Grace proposed.

"Whatever you want just do it, just keep within our budget. I don't want us out of pocket even before we're married." Jerry remarked.

Grace looked hurt after Jerry's harsh comment, showing how little he now cared for their big day. Realising how he had came across and sensing Grace's distress Jerry moved to hug her.

"Hey I'm sorry," Jerry apologised. "between the move here, starting a new job and getting ready for the wedding I'm being stretched in all directions. I really need our honeymoon vacation more than our wedding right now. This city is starting to get to me already."

"I understand, just don't shut me out if you've got problems ok? We're in this together. Try and remember why you took this job in the first place." Grace reminded him.

Jerry tenderly kissed his fiancée goodbye, soon there after leaving to go and meet up with Vincent.

Jerry drove to the new crime scene in North West Hallow, recounting the conversation both he and Vincent had had with Roberta's boyfriend David on the Monday afternoon as he went. David had an alibi from his friends who had taken him away for the weekend after Roberta had ended things between them. As her career as a professional artist had begun to flourish she had put a stop to their time together. Roberta didn't want the distraction as she had put it to him. A weekend of drunken revelry with his friends to help him forget her harsh words had resulted in a most horrid of hangovers, the reason why he was late to class on the Monday morning.

Vincent and Jerry had easily tracked him down to his family home. When he answered the door David had looked terribly ghastly indeed, the distinctive smell of alcohol still being sweated out of his pores. Jerry was suddenly no longer jealous of this fool who had damaged himself so severely, over a woman none the less. The young couple had been saving themselves for marriage, something Jerry felt a kin to, so David had taken the news especially hard. Jerry even began to feel slightly sympathetic towards this young man, once again adrift in the shallow waters of bachelorhood.

Vincent and Jerry's investigation of the slaughter house on the outskirts of the city had come up with nothing also. None of the staff had a criminal record and nothing could be seen on CCTV. The killer must have been doing their dirty work elsewhere in Hallow, down some dark secluded hell hole and away from prying eyes.

As Jerry arrived at the scene the familiar yellow police line tape spanning the outside of the shop's entrance was there to greet him. Green's Meats was definitely closed for business today. Jerry showed the officer on perimeter duty his badge to get pass.

"DI Wilder, homicide." Jerry informed the officer before walking into the store.

"You're late!" Vincent announced in greeting.

"What have we got? Is this our killer again?" Jerry asked, ignoring Vincent's remark about his tardiness.

"Sounds like it, from what Murphy told me over the phone. Shame really, this place has the best steaks in the city." Vincent added.

Both detectives stepped inside, side stepping Edward and the rest of his forensic team as they made their way further towards the back of the shop. The tinnitus inducing hum of an electric fly trap could be heard over their comings and goings. Murphy was already waiting for them inside.

"Where is he?" Vincent questioned.

"Storage freezer." Murphy simply put.

The large sliding door to the freezer was open, leaving only the thick plastic draft curtains blocking their way. Vincent removed his hat and went through first, followed by Jerry. Once inside the icy store room Vincent immediately replaced his hat back atop his head. The cold air biting at his broad nose felt very unforgiving. Laying before them was a familiar scene, only a different victim this time.

The body of a large, heavy set man in his late forties had been divided into five sections, just like the artist before him. All his wounds had been sealed with melted red plastic, not brown like Roberta's. His head was virtually bald except for the auburn mutton chop side burns that framed his podgy face. A far more rotund figure than Roberta, the years of heavy meat consumption were clearly evident. By his right hand lay an immaculately clean meat cleaver, almost brand new in appearance. To his left hand lay a long link of sausages, eight in total.

27

All around the butcher hung large slabs of frozen beef, pork and lamb. Beside these were numerous empty meat hooks, each one hungry for their own slice of death. Perhaps what was most disturbing about the butcher's fate was that his genitalia had been cut away and removed. In its place was a layer of the same melted red plastic covering his severed wounds.

"This definitely looks like the work of the same killer." Jerry announced.

"Do we have an ID on the victim?" Vincent asked aloud.

"Peter Green, he's the owner of this butcher's shop." Murphy answered.

"The figure in Roberta's mouth, the killer must have been telling us who would be next." Vincent realised.

"Why mutilate his genitals and not Roberta's?" Jerry questioned loudly over the hum of the industry freezer.

"And where would they even keep it?" Vincent thought.

"In a jar on their mantle piece, took it as a trophy probably. Or maybe our killer was jealous, making up for certain short comings." Murphy theorised.

With a creepy smile, Murphy flexed one pinky finger in front of his fellow detectives, simulating a certain unimpressive male appendage.

"Maybe our killer respects the female form more than the male?" Vincent asked himself, throwing his own theory into the mix.

"If the killer respected the female form then they wouldn't have carved up Roberta the way they did. They would have left her the way she was, perfect." Jerry said rather frustratingly.
Vincent sensed this frustration in his young partner.

"Do we have a time of death?" Jerry asked aloud to Edward as he to entered into the freezer.

The case's similarities with the murder of Roberta were all too familiar to Edward now.

"Hard to tell given the body has been in this freezer but the victim was apparently reported missing since Monday, same day we found Roberta. So within the last few days." Edward replied.

"Any witnesses or CCTV footage?" Jerry followed up.

"No, same as before with the girl." Edward replied.

"She really did a number on you didn't she!" Murphy directed at Jerry, referring back to Roberta.

"Just the fact that this sick fuck is still out there walking free." Jerry remarked.

"There will always be some sick fuck out there Jerry. Our job is to catch them before they cause any more damage." Murphy said rather defeatedly.

"Try and focus on what you can see here. Use that to help us find this 'sick fuck' as you both put it" Vincent reminded his colleagues.

Upon further examination of the body Jerry caught Vincent's eye, looking at each other and without needing to say anything more they both knew exactly where to look next, inside the mouth.

"Edward, can you check inside his mouth for us?" Vincent asked.

Edward obliged, soon returning by Peter's side. With double gloved hands Edward reached over the body, placing his left hand on the decapitated head whilst using his right hand to pry open the mouth. The head was frozen to the damp metal floor, the rest of the body too it felt under Edwards's grasp. Peter's jaw was clamped shut by frozen muscles given the icy environment.

"I can't open the mouth. It's frozen shut," Edward called out. "so we'll need to thaw out the head and the body before I can examine him properly"

"Somebody turn the damn freezer off!" Jerry shouted to a nearby member of Edward's team.

"Will do." they called back.

The tinnitus inducing hum of the freezer was quickly becoming unbearable.

"I will catch my death in here if I am not careful." Vincent complained as he walked out of the freezer.

Jerry followed soon after.

Once outside the frozen ice box of dead meat the detectives made their way back through the shop, passing the empty counters as they did. With no meat products out yet for sale the only thing on display was the sterilised green and red plastic grass barriers that lined the counter borders. There would be no business today at Green's Meats, no knowledgable friendly smile from Peter to greet his customers.

The shop hadn't been ransacked or vandalised in any way, neither had anything been stolen. With no signs of forced entry the killer must have entered very stealthily. On one shop wall hung an extensive collection of competition blue ribbons and certificates. Peter was clearly an award winning butcher and salesman. Beside these achievements were three large posters, one for each commonly slaughtered animal; a cow, pig and lamb. The posters showed the various cuts of meat you could get from each one of them and where on their body they would be found.

"I suddenly have a craving for fillet steak!" Murphy joshed, looking to the cow poster.

"The alarm wasn't triggered?" Jerry asked upon seeing the central alarm keypad.

"Looks like it. Maybe our killer kept Peter alive to get the security code from him first and keys to get into the store?" Vincent guessed.

"Or maybe the victim knew the killer. How else can no one have seen this without raising the alarm?" Jerry wondered.

As they neared the exit a couple of uniformed officers had encircled a woman roughly the same age as Peter. The shock of what had happened appearing to have kept her in a calm and surprisingly quiet state.

"This is Mrs June Green, Peter's wife. She found him this morning" Murphy introduced to the other two detectives.

"June, I am DL Harrington and this is DI Wilder," Vincent began to introduce in return. "I am so sorry for your loss. May we ask you some questions please in order to help us catch whoever did this?"

"Yes." she uttered softly, sounding completely heartbroken.

"How many people know the security code to your alarm?" Vincent asked.

"Myself, my son Gary and Peter. Just the three of us." Mrs Green replied.

"Did Peter have any professional rivalries we should know about? Any dissatisfied customers perhaps?" Vincent continued.

"No nothing like that. He was a very honourable man." Mrs Green replied.

Soon afterwards a young man frantically ran into the store, managing to barge his way past the officers supposedly on guard, cutting short the detective's questions.

"Mum!" he cried out loudly, panting heavily from running.

Gary saw his mother by the officers and ran over to comfort her. Flinging their arms around one another the pair soon burst into hysterical tears of sorrow. It appeared that Gary had only just heard the news about his father's grim fate. Vincent and Jerry moved to leave the scene, knowing full well they weren't going to get any more information from either of them, at least for today. The sight of severely distraught friends and family was an occupational hazard in this line of work for both detectives.

It was later in the day and the detectives were back at their desks, compiling the quickly mounting evidence surrounding each murder. With Hallow still in the firm clutches of a sweltering heatwave, the accompanying humidity clung uncomfortably to every pore of their bodies. With the room feeling more like a sauna than a precinct office, Jerry switched on the chilling assistance of their ceiling fan. Its five paddle-like

31

blades softly pushed down wave after wave of cooling air, only slightly relieving their discomfort.

On a large white board in the corner of their office hung photos for both Roberta and Peter's crime scenes, with notes on their murders written around them in black marker. The butcher figure, still in its sealed bag, was pinned below Peter's photo. Both men looked at the evidence on the board and speculated to each other. Vincent didn't look very well, already complaining of a cold earlier in the day. He occasionally sipped from his tea, infused with honey and lemon, whilst Jerry was on his usual coffee.

"So what's the link between these two then?" Jerry asked.

"Maybe there is not one. Christ my throat is sore." Vincent guessed, coughing shortly afterwards.

"Better take the rest of the day off old man. Can't have you dying on me yet." Jerry joked.

"Stop with the old comments ok sonny. I can still give you a run for your money!" Vincent lashed back, causing him to cough and splutter again.

Jerry returned to his paperwork, smirking to himself and admiring his partner's fighting spirit.

"Peter's surname was Green, Roberta used green paint in her art. That's a connection!" Jerry foolishly theorised to himself.

"Then why the plastic figure? Why would they tell us who they will target next?"" Vincent asked, looking to the butcher figure.

"Because it's a game to them," Jerry announced. "see if we can keep up with them. Or maybe they want to be caught"

Into their quaint yet constrictive office entered Clark and Reed. They were another pairing of homicide detectives that worked the rest of the murder and mayhem that Hallow City spewed forth. Detective Sergeant Duncan Clark was as much of a seasoned veteran of detective work as Vincent, silver haired and sporting an equally as silvered beard. He even wore a similar trench coat jacket to that of Vincent, now hooked over his arm given the sweltering warmth.

DI Natasha Reed however was not your typical HCPD detective. She was a woman for a start, a remarkable beauty with a body to match. Jerry could envision her on the front cover of some high class European fashion magazine. She made even a shirt, jacket and tie combo look good. With sumptuously full lips, lightly tanned skin, smokey grey eyes and golden brown hair, Reed was the prettiest thing in the whole building Jerry thought. It was a mystery to them all as to why such a heavenly angel would come to such a hellish city of her own accord.

Shortly after starting at the precinct Jerry had originally been promised to work with DS Clark upon his arrival, but the Chief decided to pair him with Vincent instead, something Jerry still hadn't gotten completely over. Clark was somewhat of a legend at the precinct, having brought in numerous murderers over the years. He even caught a violent rapist, dubbed the Neon God, whom had targeted Hallow's gay community. Clark had also helped bring to an end the organised crime of two dangerous gangs, known as the Gudges and the Crads, whom had previously run amok in Hallow decades earlier.

Jerry had so looked forward to learning from Clark whilst under his wing of guidance. But Jerry couldn't feel too jealous of Reed. She was a tough and determined young woman whose hatred for villainous scum rivalled that of the rest of the team.

"Any leads yet Jerry?" Reed asked hopefully.
Her golden brown locks softly danced around her shoulders with the air conditioning.

"No nothing yet, no DNA to go on either. Our killer is a meticulous non secreter. Not even a single hair sample to go on." Jerry replied.

"How you doing Vincent? Not long now huh?" Clark asked his fellow colleague, peering over his black rimmed glasses.

"Not long at all," Vincent replied, knowing Clark was referring to his retirement. "how are you two doing?"

"Fine, nothing major to report yet." Clark replied.

"Give it time. You know how this city can be," Vincent cautioned. "homicides in Hallow are like an unreliable bus service. None for ages but then they all arrive at once."

"Don't we know it huh," Clark laughed off. "well best of luck to you boys. We better get back to it also, right Natasha?"

"Yeah, we should I guess. Catch you later Jerry. You up for drinks tonight?" Reed offered, flirtatiously to Jerry's ear.

"Yeah why the hell not! O'Malley's?" Jerry rhetorically asked.

"You know it! See you both at eight." Reed confirmed with an irresistible smile as she and Clark exited the room.

This gave Jerry the brief opportunity to gaze at Reed's remarkably ample derriere once more as she walked away. Vincent caught site of this ogling behaviour and deliberately coughed louder to draw Jerry's attention back on the case. Jerry was definitely attracted to Reed. If Grace hadn't been in his life he would have definitely pursued something with Reed. Both of them were HCPD detectives and still fairly new to this strange city. Jerry had thought to himself that they might find some solace in each other's company because of this shared connection.

Jerry got up from his desk to bring himself back down to reality and approached the white board.

"There has to be something more to this figure?" Jerry wondered.

He took the butcher figure from its plastic bag to better examine it, leaving behind the tiny meat cleaver and sausage link. Having been cleared by Edward in forensics the figure was fine to handle manually now. He gripped the figure's hat between his strong fingers and without realising pulled the entire head and neck off in one piece, revealing an empty hole between the shoulders for the neck to slot into to.

"I wonder." Jerry said as he moved to pull the headless torso away from the legs. To which result they did with relative ease. The curious detective then gripped each arm individually and pulled them away from the torso also, separating halfway at the elbow. He now held in his hands five miniature pieces that when assembled would form the butcher figure; a head, torso, two arms and a pair of legs. Vincent got up from his desk to get a better look at Jerry's monumental discovery. Jerry looked to Vincent.

"The killer divided the bodies into five pieces because the figure does the same!" Jerry realised.

"We now have a motive, of sorts." Vincent announced.

"But again why?" Jerry asked once more.

"This figure is clearly a child's toy," Vincent thought. "perhaps the killer sees their victims as toys? Maybe they are trying to create their own? Devoid of any discernible adult sexual characteristics."

"Probably some creepy fuck with mommy daddy issues! You have to be pretty messed up in the head to want to cut off some guy's cock and balls." Jerry harshly put.

The phone on Vincent's desk rang out, cutting their new discovery short.

"Yes?" Vincent asked the other end of the line.
He sighed heavily like a deflating balloon and then put down the receiver.

"We have got another victim, just like the others. Our killer is moving fast." he informed Jerry

"Where?" Jerry hastened to asked.

"East Street, better go with Murphy on this one." Vincent replied as he began coughing violently again.

"You ok?" worried Jerry.

"No I feel like hell," Vincent replied as he put the back of one hand to his forehead. "jeez I am burning up. That damn freezer!"

"Shall I turn off the ceiling fan?" Jerry offered, his finger hovering over the wall switch.

"Perhaps, the mixture of cold and hot air has probably thrown my system completely out of line." Vincent admitted.

"Maybe you should go home then and rest." suggested Jerry.

"No, I will be fine, just need to soldier on." Vincent stubbornly replied.

He downed what remained of his herbal tea before shuffling through more paperwork on his desk.

"I'll call you then if there are any new developments." Jerry confirmed as he passed by his senior partner.

"Sure thing kid." Vincent coughed back.

Chapter Three

The Snake Charmer

After Vincent had received the call, Jerry and Murphy jumped into the next available patrol car and speedily drove down to East Street. Their flashing red lights and blaring siren cut through the thick city air like a hot knife through lard as then went. It was ridiculously hot inside the vehicle, the steering wheel and pleather seat surfaces felt molten hot to the touch. Simply sitting down on any of the seats inside was almost torturous. Jerry rolled down his window as they went, his skin nearly burning on the door handle.

Nicknamed 'Sleazy Street' by the wealthier types of Hallow City, East Street was more commonly known as 'Easy Street' by its main clientele. Easy Street had a reputation in the city and for good reason. Located in the darker more confined recesses of South East Hallow, Easy Street was the centre of the city's sex industry underbelly, populated primarily by flesh pedlars, pimps, whores, perverts, junkies and generally twisted fiends. Despite its name Easy Street wasn't really much of a street, more a single narrow cobblestone road with two cobblestone sidewalks either side. A dirty little cul-de-sac lay at its very end.

It resembled a concrete cavern in construction, six storey buildings either side of it acting as unscalable walls. These manmade barriers reduced the level of sunlight reaching the street floor, giving the entire area an eerily dark trench-like setting, even during daylight hours. There was only one way in and only one way out to this inner city vein of smut. To some Easy Street was a grotesque carnival of human misery, peppered with the infinite dregs of society. For others it was an escape from their typically mundane day to day existence, somewhere to expel their deepest and darkest desires. Hallow City was a labyrinth in structure, with Easy Street acting as its very own foul monstrous Minotaur.

Jerry cautiously exited the car first, with Murphy in tow. As he recounted some of the stories he had heard about Easy Street in his mind, Jerry looked up at the main entrance and exit into the street. Throughout its sordid history, Easy Street had been a rich source of numerous urban legends in Hallow. But perhaps the most well known of all these was sadly the truest. Despite being new to the city even Jerry, in his relative inexperience to Hallow, knew of this infamous tale.

The case of Lester Fenwick, the Killer Pimp, had occurred just shy of a century ago but still lingered over Easy Street and in the minds of all its inhabitants to this day. Hallow's very first serial killer, Lester Fenwick was famed for his sheer brutality and savagery towards women. After systematically hacking all of his own whores to death one evening, he suddenly vanished from Easy Street without a trace. No one knew why he did it, which only added to the mystery further. In his self induced exile, Lester turned his murderous hatred on any woman unfortunate enough to cross his path down the darkened alleyways of Hallow in the dead of night.

Even a couple of young men fell under his blade, as Fenwick's blood lust began to jump the gender gap. Their bodies bore the familiar slash marks carved across their torsos, indicating his sadistic handy work. Lester was eventually found hiding out in Hallow's sewer systems and promptly shot dead by a firing squad who were brave enough to enter his hellish domain. Even in death his actions were attributed to the unsolved disappearances and murders of between twenty five and fifty women across the whole of Hallow.

Rumours run rampant over the coming decades. That ghostly sightings of Lester Fenwick had been seen down Easy Street late at night, accompanied by a wheezy disembodied voice from around street corners, thirsting for female blood. Jerry looked to a large grated drain cover less than a metre away from his feet, fearing Lester was somehow still alive down there in the dark, watching and waiting to strike again.

Vincent had gone home in the end to nurse his cold. A few days rest in bed would soon see the old man right. It was early afternoon as Jerry and Murphy began to walk down the infamous street, passing the usual suspects along the way. Street walkers of varying ages stood around the outsides of their brothels, most of which did not appeal to Jerry's particular appetite.

"This is Skin Trap, the ass end of Easy Street." Murphy introduced.

Drug addiction was clear in some, rotten teeth and sucked in faces with cheek bones protruding. Some had needle marks clearly visible on their exposed arms, one or two with the early signs of infection starting to set in. Some of the ladies had fresh bruising around their faces, the result of unsatisfied customers or displeased pimps.

"Understandably cheaper round these parts." Murphy added.

"Sounds very inviting." Jerry sarcastically replied.

"You have to wade through all this shit before you can get to the nourishing womb further down and its nuggets of gold." Murphy slyly remarked.

He directed Jerry's attention to some very ropey looking hookers with cigarette burns on their faces.

"You sound like you know your way around here?" Jerry asked.

"I just know it's best to avoid the Skin Traps, unless you want to contract dick rot." Murphy admitted, nodding towards the nearby prostitutes.

As they kept walking down the cobblestoned street the detectives passed by more brothels, some looking far less grimy than the previous ones. The girls started getting noticeably more attractive, Jerry taking far more notice now. Some brothels had their girls inside the buildings, advertising themselves in small windowed cubicles, firmly pushing their assets up against the glass as the detectives passed by. This veritable buffet of easy young women wasn't helping Jerry in the slightest. One window

39

girl caught Jerry's eye and pressed her buttocks up against the glass, bending over and peering around her shoulder to smile at the detective. Another street girl standing outside stepped forward, her full attention on Murphy.

"Hey Murphy, who's your new friend?" she questioned him, looking to Jerry as they passed her by.

Jerry immediately took notice of the large disfiguring scar carved from the left corner of her mouth up through the cheek and towards her ear. It looked like an old knife wound of some kind. She was short, compared to the other girls, with even shorter dyed red hair. She wore black lipstick and thick black eyeliner, highlighting her large pale grey eyes. Dressed in a simple denim jacket with only a red corset underneath, this girl was cuter than the rest to Jerry. She looked very young, barely out of her teens, and the most innocent looking of all the whores Jerry had passed by so far. Her short feminine legs were topped by a matching denim miniskirt and ended in a simple pair of black knee high boots. Her speech sounded a little slurred due to nerve damage sustained on the left side of her face.

"New guy." Murphy simply put, not stopping in the process.

The detectives passed through another section of Easy Street, populated by girls just as short as the redheaded girl Jerry had encountered minutes ago. He now felt like a giant, towering over a small village of pygmies. Jerry even spied upon a couple of dwarves. All the girls looked young, too young for such a place. Some resembled school girls, others high school cheerleaders and the rest a mixture of wet t-shirt contestants from a nonexistent Spring Break competition.

"Don't be fooled," Murphy advised. "I know they look too young around here but they are all legal."

"You sure about that?" Jerry challenged.

"Yeah," Murphy sighed. "they get the more pedophilloic creeps around here, wanting the girlfriend experience, minus the jail time."

Jerry couldn't help but wonder who the girl from earlier was and why she wasn't in this particular area of Easy Street, given her youthful look. He turned to ask Murphy but sensing Jerry's curiosity and seeing the mild confusion in his peripheral vision, Murphy answered before Jerry could even question him.

"Her name is Jenny," Murphy began. "I was doing some undercover work here a few years ago on the selling off of Hu Tan properties. One day I saw a young girl being roughed up by two guys down an alleyway here. Before I could do anything one of them stuck a knife in her mouth and slit it open. He claimed it was so he could fit inside her better. I intervened but managed to hold my own against them. I had them arrested and then walked her back to her establishment but her pimp only cared about the fact that she hadn't made any money yet. I gave him the money then took her to Hallow City General."

"So thats how she got the scar?" Jerry asked.

Murphy nodded in reply.

"After my investigation was over and my cover cleared, I came by to see how she was doing. I found out she had been moved between sections due to her newly disfigured face. Her pimp's customers would no longer pay top credit for damaged goods, so she was cast out." Murphy detailed.

"What did they get for cutting Jenny up like that?' Jerry asked.

"Not enough time to rot behind bars." Murphy growled.

"How old is she exactly?" Jerry asked.

"Eighteen, going on fourteen. I know, she looks a lot younger. She's a favourite with the more, twisted types down here as a result." Murphy sighed.

"So...your relationship is purely plutonic?" Jerry coyly pried.

"Yes, I don't see her in that way!" Murphy snapped back defensively.

"That's interesting." Jerry quipped.

41

"Look pal. Jenny isn't a bad character, not a junkie, not a psycho ex, just a poor girl who sadly got caught up in the sludge that flows through this place. Once it takes hold of you, it rarely lets you go." Murphy concluded.

"Alright I'm sorry. Chill!" Jerry replied back with hands raised.

Jerry could easily see that he had struck upon an exposed raw nerve Murphy held for Jenny.

The detectives kept walking and eventually came to the homosexual sector of Easy Street, noticeably quieter and lacking fewer inhabitants. Most of the clubs and brothels were closed due to lack of business during daylight hours. One or two leather clad gigolos stood around the brothel entrances hoping to still ensnare a client at this time of day. One such brothel was called the Hammer & Anvil, another named the White Spit.

"If you ever fancy a good pounding from a power top, then that's the place for you Jerry." Murphy joked, poking fun at his partner's masculinity.

"Shut up Murphy!" Jerry snarked back.

Shuddering at the thought and envisioning his own tender posterior being invaded, Jerry subsequently began to quicken his walking pace.

The gigolos eyed Jerry up and down as he and Murphy passed them by, making the young detective feel more on edge.

"I could just eat you up little man!" one of them called out.

"Nah, I'm too chewy!" Murphy laughed back.

Jerry quickened his pace of walking, now wanting to reach their chosen destination much sooner.

"This is the territory of Lord Latex Head, the leather bound master." Murphy cautioned in Jerry's direction.

The heart of the gay community in Hallow wasn't found down Easy Street though. Just over a hundred blocks in the opposite direction was West Street, an area of Hallow bursting with colour, pride and love. Numerous bars and drag clubs could be found there, welcoming all patrons, regardless of their orientation.

Both Jerry and Murphy now came to the next section of Easy Street, Stripe Tease. After the drab and almost menacing setting of the previous sections of the street, Stripe Tease was a welcome relief.

"It starts to get 'nicer' around here now." Murphy said, motioning to the women standing outside.

The area was richly themed on Burlesque and pin up girls from the nineteen thirties. Feather boas and fans were aplenty, partially covering the already scantily clad ladies. Others adorned minuscule military uniforms to reflect the time period. Triangular bunting was hung across the narrow street, attached either end to each building. Old jazz music played overhead with the sound quality of an old record player. The central colours to the street's decor were red, white and blue, mirrored in some of the women's uniforms of victory. One such girl, wearing a blue and white striped naval uniform, saluted the men as they passed by whilst periodically marching on the spot.

"Corporal Lucy welcomes you to Stripe Tease gentlemen." she greeted.

Coming to the end of Stripe Tease, Jerry could now make out their destination in the near distance. But not before passing a small side route to his right that led away from Easy Street. Above its entrance hung a large sign with the words '*Bang'd Kok*' printed on it in Oriental style calligraphy. This side route was much narrower than the majority of Easy Street, only a car's width in diameter.

"You wanna be careful down there at night Jerry. Unless psycho Asian girls armed with knives and switchblades are your thing." Murphy cautioned.

"I thought you said it gets nicer around here now?" Jerry challenged.

"Yeah, down the main street. Bang'd Kok leads away from that though." Murphy poignantly noted.

Finally arriving at their destination, Jerry now stood in the very centre of Easy Street's cul-de-sac. He looked up at the large neon sign hanging above the building's luxurious doorway. The Fox Glove was one of the more classier strip joints and brothels at the end of Easy Street, frequented by the far more affluent human slime that visited the area. Its bright halogen lightbulb sign resembled that of a Fox, sitting in the centre of an expansive Fox Glove flower.

To the left of the Fox Glove was the Velvet Oyster, the most expensive escort and brothel establishment on the whole of Easy Street. Its own entrance was draped in flowing velvet curtains milky cream in colour, resembling the folds of the main feminine product on offer in such a place. An enormous fake pearl, bigger than a basketball, took centre stage above the doorway, signalling the clitoral treasures inside.

"It's at least six hundred big ones to hire some company in there." Murphy advertised.

To the right of the Fox Glove was Los Iguanas, another extravagant and expensive latino themed saloon brothel for Hallow City's elite clientele. Over its doorway hung the image of a large Iguana, stretching forth its long red tongue suggestively.

"The Iguana, Tyson the Tongue, runs the whole show in there. Guess how he got the nickname?" Murphy asked.

"How?" Jerry replied back.

"Bit of a motor mouth. Tends to let his loose lips run away from him more often than not." Murphy answered.

"And what about those two?" Jerry asked, directing Murphy's attention towards two other brothels in the cul-de-sac.

Similar to the Velvet Oyster, Le Fleur Rose had a very ostentatious entrance. Stretching out from around its central doorway were numerous large silken petals of varying shades of pink. It resembled an enormous flower, clearly advertising the more fleshier ones put up for sale within. The entire building was pink in colour, stencilled with extravagant flower patterns across its whole surface. Le Fleur Rose lay to the right of Los Iguanas,

44

whilst the House of Payne was the Velvet Oyster's second next door neighbour. It couldn't have contrasted more with Le Fleur Rose even if it tried.

The House of Payne was jet black in its outer appearance and furnishings, with spiked corners and jagged building edges. So absolutely black in colour, it was almost impossible to identify the intricate brick work patterning from several yards away. The only other colour besides black in the building's outward appearance was silver, which came from a collection of metallic chains hanging down over the main entrance. Some of these chains extended outwards and were anchored to the floor and building walls by an array of clamps.

"New age, hippy flower power nonsense in there! Coco la Rosa is the one to arrange some company with in there." snorted Murphy, looking to Le Fleur Rose.

"Come on in gentlemen to Le Fleur Rose, where the girls are sweet but their nectar is sweeter!" a worker called out to the detectives.

He garnered no response from them.

"What about House of Payne?" Jerry asked.

"Domination, humiliation and subjugation, Fraulein Payne's specialty." Murphy shuddered.

Jerry and Murphy were first on the scene so there were no patrol cars or police tape to cordon off the premises. They stepped towards the Fox Glove, flashing their badges to the Neanderthal looking bouncer at the entrance. He moved aside, allowing them entrance. The lights were on inside, no darkness to hide the Fox Glove's usual sleazy activities. Jerry and Murphy were immediately greeted by the owner shortly after entering, a man called Freddy Foxx but simply introduced himself as The Foxx.

"DI Murphy and Wilder, Hallow City Homicide." Murphy introduced.

"The Foxx huh? I wonder how this place got its name?" Jerry brashly joked towards Murphy.

Not acknowledging Jerry's remark the Foxx spoke to them both in an unnervingly gentle manner.

"Gentlemen, thank you for coming so quickly. I want this ugly business taken care of as soon as possible. So I can reopen and get back to business." the Foxx stated in his creepily shrill voice.

"This way please." instructed a bodyguard that flanked the Foxx.

"Yes, follow Dutchy if you please." the Foxx added.

Dutchy began leading Jerry and Murphy towards the fire exit on the other side of the room.

The Foxx was a man of small stature but none the less commanded a great level of respect from his employees. Dressed in a smart yet tacky crushed red velvet suit, he had short black hair slicked back like some old school gangster. Carrying a black cane topped with a silver handle shaped like a fox head, the Foxx walked as if he didn't need its assistance. Small brown eyes and a thin dark moustache adorned his beaten face. His hands were decorated by a couple of gold rings and had a platinum watch on one wrist. Business must have been going well for him to afford such extravagance.

Dutchy on the other hand was your typical muscle for such a place, a strong build cleverly hidden under a thick layer of body fat and another of expensive threads. Fat faced but with even smaller eyes than the Foxx, Dutchy's deep baritone voice rumbled though Jerry's chest cavity every time he spoke. He was cleanly shaven, from his dimpled chin all the way up to an uneven crown. Dutchy looked as if he could snap a man in half like a bread stick.

Both detectives passed a number of young women, evidently the resident Fox Glove strippers, causally lounging on the numerous leather seats that outlined the main stage which stretched out into the centre of the room. Business was expectedly slow due to the Fox Glove's temporary closure at this time. A long narrow stage jutted out from one side of the room, with a row of four poles running down its centre. Each one glowed intermittently from bright red to pink and so on. Evidently red and pink were the signature colours of the Fox Glove. The stage itself was edged by shiny, well polished silver bars that lined the perimeter.

A lone woman stood behind the only bar in the whole joint opposite the stage, wiping clean numerous glasses. She was dressed rather smartly in a short sleeved white shirt complete with black waist coat, her long wavy blonde hair tied back in a ponytail. On her head she wore a hair band complete with two large fox ear attachments. Her shirt was unbuttoned enough for Jerry to peek a glimpse at her ample cleavage, tenderly embraced by lacy black lingerie. As she polished the glasses her chest gently bounced ever so slightly from side to side.

Entranced by this captivating sight Jerry noisily fell into one of the bar stools, causing her to look up and peer over her red rimmed glasses at him. Jerry clumsily replaced the over turned stool, causing her to softly giggle at his foolishness. All he could do was smile back, before continuing his approach to the fire exit. Murphy had witnessed the whole incident.

"Eyes on the prize there chief." he reminded Jerry.

"My hens are certainly very distracting, huh detective?" the Foxx smirked back at Jerry.

Dutchy held the door open as the detectives stepped out into the alley way that ran behind the Fox Glove. The early afternoon sunlight only just managed to shine down into the deep alleyway. Jerry peered up at the sky, partially hidden by the high-rise buildings either side of him. Despite the daylight it was still dark in the alleyway and smelled of urban decay and detergent.

"Over there." Dutchy rumbled, his right arm gesturing in the same direction he was looking.

Jerry and Murphy walked slowly towards the dead end of the alley. As they got closer an all too familiar sight came into focus, partially obscured by large garbage bins. The naked body of a young women lay on the dirty concrete ground, divided into five sections just like the other two victims. Her wounds had been sealed with melted green plastic this time.

"This is our killer again." Murphy sighed.

"A different colour plastic for each victim also!" Jerry remarked.

Jerry crouched down to have a better look at the girl. Early twenties maybe with blonde hair tinted by a pink rinse, she had a slim to medium figure with slightly freckled skin. A long snake tattoo extended all the way from the top of her left foot, round her leg and up towards her thigh. From there it continued to move off round her lower back, wrapping around her middle before moving further up her front, between her chest and stretching across her left shoulder. The tattoo then moved down her left arm before finally ending with the snake's head on the back of her hand. The snakes fiery red eyes drastically contrasted with the numerous greens that comprised its body. Jerry could only discern jade, lime, artichoke and even turquoise. The impressive snake tattoo had been cut in half along with her body and then beheaded with the severing of her left arm.

Just like Roberta the artist, her womanly regions had also been mutilated, her nipples having been sliced off and removed, whilst her vagina had been sealed shut with a layer of melted green plastic. Her large breasts, the result of surgical implants, still wore the scars of a surgeon's scalpel underneath them.

"Do we have a name for her?" Jerry asked aloud to the Foxx who had followed them outside along with Dutchy by his left side.

"Rebecca, Rebecca Childs I believe but we all just called her Becky." the Foxx replied.

"Anything else you can tell us about her?" Murphy further questioned.

"She joined us only a few months ago, after leaving The Black Octopus. Cute girl, twenty two, thirty six Double E, already a hit with my customers, already making me a lot of money and raising my profile. My favourite new hen." the Foxx clucked.

Jerry took out a pair of forensic gloves. He knew where to look straight away. Taking a firm hold of Becky's severed head with his right hand Jerry reached into her mouth. Her jaw had undergone minor riga mortis but it was far easier to manipulate than the butcher's. After prising it open he pulled out a little plastic figure in the same design as the butcher figure.

In his hand was what appeared to be a surgeon. The figure was green in colour, resembling surgical overalls, with little white hands. A surgical hat piece adorned its head, with a surgeon's mask printed over the mouth. In one hand was a miniature stethoscope. In the other hand was a tiny grey scalpel.

"What's that?" the Foxx couldn't help but wonder aloud.

"We're not sure.'" Murphy said to him.

"A doctor?" Dutchy chimed in with his booming voice that echoed down the alleyway.

"We really don't know yet." Jerry admitted.

"This kind of work must require a good knowledge of human anatomy. But why cut off her nipples and seal her vagina shut?" Murphy wondered.

"Our killer means to desexualise their victims," Jerry thought. "they did the same with Peter the butcher and with Roberta the artist."

"Marvellous. A psycho doctor is on the loose and I'm going to be out of pocket more than before." the Foxx complained.

"A young women has been brutally murdered and all you're worried about is how much money you're losing!" Jerry angrily snapped at the Foxx.

Dutchy quickly stepped forward with intention, only to be stayed by the slightest raise of the Foxx's left hand.

"It's alright Dutchy, no offence taken." the Foxx softly uttered.

49

Dutchy slowly stepped back to his position at the Foxx's side. The bodyguard's sudden advance made Jerry immediately see the influence the Foxx held over his employees and his territory. The detective realised he should watch himself more carefully around this man now.

"My sincerest apologies for my earlier comment." the Foxx whimpered, with no sign of remorse in his shrill voice.

"Who found her?" Jerry asked.

"I did, when I came out here for a smoke earlier. Must have been around lunchtime." Dutchy confessed.

"Did you move or touch the body?" Murphy asked Dutchy.

"No of course not, freaked me out just seeing her that way." Dutchy replied.

"And no one else was in this alleyway until then?" Murphy followed up.

"No, the garbage bins are emptied on Monday I believe. Until then this alleyway is pretty quiet." said the Foxx.

"Boss, what should we do with her snake?" Dutchy asked the Foxx.

"I don't care. Just get rid of it. We've no need for it now." the Foxx uttered menacingly.

"Snake?" Jerry repeated.

"Becky keeps, sorry kept her python here. She used it in her performances now and again, especially in her one to one meetings." Dutchy filled in.

"She used this snake in her one to ones?" Murphy repeated.

"Indeed. If my clients like what they see they can arrange a private meeting with my hens in a room upstairs. Far more privacy in there." the Foxx grinned suggestively.

"Away from the usual drooling goons." Dutchy added.

"We'll need to take it for evidence. If this snake has been in contact with her regular clients, we could have DNA evidence for a potential suspect on our hands." Jerry theorised.

"Impressive thinking detective," the Foxx complimented. "by all means take the beast. I've no use for it now. The rest of my hens are too terrified of it anyway. Without Becky it's just a potential belt to me now." the Foxx cruelly added.

"You mentioned The Black Octopus earlier. What's the Black Octopus?" Jerry asked, trying to ignore the Foxx's cold attitude to the situation.

"The Black Octopus is both a place, and a person my dear boy" the Foxx chuckled, looking to Dutchy to join him in his amusement.

"Madame Wu, she's the owner of The Black Octopus. It's an Asian rub and tug joint just down the way in Bang'd Kok. Well it fronts as a massage parlour anyway." Dutchy added.

"In her basement supposedly lurks a whore house that caters to, shall we say, a number of peculiar appetites. I try not to get my business involved in her's, and if the rumours are true I'm certainly glad I still don't." the Foxx finished.

"So why was Becky there before coming to you?" Jerry enquired.

"Young pretty little thing, looking to make serious bank off her assets, as they all do. Some go to Madame Wu first, despite her reputation, because she pays far more than most places around here. But only if the girls do one thing for her. I guess Becky couldn't go through with it." the Foxx detailed.

"And that is?" Murphy asked.

"I'm not sure detective. You'll just have to go ask Wu herself. If you can get anywhere near her that is, she's well protected. Besides she'll be one of your prime suspects I'm sure." the Foxx teased.

"You holding out on us Fred? Got something else to tell us have you?" Jerry forcefully questioned.

"Let's just say not many girls escape the clutches of The Black Octopus. Those that do don't stay around here for very long." the Foxx said, amused by his own foreboding comment.

51

"Madame Wu is someone you don't want to get involved with detectives. Believe us when we say that." Dutchy cautioned.

"I didn't realise you cared so much for us Sir." Murphy quipped.

"I don't, no offence. I've just seen tougher men than you be reduced to nothing because of that woman." the Foxx ominously added.

"Call in Edward and the rest of forensics Murphy. We'll need to pay this Wu a visit." Jerry said aloud.

Murphy stepped back inside the Fox Glove again, taking out his phone in the process.

"Her place won't be open until early evening detective." the Foxx advised Jerry.

"Best try after dark." Dutchy suggested.

"After all, that is when octopuses are most active. Or is it octopi?" smirked the Foxx

"I don't quite rightly know boss." rumbled Dutchy.

"In the mean time if you see anymore of Becky's regulars please get in contact with us." Jerry instructed, handing the Foxx his card.

"I'm sure we'll be seeing you gentlemen again real soon." the Foxx coyly grinned as Jerry left the alley way and its macabre scene.

"The Octopus. The Fox. The Iguana. Are all the brothel owners around here nicknamed after animals?" Jerry asked Murphy as they travelled back through the Fox Glove.

"Pretty much. The Velvet Oyster's Madame is known by many as Pam the Clam. You wanna know why?" Murphy asked.

"Not really" Jerry quickly replied.

"Because she has a fishy smelling..." Murphy began.

"Don't even say it!" Jerry interrupted, cutting Murphy's childish joke short.

Murphy laughed to himself as they kept walking.

"You're no fun," Murphy complained. "anyway it's Easy Street Jerry. It's best not to ask too many questions here."

"Well that kinda defeats the whole point of our investigation doesn't it." Jerry said.

The two detectives exited the Fox Glove and passed by the Neanderthal looking bouncer from earlier. Jerry could easily imagine him being a relative of Dutchy's, at least a brother or a cousin.

"This Wu sounds like a real piece of work anyway. You didn't hear anything about her when you were undercover here?" Jerry asked.

"I heard things. Somethings I wish I hadn't." added Murphy, a nervous tone to his voice.

As they exited Easy Street and walked back to their car, Jerry couldn't help but feel the air get much cleaner and thinner. It was almost as if the street had its own smog like atmosphere, the air thick and heavy, comprised of depravity and sin. Just as they got back to the car Murphy's phone rang out, which he quickly answered. After a few moments he looked at Jerry with a look of bewilderment.

"OK thanks for the update." Murphy answered as he hung up.

"That was Edward?" Jerry guessed.

"Yeah. He finally finished with the butcher's body. Same thing as Roberta. No organs taken, same method to bleed the body and seal it, traces of chloroform around the mouth and more importantly there was another figure in his mouth." Murphy informed.

"Well what was it?" Jerry eagerly asked.

"Ed described it as a woman with two smaller plastic snake pieces, possibly a snake wrangler or charmer." Murphy summarised.

"Son of a bitch!" Jerry loudly exclaimed.

He slammed his fists down hard on the car's bonnet in dismay.

"The fucker really is telling us who is next with each new victim!" Jerry added.

"We officially have a serial killer at work ladies and gentlemen." Murphy announced to a non-existent audience.

"Vincent was right." Jerry softly giggled to himself as he fell back against the side of the car.

"About what?" Murphy asked.

"This is just the beginning." Jerry answered forebodingly.

"We're missing Roberta's artist figure though. We haven't found a body yet to link to her murder!" Murphy suddenly realised.

"Yet. We haven't found it yet. The killer must be building towards something Murphy, the only question is what?" Jerry wondered with dread in his voice.

Chapter Four

The Black Octopus

Night had finally fallen over Hallow City's Easy Street, and with the returning darkness came Jerry and Murphy once more. The evening felt even more airless than during the day, warm and sticky with uncomfortable humidity. Despite this Jerry still wore his thick leather jacket to help conceal his weapon, just incase things went array.

"Better watch ourselves around here now. This place gets much rougher after dark." Murphy cautioned Jerry yet again.

The young detective began to sense some palpable tension, that entering Easy Street now was like entering a deeper circle of Hell. The stain left on Easy Street by Lester Fenwick certainly added to the dire setting Jerry was venturing into again.

As the men retraced their steps from earlier in the day there was far more activity happening on Easy Street. Jerry and Murphy passed the same whores from earlier, still in exactly the same place and clothing as before, even uttering the same tired old pick up lines. They seemed zombified, perpetually stuck in the same locale and situation for all time.

Customers were standing around admiring the merchandise, before making quick deals and exchanging handfuls of cash with the nearby pimps. Several of the ladies aimlessly reached out at the crowd of numerous passing customers, hoping to ensnare some business. Jerry spied the young redheaded girl Jenny again, she appearing to have keen interest from a number of disheveled looking clients. It pained Murphy to see her stuck in this situation still.

"Hey sugar, wanna date?" one nearby hooker asked Jerry.

"No, I'm only here on business." Jerry quipped.

He could easily imagine this wretch being one giant walking STD in clothing.

"Aren't we all." she retorted, sparking up a cigarette in the process.

Her severely weakened lungs from years of smoking wouldn't allow her the simple pleasure of this nicotine hit as she immediately began gagging on the choking fumes.

As the detectives kept walking they steadily garnered more and more offers from the ladies, slowing their progress down the street. Asian girls, African girls, Hispanic girls, Blondes, Brunette, Redheads, all and much more were on offer down Easy Street this night. Hallow really was a city that worshipped flesh. Jerry had no time for this delay, reaching into his jacket and pulling out his badge to hold it up for all to see. The human traffic of Easy Street slowly took notice of the young undeterred detective and his associate.

"Police business, move aside." Jerry announced over the noise of the crowd.

Almost without having to slow his walking pace, the throbbing population of Easy Street moved either side of him and Murphy. Jerry almost felt like Moses, parting the Red Sea for the Israelites, but there was no promised land at the end of Easy Street. Or perhaps there was for some, a short lived state of euphoric release.

The detectives came to the homosexual sector of Easy Street once again, Jerry spying several leather clad men groping one another outside the brothels. Loud bass heavy music thundered around them with the occasional strobe lighting momentarily escaping out of the brothels with the mere opening of a door. Some men had others chained up like animals, wearing unsettling zippered masks and crouching down on all fours like a dog. One of them made a pass at Murphy.

"You're barking up the wrong tree there Fido!" Murphy nervously remarked, side stepping his new admirer.

Jerry and Murphy passed through Stripe Tease once more, the music now playing louder over the speakers. Wartime radio songs now accompanied the earlier jazz percussion tunes. Stripe

Tease had far more of a party atmosphere than anything Jerry had passed through already. The decades old big brass band tunes were the life and soul of the street. Jerry made his way through the crowd, no longer needing his badge. Some of the women danced in the street with their feather fans, teasingly providing a sneak peek at what they would offer that evening. Nipples momentarily caught Jerry's eye as they appeared from behind multiple swishes of feathery boas.

Jerry thought of Becky and how her barbaric death hadn't impacted on Easy Street in the slightest. The detective then thought of the Killer Pimp, Lester Fenwick, and what his crimes must have really done to Hallow.

"Hey Murphy, where was Fenwick's old whore house?" Jerry asked his colleague.

"The entire cul-de-sac! It use to be one large brothel but got divided up after his death!" Murphy cried over the music.

Once free of the crowds in Stripe Tease, the detectives soon came again to the gateway leading into Bang'd Kok. Jerry could just make out the entrance to the Fox Glove in the near distant, wondering how much attention his blonde barmaid would be getting this evening. Rising up over the hustle and bustle of Easy Street's cul-de-sac, a single male voice could be heard, crying out his words of warning. He sounded like a warped preacher, declaring the coming of an apocalypse brought about by the sin on Easy Street.

"He will return again! Mark my words brothers and sisters! Lester Fenwick, he will return for us all!" he warned.

"Crazy nut heads," Murphy shrugged off. "can't believe they still get them around here, even on the busiest nights. Pay no attention Jerry."

Ignoring Murphy's caution, Jerry's attention inevitably returned to the man in the distance.

"Beware the signs of his coming! Bodies will litter the streets, both of man and beast. The sky will darken as fire reigns down from above. Beware the twelve signs of the zodiac when

57

the planets align, and the moon turns red with blood!" the man warned.

"Silly fucker." Jerry chuckled, confident in the man's delusional rantings.

Jerry looked again to the entrance of Bang'd Kok, momentarily stepping aside as a wave of bodies pushed past him and Murphy to get to the cul-de-sac.

"Here we are then," Murphy ominously announced. "you ready for this?"

"Lets do this then." Jerry replied.

Jerry looked up at the large sign above the entrance again before walking through first, almost immediately attracting the attention of three Asian beauties, each one lining either side of his path. They had initially been hidden by the shadows, their sudden appearance catching Jerry off guard.

"Hey there sexy. I'm Jade and these are my sisters Ruby and Sapphire. You looking for good time tonight?" one of the ladies asked Jerry in a girlish sounding tone.

She stepped forward to clutch hold of his forearm with her small, dainty hands. Jerry looked between the female faces now staring intently at him. All three young women looked remarkably similar, appearing to be identical triplets. They all wore exactly the same outfit, a tight fitting boob tube and very tight fitting short shorts. The triplets even shared the same outlandish hairstyle.

Their incredibly short fringes were cut straight across, with the hair on the back of their heads kept long and spiked like a horse's mane. The remaining hair at the sides was kept long also, hanging down past their ears and delicate necks. The only way Jerry could tell them apart was by the colour of their outfits. Cleverly colour coordinated, Jade wore a pastel green, Ruby adorned a pinkish red and Sapphire a Robin's egg blue.

"No I'm not and take your damn hands off me you little whore!" Jerry snapped.

One more proposition had finally proved too many for him. Jade's friendly greeting smile quickly melted away into a look of disgust, as did her sisters'.

"Oh honey! Such rudeness in the presence of us ladies." Jade responded unnervingly, producing a large flick knife from betwixt her posterior.

"Hey look we don't want any trouble!" Murphy pleaded, holding up his hands in defence as Jade flicked the knife open.

She squinted at Murphy before turning her attention back to Jerry, one hand still holding his arm. Ruby and Sapphire had also produced large intimidating knives from somewhere on their person.

"You threaten our sister? Not very wise." Ruby assured Jerry.

"You now pay entrance fee to get past!" Sapphire instructed, pointing her knife at Jerry.

"I'll teach you some manners with my little friend here. Now then, let's try this again. Thanks to your rudeness the price just tripled. How about it? I'll show you mine if you show me yours." Jade propositioned.

"Very well. I'll show you what I've got." Jerry calmly returned.

With his free arm Jerry took out his badge again and held it up for the ladies to see.

"Law!" Jade alerted her sisters.

"Precisely. DI Wilder and Murphy of the HCPD. Now you try this again, Jade. Let go of my arm, move aside or I'll have you and your sisters thrown into a cell for threatening an officer of the law, assault of an officer and obstruction of justice." Jerry confidently threatened.

With a look of surprise Jade immediately put away her knife and sheepishly stepped away from Jerry and Murphy, releasing her hold on his arm.

"Sorry officer, we didn't know. Some men ya know, they come and try to take by force. We have to protect ourselves ya know." Jade apologised and then tried to justify.

Ruby and Sapphire moved aside also, having seen the altercation between them. Jerry calmly tucked his badge back into his jacket pocket, adjusted his sleeve that Jade had crumpled under her grip.

"Why you come here then?" Sapphire enquired in broken english.

"We've come to speak with Madame Wu." Murphy replied.

"Ah, Madame Wu." Ruby smiled.

"She take good care of you!" Sapphire assured.

"Madame give you good time." Ruby added.

"You stay safe now ladies." Jerry slyly uttered as he passed them by.

"You too detectives," Jade politely called after them. "you're gonna need it."

Jerry continued onwards, but not before overhearing Sapphire's comment to her sisters.

"He have nice butt." she whispered.

Jerry had to admit that he secretly enjoyed the misguided compliment.

Now finally outside their destination, Jerry surveyed the front of the building. The Black Octopus was the central building of Bang'd Kok. It had extensive blue lighting around its windows, highlighting the wave like patterns frosted on to the glass. A nautical theme was heavily present in the general image of the place, with the outline of an octopus at the centre of each window. Unlike the Fox Glove with its large red worded sign, the Black Octopus noticeably lacked any written advertisements out front. It seemed as though people knew what they would be in for before stepping inside.

Either side of the Black Octopus were a number of other Asian themed strip joints, saloons and brothel houses. The veritable banquet of young Asian women on offer in these places even tempted Jerry to reach for his metaphorical wallet. Bright halogen lighting was strung up everywhere, making it very hard to hide in the shadows of this default appendix of Easy Street.

"How bad can this Wu be?" Jerry turned to Murphy and joked.

Murphy fell silent, taking in a deep breathe as if to mentally prepare himself for what was to come. Jerry could see the anxiety in his partner's eyes so entered first, not wanting to waste anymore time on the investigation. Murphy following him soon after.

They entered into a heavily air conditioned narrow hallway, dimly lit by further blue fluorescent lighting. The chilled air helped Jerry cool down after his hot and sweaty walk down the confined street. A few wafts of his cumbersome leather jacket further accelerated his cooling down. Almost immediately to their right was a small booth, in it was a young pretty Chinese girl in her late teens. With dark hair tied back into youthful pigtails and wearing a tight fitting blue tank top, she greeted the two men.

"Welcome gentlemen, Madame has been expecting you." greeted the girl.

A fake smile across her face exposed her teeth.

"We're expected?" Jerry asked.

He took a quick glance at the girl's erect nipples trying to poke through her thin top, a result of the cold interior no doubt.

The girl nodded, her fake smile hiding her teeth this time.

"Word travels fast around here." Murphy confirmed.

"Now you tell me!" Jerry exclaimed.

"Madame will see you now." the girl spoke again, her English sounding better than Sapphire's.

Jerry's frustration was becoming too great, objectifying nearly every pretty woman he now came across.

"This way please." instructed another young Asian girl.

61

She appeared suddenly from behind the entrance to the booth, her outstretched arm beckoning the detectives to follow her.

Dressed in the same tight fitting blue tank top and matching miniskirt, the girl stood almost as high as Jerry's shoulders, yet another pretty thing for him to look down upon. Jerry's gaze returned to the girl in the booth as he walked away, her smile nervously wobbling into a look of worry and unease. As the girl rustled through the paperwork in front of her in a somewhat failed attempt to look busy, Jerry suddenly noticed that she was missing most of her left arm. How he had missed this earlier was no surprise, given his initial interest in her before. Her arm looked as if it had been cleanly amputated just above the elbow. Tattooed on to her stump was the image of a small black octopus. Entranced by her choice of tattoo, Jerry continued on after his diminutive escort.

As Jerry and Murphy followed the second girl down the corridor they passed a number of rooms on either side of them. Although the doors were closed shut, that didn't stop the muffled orgasmic groans of Madame Wu's clients receiving their happy endings from passing through the walls. One such client was so comically vocal Murphy smirked to himself.

"Sounds like someone is having a good time in there!" he joked.

"Oh my yes, we always aim to please here." the girl assured, looking over her shoulder at Murphy.

The detectives continued to follow her, Jerry now noticing this girl had the same octopus tattoo as that of the girl in the booth, but on the back of her neck. It appeared as though this Madame Wu liked to brand her employees with her own logo. Gazing down her back and then to her bare legs, Jerry couldn't help but undress this young girl with his eyes. As they reached the end of the corridor the girl turned around, hands clasped together in front with her elbows outstretched. Jerry snapped out of his adulterous fantasies.

"Please enter." she instructed, the same fake smile across her otherwise angelic face.

"What's inside?" Murphy cautiously asked.

"Madame's office. She waits for you inside." the girl informed.

Jerry stared at the door, a large outline of an octopus was all that stared back at him. His gaze returned to the girl, her forced smile starting to waver due to his momentary hesitation. Jerry grasped the handle, turned it open and stepped inside.

There before him, behind a small but impressive mahogany desk, sat an elderly Thai woman. She was in her late fifties, dark hair tied back in a bun which was starting to grey in areas. Her wrinkled miserable expression surrounded two menacing dark eyes that glared at the detectives as they entered, closing the door behind them. Draped in turquoise silken finery she wore little makeup and adorned two pearl earrings.

On the desk in front of her was a large glass jar half filled with water and contained what appeared to be four black octopuses. They lay motionless on the bottom, each one no bigger than a golf ball. The air was thick with the smell of burning incense, small pillars of smoke rising up from an octopus shaped holder on her desk, one tentacle for each incense stick. Jerry had no choice but to breathe some of it in, choking a little on the thick fumes.

Behind this seemingly feeble old woman towered two bodyguards, a must have accessory it seemed for anyone in power on Easy Street. Both had buzz cut hair styles and wore narrow sunglasses, despite the dim lighting in the room. They were both dressed in the same expensive looking grey suits with black shirts underneath, unbuttoned at the top due to the thickness of their necks. With impressively broad shoulders and visible upper body strength Jerry knew he wouldn't stand a chance against one of them if things went array.

But perhaps what first grasped Jerry and Murphy's attention the moment they entered was the half naked Asian woman cowering on her knees to the side of the old woman. Slightly hunched over with her arms in her lap, the woman's face was obscured by the top of her head which was crowned by long black hair. She was clothed in only skimpy black lingerie. A studded leather dog collar around her neck was in turn attached to a long silver chain, the end of which grasped firmly in the old woman's boney left hand.

The old woman spoke briefly in her native Thai tongue.

"Madame Wu welcomes you both gentlemen and asks why you have come to her?" the cowering woman questioned.

She didn't look up from her position on the floor. This woman was evidently Wu's translator, albeit being in a somewhat pet-like role.

"You know why we're here Wu. Tell us what you know about this girl." Jerry impatiently asked.

He held up a recent photo of Becky that he produced from inside his jacket pocket.

Madame Wu glanced at the photo then back to him. She spoke once again in Thai. Jerry and Murphy were unable to understand a single word she said, which seemed to be the whole point.

"Madame Wu says that is Becky, a young girl who came to her only a couple of months ago for work in her parlour." the woman interpreted.

"She wasn't here for very long. Why did she get canned then?" Murphy asked.

"She...no...swallow." Madame Wu crudely said in broken English.

"Is that what you get your girls to do then?" Jerry immediately followed up.

"So you do understand English? In that case word of advice sister. Tone down on the level of incense in here next time." Murphy joked.

Madame Wu looked to Murphy, unamused by his comment. He expected a comeback of some kind but was met with steely silence. She instead calmly reached over to unscrew the large jar

64

of octopuses on the desk, sticking her hand in and grasping hold of one as it appeared to struggle between her fingers. Yanking on the chain, Madame Wu pulled the woman closer to her. She grabbed the chain closest to her neck and pulling her head back. A look of panic spread across the woman's face, tears beginning to form in the corners of her large eyes. Wu spoke a single word to the woman as she moved the octopus closer to her face.

The woman pursed her lips firmly closed and shook her head in a desperate plea of refusal as Wu repeated the word again. This time the woman appeared to comply as she opened her mouth, tears now running down her face whilst she softly whimpered. The thick incense smoke clung uncomfortably to Jerry's dry tired eyes. He rubbed them firmly to help relieve some of the discomfort. The choking cloud of incense began to impair his vision and play tricks on him. Wu's face showed no emotion as she moved to shove the struggling creature into the woman's gaping maw.

"Enough!" outburst Jerry.
This surprised Wu, causing her to stop what she was doing and let the woman go.

The crying woman stopped her whimpering also, looking to Jerry whilst closing her mouth. Wu recoiled the octopus from her face.

"Cut the bullshit games Wu and tell us what you really know!" Jerry firmly questioned.
The old woman looked surprised by his aggressive outburst.

"Why is Becky dead? Answer us that at least!" Jerry demanded, but this time directing his enquiry at the sobbing woman on the floor.

A stunned silence spread throughout the room, one bewildered bodyguard looking to the other as the old woman relaxed her hold on the chain. She looked to the younger woman cowering on the floor. The young woman stopped her act immediately, her sad expression quickly turning into a look of impressed annoyance.

She reached up to her head and pulled off her hair, now revealed to be a wig. Underneath she was completely shaven, with a large octopus tattoo etched in black ink spread across the left side of her cranium. She also unhooked the chain from the dog collar around her neck.

"Very clever detective." she spoke.

Her voice now sounded like a completely different person, no longer the meek simpering character she had been portraying.

Her attention returned to the octopus in the old woman's hand, grabbing it from her. Popping it into her mouth, she began to chew the creature loudly. Its ink defence proved useless, squirting out the corners of her mouth on to the floor, whilst dribbling down her lips and chin. Jerry could only look on repulsed by the grim scene before him. After what seemed like several minutes she finally stopped chewing and noisily gulped down the mass of tentacles, completely unfazed by her actions. Jerry felt dizzy from the spectacle, as if something was laced in the burning incense, impairing his judgment. The room's contents appeared slightly blurred as a faint ethereal haze began to outline everyone and everything in Wu's office.

Standing up from the floor, the real Madame Wu commanded something briefly in Thai at the old woman. She in return responded by standing up from her chair, at first struggling to haul herself up. One bodyguard assisted her whilst the other handed her a walking stick that had been hidden behind him. Now on her feet she moved to leave through a door on the left hand side of the room. As she exited the room the bodyguards returned to their original positions. Jerry also noticed a third door to the right and wondered where both these doors led to.

"Not many men see past this little façade." Wu commented.

"Well I am a detective!" Jerry quickly retorted, annoyance beginning to creep into his voice.

Now that she was standing in front of him Jerry could get a better measure of this woman. Unusually tall for her ethnicity,

Wu was very slim figured with ghostly pale skin. She had high cheek bones crowned by a pair of very dark piercing eyes. She looked almost alien-like, with her angular face exaggerated by her shaven head. Wu adjusted both sides of the black thong she was wearing, carefully running her fingers along the insides of each strap, whilst looking Jerry deep in the eye, before audibly pinging them back into place.

All up and down the insides of her arms and the palms of her hands were what appeared to be numerous tattoos of octopus suckers. As she turned round to replace the lid on the jar of the surviving octopuses, she seductively bent over the desk, revealing the rest of her minuscule garment nestled between her cheeks. A much larger and more detailed tattoo of an octopus stretched upwards from her lower back to the middle of her spine.

Murphy couldn't help but sneak a peek of her quite stunning rear end, smooth and well curved. Jerry couldn't resist a look either, not even Grace had a figure like this woman. Wu turned her head round at that exact moment, anticipating their lust as if she had eyes on the back of her head. Jerry's gaze quickly darted away, trying to hide his interest but it was too late. Wu knew he had admired her physique and she coyly smiled back at him, her teeth now slightly blackened by the octopus ink. Wu stood up and turned around to sit on her desk, now facing the detectives again.

"You speak many languages?" Jerry asked, noticing her bilingual skills.

"Oh yes, I have a very flexible tongue detective. But my favourite has to be body language. Now there is a form of communication that transcends mere race." Wu flirted.

"Must have been painful," Murphy began. "getting those tattoos on your palms?"

"It was yes, but an enjoyable pain." Wu calmly and unnervingly replied.

Wu shuffled on the spot enticingly, her eyes set on Jerry during her words.

"So what do you want to know? That sweet Becky came to me a couple months back?" Wu hastened to ask.

"Yes, start at the beginning." Murphy confirmed.

"Becky was young, full figured, tits I could worship for days on end. She impressed me enough in her initiation feed, I was deeply disappointed when she refused to join me in my bed. I guess she preferred wrestling big muscular snakes to opening juicy oysters." Wu cryptically spoke.

She crossed her legs and placed her hands on the desk to support her upright posture, pushing out her small yet tantalising chest that only Murphy looked at.

"Initiation feed?" Jerry wondered to himself, before remembering the jar of octopuses by Wu's side.

"So if one of your new girls doesn't sleep with you you kick her out? Sounds like quite the job interview! When can I start right?" Murphy jabbed.

"I didn't fire her detectives, she quit. Besides hardly any girls refuse me these days. So you could say I was a little insulted." Wu said.

"Insulted enough to have her killed? Didn't want word of your failing appeal to get out on to Easy Street?" Jerry asked, hoping to provoke a reaction.

Wu glared at Jerry after this line of questioning. She stood up to walk over to him, her hips sensually swaying from side to side with each step. Stopping only a few inches away from his face Wu looked deep into Jerry's eyes again. Jerry stood his ground, knowing this was a power play. She was close enough that he could feel her breath on him, the salty yet sweet smell of seafood filled his nostrils. She reached round her back to unhook her bra. Dropping it to the ground, Wu now stood completely topless in front of the detectives, watching to see if Jerry would be bold enough to take a look at her bare chest. Jerry locked his gaze with Wu's, her eyebrow raised as a smile slowly grew.

So captivated by Wu's alluring presence, Jerry had failed to notice the two statue like bodyguards behind her had reached into their jackets to clasp a weapon of some kind.

"You don't find me appealing detective?" Wu softly questioned, hoping he would crack under pressure and look down.

"No." Jerry lied, feeling a rush of blood to his loins.

The smell of incense encircled him further, filling his lungs before going straight to his already weary head.

"A girlfriend you have? Wife maybe?" Wu coyly pried.

"No." Jerry lied again, trying to keep his mind on Grace.

"I bet you taste good regardless" Wu pried further, seductively licking her lips.

"So Becky quit and went to work for the Fox Glove instead?" Jerry asked, trying to get his enquiry back on track.

Ignoring this question Wu leaned closer to Jerry's left side.

"I could make you very happy." Wu softly propositioned into Jerry's ear.

"No you couldn't." Jerry replied.

"Liar. I bet you I can. Again and again…and again." Wu whispered further.

As she moved to face him again Jerry's eyes fell to the dribbles of ink staining her lower lip and chin, struggling to hold back his arousal quickly growing down below. Wu cocked her eyebrow upwards again, trying to get a rise out of Jerry but seemingly failed. She sighed and slowly stepped away, each bodyguard returning their arm to their sides empty handed.

"You don't scare easily do you detective." Wu noticed.

"Why should I be scared?" Jerry quickly returned.

"Most men are." Wu proudly admitted.

"You know better than to threaten an officer of the law Wu." Murphy finally chimed in.

"I don't hurt my girls detectives and you won't find any of my DNA on our poor unfortunate Becky. I was so saddened to hear of her demise, I certainly hope you catch this maniac soon. I want my girls to feel safe when they walk home at night." Wu worried.

She returned to sit on her desk, placing one hand on the jar of octopuses and lightly drummed her fingers on the lid.

"You'll be hearing from us soon." Jerry said, hoping this was the end of their enquiries.

"My memory can be a little hazy these days. Maybe you'll come back to see me again detective?" Wu teased.

"Here's my number, just in case you remember anything else." said Jerry.

He tentatively handed his card to Wu, locking her gaze instead of looking at her chest. He didn't want to give this creature any more access to him but it was standard procedure.

Wu reached out to take the card from his hand, her index finger softly stroking his. Jerry recoiled and went to make for the door, side stepping her bra on the floor.

"And no more octopuses! Or else I'll be back here to issue you with charges of animal cruelty Wu!" Jerry firmly cautioned.

"Wu? Who said I was Wu?" questioned the woman sitting on the desk.

A confused Jerry turned around to face her, again resisting the allure of her naked upper body.

"How'd you know Wu wasn't the elderly woman earlier? Or the girl who led you to this room? Or the girl in the booth?" the inked soaked woman teased the detectives further.

"No more octopuses." Jerry repeated as he and Murphy left the room to exit the building.

The sound of the woman's mumbled laughter mixing with the groans of men being massaged either side of them chased the detectives down the corridor as they left.

Once both men tripped back outside into the hot sweaty night air, Jerry began to feel far less disorientated and light headed. Even the foul smelling air of Easy Street wasn't as choking as that of Wu's office.

"What the hell was that all about?" Murphy exclaimed.

"She's quite something that woman." Jerry remarked.

"She took quite the shine to you! How did you know she was Wu?" Murphy asked Jerry.

"I'm not quite sure who she was pretending to be in there Murphy, but I've seen that sort of thing before. Falsely staged meetings so the gang leader can get a measure of their enemies. I took a risk and well it paid off." Jerry said.

"It certainly seemed like you ruffled some of her feathers!" Murphy acknowledged.

"What stories did you hear about her exactly?" Jerry once again asked.

"Well they're only stories, urban legends if you will. But after what we just went through in there I wouldn't be surprised if they were all true." Murphy pondered.

"Did you feel light headed in there? Like something was in the incense?" Jerry asked.

"Now that you mention it yeah, a little. My vision went a little cloudy." Murphy admitted.

Jerry and Murphy began walking back down the narrow alleyway to rejoin Easy Street once again, passing Jade and her sisters along the way.

"That was quick." Ruby noticed.

"Madame is always quick to please" Sapphire smirked.

"Did you get what you came for detectives?" Jade asked aloud to them.

"Not exactly." Jerry politely replied, remembering the knife she held.

"Well if you ever fancy something new, we'll be waiting." Jade coyly propositioned.

Only then did Jerry notice the same black octopus tattoo on the back of Sapphire's neck, before seeing it again on both Jade and Ruby.

"I bet that would be one hell of a threesome, or would it be a foursome?" Murphy joked as they kept walking.

71

"What do you mean?" Jerry asked.

"Three of them, one of you." Murphy prodded, looking to Jerry.

"Me? Why not yourself?" Jerry asked back.

Murphy didn't reply, as if ignoring the question entirely.

Curiosity however crept into Jerry's mind, his lust proving unbound to anything, even knife wielding triplets and octopus eating harlots. Jerry and Murphy briskly passed through Stripe Tease, then the homosexual sector again and then past the earlier whore houses. This time Jenny was nowhere to be seen. She must have snagged herself another client for the next hour. Murphy appeared to be looking for her as they walked on by, before sighing in solemn defeat. Both men returned to the patrol car outside the entrance to Easy Street, narrowly avoiding the Skin Traps.

Jerry climbed into the driver's side and Murphy into the front passenger seat. Murphy sighed loudly to himself again

"Everything alright?" Jerry asked him.

"Legend has it Wu was the personal sex slave to crime boss Hu Tan, big ugly prick who owned nearly all of Bang'd Kok. Chaining her up during the day he had his way with her most nights, with occasional beatings thrown in when he was drunk and violent, or just plain bored. Until one day she finally had enough. Whilst 'taking care of him' she bit it off and ate it right there in front of him. He bled out in minutes as she watched him die." Murphy recounted.

Jerry shuddered at the thought, picturing Wu's lips and chin stained red with blood instead of black with ink.

"She took over his business, no man dare go near her after that. She sold off nearly all his properties, erasing his footprint in Bang'd Kok but kept the Black Octopus for herself. Since no man would go near her personally, her appetites turned to women but her abusive past caught up with her. Any girl or woman who betrays her or tries to leave her would have a limb removed as punishment." Murphy detailed further.

72

Jerry immediately thought back to the one armed girl in the booth.

"So she knows someone or has access to someone who can perform surgical procedures?" Jerry guessed aloud to himself.

"Maybe, but that's not the worse I've heard." Murphy shuddered.

Jerry continued to listen on with worrying interest.

"Some say she is trying to build an immunity to octopus venom by injecting herself with small amounts, numbing herself to pain in the process. Others say she has a dungeon underneath the Black Octopus, where she dabbles in sexual acts involving octopi, holding down her girls as they slide all over them, and sometimes into them! Or her! She's a monster Jerry!" Murphy finished.

"Why has no one reported this?" Jerry asked, with Murphy looking surprised at his comment.

"Because it's Easy Street Jerry. We barely have enough control down here as it is and besides lack of physical evidence. Snitches get stitches remember! These are just rumours after all." Murphy replied.

"So what happens on Easy Street, stays on Easy Street huh?" Jerry shrugged off as he started up the car's engine.

"She's a good prime suspect already though, don't you think?" Murphy asked.

Jerry agreed, now feeling a great need to finally remove his thick heavy jacket, its assistance in concealing his primary weapon no longer necessary. His shirt underneath was soaked through with sweat in numerous patches including under his armpits, lower back and chest. Whether it was due to the night's humid air or Wu's lustful advances Jerry pulled the car away regardless. Taking one final look down Hallow's notorious and sin filled street, he was happy to be leaving it behind.

Chapter Five

The Surgeon

The precinct bull pen was bustling with activity, the crowd mainly comprised of on duty uniformed officers and their arrested perps in tow. Most were still proclaiming their innocence even as they were being processed by the several desk bound clerks, who busily typed their information on to precinct reports. Elsewhere a rag tag collection of handcuffed suspects from other cases awaited their turn in the quickly lengthening queue of perps.

Jerry watched this ensuing hive of ordered chaos whilst he fumbled for some coins in his pocket, before flinging them into an adjacent vending machine. A few hums and clicks later a plastic cup of steaming hot coffee emerged. Jerry took relative caution as he picked up this beverage, along with a second for Vincent made earlier.

Jerry held both cups out in front of him as he precariously carried the hot liquids through the jostling crowd, narrowly avoiding spilling the contents on himself. He was glad to finally reach his office, closing the door behind him and sealing himself off from the noisy going ons outside. Vincent was back sitting at his desk opposite Jerry's, removing his reading glasses and looking up from his paperwork. His bout of the flu had finally subsided.

"Here you are partner," Jerry said, handing Vincent his tea. "how you feeling?"

"Much better thanks. Back from the dead so to speak." a hoarse sounding Vincent chuckled, causing him to hack and cough loudly.

After a minor coughing fit and spitting forth mucous into a tissue, Vincent finally composed himself.

"Sounds like you're not completely over it yet old man. Do I need to book you in for your free flu shot? A man of your advanced age can't be too careful now." Jerry joked.

"Did I miss anything important?" Vincent questioned, ignoring his partner's light hearted jab.

He thumbed through the small pile of paperwork on his desk, hoping to find the piece he needed.

"Yeah quite a bit," Jerry began. "looks like we have the makings of a serial killer on our hands after all, using those plastic figures to tell us who will be their next victim."

"It says here the latest one was a surgeon, any connection to the victim?" Vincent read aloud from the report he was able to finally find.

He peered over his reading glasses at Jerry judgmentally, like a stern librarian distracted by a troublesome noise maker.

"Not yet. We're waiting on lab reports from Ed. We even took a python as evidence." Jerry chuckled, seeing the funny side to the unorthodox situation.

"Yes it says here that it belonged to the most recent victim, Rebecca 'Becky' Childs." Vincent read.

"She was a stripper at the Fox Glove, after leaving the Black Octopus a few weeks prior." Jerry recounted.

"The Black Octopus," Vincent mused. "I have heard things about that place."

"Murphy and I went to question the owner about Becky, well who we thought was the owner anyway, Madame Wu." Jerry informed.

"You actually met her?" Vincent said, sounding surprised.

"Sort of. Anyway Murphy and I thought that as the snake may have been in contact with Becky's clients it may still have traces of their DNA on its skin, pointing us towards a potential suspect. My guess is the killer knew her somehow." Jerry said.

"You know that snakes shed their skin right?" Vincent rhetorically asked.

Jerry felt a sinking feeling in his stomach as his momentary hopes of having a suspect were quickly quashed by Vincent's knowledge of basic reptile biology.

"Chances are that any DNA evidence on the snake may have been lost days, maybe weeks ago." Vincent added.

"Well let's just hope that Becky's snake didn't feel like shedding this time huh!" Jerry retorted.

"And what of the figures? Anything on them?" Vincent followed up.

"No, nothing on record yet," Jerry said. "the killer could be manufacturing them by themselves."

"So look into model repairmen and toy makers in and around the city," Vincent instructed. "we have a possible lead there."

Their deducing was suddenly cut short by the loud ringing of Vincent's desk phone. Being the superior officer working the case he once again answered. After a minute of silence he put the phone down, stood up and began to get ready to leave.

"Let's go. That was Edward down in the morgue. He says we have some new evidence." Vincent announced.

Jerry followed suit, taking his cup of milky coffee with him.

Back down in the precinct's morgue both detectives were greeted by Edward once more. Becky's body was on the table next to him, partially covered by the thick body bag she was in.

"Good thinking on taking the snake for evidence Jerry." Edward smiled, showing his irregular teeth.

"You got something for us Ed?" Jerry asked.

"Oh my yes! We dusted it for fingerprints and came up with two sets. Even managed to find a minute semen sample." Edward cheerfully responded.

"Gross." Jerry gagged.

"How did you manage that?" Vincent wondered.

"Well the slippery devil gave me quite the run around, even snapped at me a couple of times." Edward recounted,

76

looking over at a large glass vivarium that housed the snake in question.

Jerry walked over to inspect the large serpent once more. Its lifeless yellow eyes had now clouded over into a light grey colour.

"Why are its eyes grey? Is it dead?" Jerry bluntly questioned.

"No, Jerry. Samson is just getting ready to shed. Looks like you got him here just in time." Edward said.

"You named it?" Vincent asked puzzled.

"What? It's not like Samson is going anywhere soon. Do you think the department would let me keep him?" Edward childishly asked.

"I have no idea Edward." Vincent said.

"How do you even know it's male?" Jerry asked.

"I probed him." Edward responded rather innocently enough.

This remark caused Jerry to snigger at his easily misleading choice of words.

"You what? Ed, I didn't know you were...like that!" Jerry prodded sarcastically.

"What? Oh haha, very funny Jerry! I'd expect that sort of school boy humour from Murphy, not least of all you." Edward snorted.

"Anyway back to the case." Vincent spoke aloud, ushering the conversation back on to the topic at hand.

"One set of prints belongs to the victim Rebecca and the second we're running now. Plus the semen and hair sample I found embedded under one of Samson's scales. Results should be ready soon enough." Edward summarised.

"Looks like me may have a suspect then." Vincent said upbeat.

"Or another dead end lead." Jerry pessimistically replied.

"I'll let you know as soon as we get a match." Edward reassured.

As the detectives turned to leave the morgue Jerry suddenly stopped as if something had caught his attention, looking to Vincent, then at Edward, before back to Vincent.

"What is it?" Vincent asked, seeing the concern in his young partner's eyes.

"I just have this feeling. Most serial killers like to take something from their victims, either a possession or body part as a sort of trophy." Jerry detailed, looking again curiously at Edward.

"You don't think Edward could be the killer?" Vincent asked.

"He did ask to have Becky's snake, has knowledge of human anatomy and has access to tools needed to dissect a body." Jerry said.

Jerry looked again at Edward as he zipped up Rebecca's body bag, starting to think he could very well be a killer. He fitted the usual serial killer profile; Caucasian male, aged between twenty and thirty five, a loner and even surrounded by death on a professional basis. There was nothing really to stop Edward from taking his work home with him.

"Should we keep an eye on him then you think?" Jerry pondered.

"No I don't think we need to. I like your train of thought on the matter kid but I've known Edward for some years now. He's definitely not the kind of person to go out and do this sort of thing" Vincent reassured.

At that moment Jerry's phone rang out. On the other end was the Foxx, to Jerry's surprise.

"Good day detective." the Foxx beamed in his shrill tone.

"What can I do for you Fred?" Jerry replied.

"I just thought you'd like to know for your investigation that one of Becky's regulars hasn't been coming as often to the club since he heard the news. He was her biggest tipper. Some of the girls here referred to him as Dr Cock" the Foxx detailed.

"Is he a doctor?" Jerry quickly asked.

The loathsome Foxx could very well have a big lead here Jerry thought.

"I haven't the faintest idea detective, sorry." the Foxx apologised.

"Did you see him? What does he look like?" Jerry questioned.

"Quite tall, athletic, good looking chap, a real lady killer if I dare say so. Excuse my phrasing there. Some of my hens say that he was always interested in her implants, more than the usual lot!" the Foxx laughed to himself.

"Can you give me a full name or even surname?" Jerry probed further.

"That's all I know detective. The men they come, they pay, they drink, they look at the girls, some cum again and then leave. None stay long enough for idle chit chat with either us or one another." the Foxx summarised.

"Well if you or any of your staff see him again you let me know immediately!" Jerry firmly instructed.

"Can do sonny. Good day to you." the Foxx replied, sounding almost charming.

Jerry hung up the phone and turned to Vincent.

"Do we have a lead then?" Vincent asked.

"We do, a 'Dr Cock', good with women, potential knowledge of human anatomy. Could be promising." Jerry said, sounding optimistic.

As the detectives moved to leave the morgue Edward came running over to them.

"Detectives we just got the results through! Brilliant timing. We have a match on the hair sample and second set of prints! A Dr Joshua Langland MD. He is a plastic surgeon over at Hallow City General Hospital!" Edward frantically filled in.

"Son of a bitch!" Jerry exclaimed loudly.

Vincent got on his phone to immediately call in support, thinking they could still have time to save or arrest him, whether he was guilty or innocent.

"What's he doing on the system?" Jerry asked.

"Past record of domestic abuse against his fiancée," Edward informed. "slapped her around pretty good by the sound of it. He was arrested but she never pressed any charges against him."

Jerry immediately thought of his own fiancée Grace and how he would never harm her in such a way. He had no patience for men who beat women.

"Ok thanks." Vincent said over the phone, before hanging up.

"And?" Jerry motioned.

"We have a SWAT team heading over to Hallow City General now and another heading to his home address" Vincent informed.

"Let's go then!" Jerry insisted.

The detectives followed closely behind the first SWAT van, their combined sirens blaring through the city as they speedily made their way to the address Edward had provided.

"What do you think? Guilty or innocent?" Vincent asked Jerry, referring to Dr Langland.

"Guilty I hope, so we can finally catch this killer and end this!" Jerry answered.

Joshua's home address was on the Western outskirts of the city, in a quaint little housing district. Evidently he had planned to marry his fiancée then set up home there. The armoured SWAT van pulled over and immediately the back doors exploded open as the entire team quickly exited the vehicle. All eight of them were heavily protected with Kevlar body armour, helmets and armed to the teeth with semi automatic firearms, with a few shotguns and a couple of handguns between them. They weren't taking any chances it appeared.

Leading the operation and exiting the vehicle last was Commander Randall Briers, a large, muscular and quick tempered man whose fuse was as short as his bright red hair.

Adorning his slightly scarred face from years of brutal combat service was a handle bar moustache and goatee combo. Commander Briers was a man not to mess with, his knowledge of firearm usage, self defence and martial arts deeply ingrained into his very genes. The eight members of his team moved quickly to surround the house, in turn drawing a crowd of neighbourhood spectators.

"Y'all stay in ya houses now ya hear!" Briers commanded at the top of his lungs to the neighbours in his southern drawl.

At the risk of announcing his teams arrival even further, Briers was confident he would catch his man regardless.

Vincent and Jerry exited their own car and waited for orders themselves. The Commander was running this show and his word was law. Once the entrances and exits to the house were guarded Jerry could hear all the SWAT team members call in their positions over Briers' radio.

"Ok move in," Briers instructed his team. "decks you follow!"

Jerry couldn't help but smirk to himself at the abbreviation the Commander had given to his accompanying detectives. One SWAT personnel caved in the front door with a miniature battering ram, then moved aside for other team members to enter. As the men charged around the house shouting instructions to one another a woman's screams could be heard over the commotion. Vincent moved in first, his gun in his hand ready for any violent resistance that could follow. Towards the back of the house in the living room was a young terrified woman, completely bewildered by what was going on.

"Who are you? What's going on? Get out of my house!" she brashly shouted back.

Her hands were raised up in defence, ideal given the number of guns now pointing at her.

"Mrs Langland?" Jerry asked.

"No, Miss Cohen! Wrong house you moron!" she replied, hands still raised.

"Does a Joshua Langland live here? Where is he?" Vincent followed up.

"The hell should I know! I kicked that son of a bitch out months ago!" she yelled back.

"He doesn't live at this address?" Jerry asked.

"No, what's this all about?" Miss Cohen questioned.

It was quickly clear to the detectives that she had not married Joshua after all.

"Miss, do you know where he is? Can you get into contact with him?" Vincent asked her again.

"No I cut that arsehole out of my life the minute he laid a finger on me!" the distraught yet angry woman replied.

Commander Briers suddenly got a call from his second SWAT team over at Hallow City General and answered.

"Seriously?! Fuck! Well where then?" Briers yelled out.

Jerry looked over in his direction to try and listen in on what was going on.

"Decks! Get over here!" Briers called out to them.

Jerry and Vincent left Miss Cohen in the company of the SWAT team to answer the call from Commander Briers.

"That's some real fuckin' great intel you decks gave us! Langland ain't at the hospital, his damn day off. Silver lining however. Staff records confirmed his new home address for us." Briers informed.

"Our records must not have been updated." Vincent muttered to himself.

"Go to that address and wait for my arrival. Team we're moving out now!" Briers commanded down the phone before hanging up.

The Commander's team stormed out of Miss Cohen's home, followed by Jerry and Vincent and then Briers himself.

"Hey wait! Who's going to pay for the damage you big apes did to my house?" Miss Cohen shouted from her front porch.

"Send your bill to the HCPD. I'll see to it that those two deck heads over there get it taken care of. But right now we gotta move!" Briers shouted back.

He continued to strut powerfully towards the van, giving both Jerry and Vincent a look that would kill. Jerry could practically smell the testosterone oozing out of him, making the young detective feel very inadequate.

Jerry, Vincent and Briers soon arrived into central Hallow, only a few blocks away from the river. Outside the apartment building that housed Doctor Langland's new address, the SWAT van screeched to a halt. The van's back doors exploded open once more and the team yet again quickly poured out on to the street. The second team was already there waiting. Commander Briers swaggered over to them to detail his next plan of attack.

"We have all the exits guarded sir, no visual on the suspect just yet." one SWAT personnel informed Commander Briers.

"OK good. You, you and you come with me." Briers instructed, pointing a stern finger at the remaining members of team two.

Vincent and Jerry both surveyed the outside of the apartment block, the doctor's own apartment was located on the twenty first floor. Some of the building's many windows were now filled by dozens of worried faces, curious to know what the commotion was about down on the city streets.

"Let's move in!" Briers ordered.

He motioned for both teams to enter the building by circling his hand above his head.

Some SWAT members moved to climb the fire exits on the outside of the building. Briers and the rest of his team moved to enter through the front lobby. Some branched off to climb the flight of stairs whilst other used the only elevator. Jerry and Vincent were the last two into the building and so missed the elevator going up.

"Looks like we are climbing kid." Vincent directed at Jerry.

As Jerry quickly ascended the long spiralling staircase, the sound of the SWAT team's heavy footsteps and gun clips jangling against the steel railings echoed down from above like metallic rain. After several minutes of puffing and panting up the stairs the detectives finally arrived on the twenty first floor. They moved into the hallway and down towards the doctor's apartment, passing by numerous other apartment doors.

In an almost deafening silence several SWAT members were crowded around one door in particular, labelled 21A. All Jerry could hear was the sound of his pulse racing either side of each ear, along with the deep breaths he was inhaling and exhaling.

"Ok go!" Briers ordered.

The same battering ram from earlier was now being used again to knock in this particular apartment door.

In went the SWAT team as Vincent and Jerry waited outside in the hallway. After some initial noisy shouting and commotion from the SWAT team an eerie silence filtered out of the apartment. The unsettling silence continued to grow, like an inaudible cancer. A few moments later the only sound Vincent and Jerry could hear was the Commander's hoarse voice calling out for them.

"Decks! Ya'll better get in here!" ordered Briers from inside.

Vincent entered first, gun in hand, and followed the trail of the Commander's call into the only bedroom. Jerry entered second and tailed Vincent's path. There on a pristinely clean white bed was Dr Joshua Langland, only he was dead. The detectives were too late to save him. Divided into the killer's trademark five sections, Joshua was slightly different to the other three victims before him.

His hands had been cut off from the wrist and lay a few inches away from where they were once attached. All the main cutting areas, as well as the wrists and hands, had been sealed in the expected melted plastic, this time white in colour. To his left hand was a scalpel and to his right a stethoscope, mirroring the figure from Becky. His genitals were also noticeably absent, having been previously cut away and removed.

"What the fuck is all this? I was expecting a living perp or body at least...but this! They took his dick and nuts?!" Briers exclaimed as he looked down upon this sterile scene.

"We're still not really sure what this is." Jerry replied honestly.

"Well it's nice to see you decks are doing ya job properly!" Briers sarcastically snorted.

"This is slightly different to the others. The killer is trying out new things to see what they like and what they don't." Jerry said, noticing the hands.

"They are evolving." Vincent poignantly added.

Jerry moved to look inside Joshua's mouth, so eager to see what was inside he almost forgot to put on gloves. Dr Langland had a very angular jaw line ending with an amusing baby's bottom chin. His forehead was smooth and lacked any wrinkles, even for his middle age. It appeared he had been dipping into his own supply of Botox injections. Short brown hair and an athletic physique, he looked very much like the description the Foxx had given Jerry over the phone. His midriff was a six pack collection of highly defined abdominal muscles, even with the main severing of his two halves.

Despite his chiselled adonis frame, the surgeon's body was not entirely without its flaws. Numerous bite mark scars decorated his chest, shoulders and arms. The indentations of each singular tooth could be easily distinguished.

"Who do you suppose made those then? Our killer?" Jerry asked Vincent.

"Unlikely. We would be able to take an impression from the scarring and narrow down a suspect through dental records. Our killer would not be that stupid surely?" Vincent wondered.

Once gloved Jerry reached inside the mouth to pull out yet another small plastic figure, this one appearing to be a merman. It had a long dark brown beard with long brown hair, a fish tail instead of legs and a three pronged trident accessory.

"Looks to me like either Neptune or Poseidon. I forget which is Greek and which is Roman" Vincent admitted whilst admiring this new figure.

"So maybe we should go question a professor of archaeology and see if he likes to cut people up in his spare time" Jerry retorted.

"That ain't a bad idea Deck, although archaeology is the study of ancient buildings and structures. Ya'll want a professor in Roman or Greek history slash mythology instead." Briers quipped, amused by Jerry's minor misunderstanding of archaeology.

"Ah hell." Jerry huffed.

"Looks like our killer cut off his hands possibly to spite him being a surgeon, no longer holding people's very lives in his hands." Vincent guessed.

"He was a plastic surgeon Deck. Boob jobs, face lifts and tummy tucks ain't exactly life saving surgery!" Briers chimed in.

"Perhaps for some people they are." Vincent responded.

On the other side of the room, opposite the bed, was a large television set, a video camera complete with tripod for filming and a video cassette player. On top of the cassette player were several blank tapes, each one labelled down the spine with a number and woman's name in bold black marker. Jerry walked over and read the names aloud.

"1 Rosie, 2 Mary, 3 Tracey, 4 Candy, 5 Gypsy, 6 Judy and 7 Rebecca." Jerry recited aloud, stopping at Rebecca.

"Rebecca?" Vincent asked.

"Could be our Becky Childs maybe?" Jerry replied hopefully.

He turned to look at the stethoscope laying next to the doctor. Jerry picked it up to better examine it.

"I don't get it. Roberta was in an art studio, Peter was in his butcher's shop, Becky was near her snake charming profession but Joshua isn't in the corresponding location to his figure. Why?" Jerry questioned.

"Greater risk of being seen in a hospital. My guess is that the killer is adapting to what is available." Vincent theorised.

"True, but surely this disrupts their usual pattern of work?" Jerry wondered.

"Call in Edward and forensics. Do not touch anything else until they are here." Vincent instructed.

He motioned for Jerry to replace the stethoscope back on the bed.

"No need for my team and I to stick around any longer. You decks and ya lab tech geeks have fun with...this!" remarked Commander Briers.

He circled his highly defined knuckled hand over Joshua's divided body. Briers and his SWAT team soon exited the apartment to head back down to the ground floor, leaving Vincent and Jerry alone with the corpse of Dr Langland.

Back at the precinct the detectives came to learn the connection between Becky and Joshua. Hospital records showed that Dr Langland was Becky's consultant plastic surgeon for her breast augmentation. After the surgery Dr Langland would apparently go to visit her quite often at the Fox Glove, obviously taking great pride in his work. This it turned out was what led to his engagement ending with his fiancée, that and his momentary abusive ways towards her. The detectives sat down to watch the tapes from Joshua's apartment but by the end they wish they hadn't.

Starting in numerical order with Rosie, each videotape contained a violent sexual encounter, filmed by Joshua on the very bed the detectives found him. The videos appeared to have been filmed in secret from a hidden location on one side of the room. It all started innocently enough, each girl appearing to be there of her own free will, even smiling and joking with the quite charismatic man. All of the women appeared to be prostitutes.

The doctor started by undressing each woman and then giving his honest opinion on any work their bodies needed. He took a black marker and outlined the areas where he thought they needed work done. Some needed liposuction, others nose jobs, excess skin removal or breast enhancement. Joshua would then go over price and contraception for the evening. The woman would then undress him before the pair moved on to various sexual acts.

This didn't last long as the doctor soon decided to take things in a far rougher direction, insisting he tie the women up and gag them. When he ignored their requests for more payment or the girls refused his advances he became more forceful with them. He called them vile names before proceeding to beat and then violently rape them. The sound of their terrified screams and cries of agony proved too much for Vincent, causing him to turn the volume to mute.

"Another serial rapist escapes true justice." Vincent sighed.

"Well at least he got some comeuppance in the end." Jerry replied.

"How did none of his neighbours hear any of this?" Vincent asked himself.

"Maybe sound proofed walls. Why haven't any of the girls come forward about this yet?" Jerry asked also.

The detectives finally came to the seventh tape labelled 'Rebecca', hoping it might hold some answers to all this. Same as the other girls before her, Becky appeared to be there of her own free will, playfully flirting and groping the beast of a surgeon. The two engaged in some oral foreplay, with Jerry struggling to control his arousal upon viewing this. It was nice to see Becky alive, even if the knowledge of her impending death loomed over the situation. The image of her body writhing around and cavorting gave the impression that her snake tattoo had come alive. However this encounter was unlike the others. There was no mention of money just contraception. Dr Langland didn't get violent towards Becky or force her down to rape her. Instead the two just lay there after the sex and just talked, the doctor appearing to be almost in love with her. He commented a lot about her breasts, evidently he was still egotistically proud of his work. With the sight of them just laying there the tape's footage came to an abrupt end.

"Becky wasn't a prostitute though. And where are these girls now? He turns off the camera after the rapes but not with Becky!" Jerry remarked aloud.

"Maybe that is why she was spared. I also did not see any of the girls actually bite Joshua." Vincent noticed.

"Me neither. So whoever made those marks on his body remains a mystery for now." Jerry replied.

"We will get Edward to take an impression of each, see if they are all the same or different." Vincent added.

"The footage shows the date and time in the corner. Rebecca's footage was only a few weeks ago but Rosie's was months back." Jerry noted down.

Jerry went through all the tapes again to make a more accurate note of the date and time for each of the victims.

"See! There is a pattern. The footage of Rosie's rape was nearly three months ago and the following girls every two weeks afterwards." Jerry declared.

"We should check missing persons." Vincent instructed as he got up to leave the room.

Once Vincent was gone, Jerry replayed the tape with Becky on it again to try and understand why she was spared the doctor's darker tastes. The only reason Jerry could fathom was that Dr Langland was just so proud of his work on Becky's breast enlargement. Murphy entered into the room as the footage came to when Becky was giving the doctor oral. Jerry immediately stopped the tape's footage, Murphy's sudden appearance catching him off guard.

"Should I leave you alone to finish then clean up?" Murphy joked to Jerry.

"Shut up Murphy. You wouldn't be making jokes if you had seen the footage of the other girls!" Jerry snapped.

"Let's have a gander then." Murphy suggested.

Murphy sat down to view the footage from the other tapes. After watching only Rosie's footage, Murphy stopped the tape and sat in stunned silence for a moment.

"Are they all like this?" he worryingly asked, the shock of the footage apparent in his trembling voice.

"All except for Becky. The doctor seemed to like her too much to do anything else." Jerry replied.

"Well at least this twisted bastard got what he deserved!" Murphy retorted.

"Are you saying we should be thanking the real killer here?" Jerry asked.

"Not necessarily. All I'm saying is that sometimes it takes another monster to take down an even greater monster." Murphy philosophised.

Murphy got up to exit the room, leaving his somewhat profound words to stew inside Jerry's mind. He had to admit that Murphy made some sense. The killer must have known the doctor and what he was secretly doing. It was too much of a coincidence that the killer had targeted this vile rapist. Even the tapes in the apartment had been laid out in a sort of presentation for the detectives to more easily discover them.

Back in their office, after a sweltering weekend, Vincent and Jerry continued to amount the growing evidence in regards to the figure killings. No clues or leads were found in any of the city's toy stores. Not one person recognised any of the figures found with each of the victims. Their design and manufacture still remained a mystery.

On their white board, hanging alongside photos of both Roberta and Peter, were now photos of Becky and Joshua with their corresponding figures. The girls from the footage found at the apartment had not been reported missing. After questioning the Skin Traps working Easy Street's entrance and presenting them with photos of the girls, the detectives soon discovered the girls from Joshua's tapes to have been Skin Traps themselves.

Vincent deduced this to have been the main reason why Joshua had targeted these girls, knowing full well that no one would go looking for them or even care about their sudden absence from Easy Street .

"So those poor girls were definitely Skin Traps then, prostitutes without a pimp or establishment to work for." Vincent summarised.

"Yes. Ed's examination of Joshua's body came up with nothing we didn't know already. But again why the melted plastic?" Jerry asked aloud.

"Well Edward said the plastic is melted acrylic. The killer is trying to preserve the bodies further some how, turning them more plastic, like the figures." Vincent said.

"The key factor in all this are the figures. Why is the killer using them and not something else?" Jerry asked.

"We also have a pattern to the victims. Female, male, female then male again." Vincent noticed.

"You think our Merman victim will be a woman?" Jerry asked.

"Mermaid maybe?" Vincent guessed, rubbing his stubbly chin in thought.

All of a sudden the detective's office door burst open and a man roughly older than Vincent rushed in, slamming a newspaper down on Vincent's desk.

"What the hell is this?" he asked angrily.

Vincent picked up the paper and read aloud the front page headline.

"Figure Killer Prowls Hallow." he read.

91

"You went to the press with this?!" the man asked.

"No of course not Glenn." Vincent pleaded innocently.

"Then how did they get hold of this information? They got the names for some the victims! Answer me that!" the Chief snapped, a big ugly throbbing vein appearing on his forehead.

Chief of Police Glenn Matthews was typically an even tempered man, with his narrow nose firmly pressed against the proverbial grinding stone. He was a stickler for the rule book and was prone to letting his thirst for justice get the better of him now and again, presenting an almost schizophrenic quick temper.

Chief Matthews was a man slightly older than Vincent yet somehow still in peek physical fitness. He had a muscular build, which Jerry attributed to his strict swimming routine, and a head full of slightly upturned thick white hair. The Chief wore an equally as thick greying moustache below his protruding nose and small tired eyes.

Having been promoted much later in his career than he had hoped, the Chief was far more of a General than Chief of Police, barking orders at his constituents daily. Jerry remembered his first interview with this man and all the difficult questions he had been asked. The Chief knew 'his' city was a cess pool of crime and wanted the best men for the job, 'no limp dick pansies' as he put it.

Jerry could tell the Chief wanted to clean up the city as much as he could within the brief window of time bestowed upon him and his title. The young detective respected this fact about the man, Jerry himself undertaking his new position at the precinct for exactly the same reason as the Chief.

"I know you've already got one foot out of the door here Harrington, but that doesn't mean you can coax by with your eyes closed until then got it?" the Chief warned.

"Honestly we have no idea how this info got out Sir." Jerry pleaded his innocence also.

"Well somebody must have talked! And I want to know who by the end of today or heads will roll! Starting with yours!"

the Chief ordered Vincent, pointing an angry wavering finger at him.

The Chief turned to leave the office, before slamming the door behind him as he left. Vincent appeared unfazed by this empty threat, but Jerry immediately began to worry over the loss of his job. Never the less Vincent held relative distain for his over bearing superior.

"The Figure Killer," Jerry repeated as he read aloud from the newspaper. "catchy name."

"Well it was only a matter of time until the press got wind of all this. They always do somehow." Vincent uttered downbeat.

"Ah hell!" Jerry all of a sudden remarked at himself.

"What is it?" Vincent asked concerned.

"When Murphy and I went to investigate Becky's body at the Fox Glove, the owner and his bodyguard were there too. They might have overheard details about the figures from Murphy and I. Maybe they went to the press." Jerry admitted.

"Get down there now and find out for certain," Vincent asserted. "I will keep digging to see if I can find anything more on these figures."

Jerry soon found himself dubiously back in the Fox Glove again to speak with Freddy Foxx personally. Walking back and forth down Easy Street was starting to become a regular occurrence for the detective. During his travels he had nearly always noticed Jenny, Murphy's young friend, even greeting her every now and then. When Jerry had passed by the entrance to Bang'd Kok he had nearly always received three girlish waves from Madame Wu's guardian triplets.

The Fox Glove was back in business and Jerry found himself to be surrounded by its numerous male clients, most of whom were staring at the young women on stage. Whilst waiting at the bar for the Foxx's arrival Jerry noticed the buxom barmaid from his first visit had been replaced by another beauty, but she didn't appeal to the young detective as much as the previous one did.

The strange music of the Fox Glove in no way matched the beat to which the women were dancing to on stage. Jerry looked around at the range of male clients, also several female ones, that had come here for their own release. As Jerry watched one man sipping his Bourbon on the rocks at the bar he noticed the wedding ring on his left hand. It was early afternoon on a weekday. So this man was either skiving off work or worse, time away from his wife and family.

Jerry knew he was better than that, even if his loyalty to Grace had recently wavered now and again. He would never cheat on her for some fling with a cheap floozie. At that moment Jerry wanted to leave the Fox Glove as quickly as he had arrived, he didn't want to spend another minute in there.

"Ah detective! What can I do for you?" the Foxx spoke aloud over the dreadful music.

The massive mountain of a man known as Dutchy closely shadowed the Foxx from behind.

"Skip the pleasantries Fred! Why did you go to the press with Becky's murder?" Jerry forcefully asked.

"Very direct. I like it. Well they came by one day. You see the press pay good money for information in this city detective. I do well with my hens here but it never hurts to have a little more loose change in your pocket. You're new to Hallow but you'll soon come to realise how things really work around here." the Foxx advised.

"Do you realise what you've done? Now the whole city will be in a panic over yet another serial killer stalking the streets!" Jerry yelled over the music, but somehow not drawing any attention to him.

"Isn't that a good thing sonny? Letting the people know that there is another maniac out there so they know to stay alert, ever watchful for danger?" the Foxx justified, making some sense in Jerry's mind.

Jerry didn't say anything in return, looking as though this pimp had made some sense, and the Foxx had seen it.

"Here detective. Grab a seat, stay a while and take the load of your feet. Have a drink on the house!" the Foxx politely offered.

He snapped his fingers in the direction of the barmaid.

"Sybil! A drink for this fine young man here, what ever he wants!" the Foxx instructed.

The new barmaid approached Jerry with a second snap from the Foxx's stubby fingers.

"What'll it be handsome?" Sybil asked.

"Orange juice" Jerry replied, figuring a free drink wouldn't hurt.

"No liquor?" the Foxx scoffed.

"I'm on duty" Jerry quipped.

"That never stopped some of your peers" the Foxx smirked.

"Coming right up." Sybil answered, before turning around to prepare his drink.

Sybil wore the same barmaid outfit as the girl from before, complete with the same Fox ear hair band. She was a little more built than the last girl, more meaty, with even the same long blonde hair. The Foxx appeared to have a particular preference for blondes, seeing as most of the girls working for him were blonde, either natural or dyed.

"She's' nice huh?" the Foxx gleefully commented to Jerry. His creepy smile returned as he looked Sybil up and down.

"Where is the girl from before?" Jerry couldn't help but blurt out.

"Who Claudia? Oh she's over there" the Foxx said, directing Jerry's attention back to the main stage.

The buxom barmaid, now known as Claudia, was swinging around the end pole at the very front of the stage. Gone was her smart but professionally sexy barmaid uniform, now replaced by flimsy green netting which encased her entire body. Jerry was immediately captivated by her again, unable to take his eyes off her naked form. Her hair was no longer tied back. Instead it now cascaded down over her milky shoulders and circled around her delicate face as she swung around. As the pole she was swinging on periodically changed colour from red to pink, its luminous glow further enhanced all her natural womanly curves.

Now being showered in singles from her nearby punters, Claudia climbed further up the pole, before wrapping her well toned legs around it and sliding slowly down head first. Her minuscule green casing suddenly made Jerry think back to Becky's tattoo, along with Green's Meats and the green paint on Roberta's pallet.

"It couldn't be that simple of a link could it? Green?" he thought to himself aloud.

"What? You like her?" the Foxx guessed.

He could clearly see Jerry's interest in his hen Claudia.

"She's very good, if you know what I mean. She can suck the peel off an apple, or a golf ball through a length of garden hose." the Foxx gushed.

Jerry was once again completely mesmerised by this woman.

"I like you detective, so if you ever want anything more with her I'll give you a good discount price ok?" offered the Foxx.

"Thanks for the drink." Jerry replied without answering.

He got up to leave, but not before quietly contemplating this offer and downing the rest of his orange juice.

"Ok, well if you ever change your mind then another time perhaps?" the Foxx pitifully tried again to reel in Jerry's business.

"I'm engaged so no thanks." Jerry remarked,

"Like that ever stopped a man," the Foxx mused. "just remember to glove up before you love up my hens."

Jerry turned to leave the Foxx and his sleazy ways. But as Jerry left he couldn't help but take one final look back at Claudia. She recognised him this time, smiling and waving before blowing him a kiss from across the room. Temptation it seemed was everywhere for the young detective and just as inescapable.

Jerry could feel the bass from the music ripple up through his body from the floor, before lingering in his pocket. He quickly realised it was his phone that was now vibrating. Vincent was calling him from the other end of the line.

"Yeah?" Jerry answered, covering his other ear with his hand to shield from the loud music.

"We have got a potential lead. Head back to the precinct now." Vincent instructed.

Chapter Six

The Merman

The detectives had scoured Hallow City for any clues or locations that could be linked to a merman, mermaid, Poseidon or Neptune but they had come up with nothing solid. They were into week two of their investigation and the closest lead they had come to was a former sea captain named William Simmons, who had taken ownership of a small bar near to the river, renaming it The Mermaid's Purse. He and his family had been placed under police protection, hoping the Figure Killer wouldn't strike them in any way. Vincent and Jerry had gone to investigate this drinking establishment before all this.

It was a quant little bar, rather heavy on the sea faring theme, even more so than the Black Octopus Jerry had thought when he first visited. An old wooden steering wheel for a large sail boat hung over the bar, draped in an expansive blue fishing net. Entangled within it were numerous plastic fish and buoys. There was even an old antique harpoon hanging on the wall, accompanied by a collection of artworks depicting giant whales sinking mighty whaling ships. But there was no trident to be seen. The busty mermaid on the bar's logo was just as voluptuous as Mr Simmons's barmaid daughter, but she was definitely hands off given the dirty look the former sea captain had given Jerry when the young detective mistakenly ogled her.

A day later a call came into the precinct with a far more promising lead. It was from an elderly woman saying that her husband had not returned home after the evening before. His name was Dr Harold Remington. He was a consultant cardiologist at Hallow City General, the same hospital Dr Langland had previously been working at, before his somewhat karmic death. Vincent and Jerry went to question Mrs Remington further at her stately home on the very edge of North Hallow, hoping she might provide some further clues to her husband's mysterious disappearance.

"When did you last see your husband Mrs Remington?" Vincent began his questioning.

"Last night, before he went out to play poker with some friends of his." she replied.

Her prim and proper accent was heavily laden with snooty overtones, typical of the wealthier upperclass of North Hallow.

"Mrs Remington, does your husband have any connection with someone or something to do with Neptune, Poseidon, a mermaid or even a merman?" Vincent asked.

"What do you mean detective?" Mrs Remington asked back.

A blank expression came across her tired old face, bewildered by Vincent's choice of words.

Jerry couldn't help but behold the extravagant living room he now found himself and Vincent to be sitting in. The whole house reeked of opulent decadence, a fact only further cemented by the detectives having been greeted by the Remington's own personal butler named Wallis upon their earlier arrival. The Remington's were certainly well to do people, nearing the top of Hallow City's financial pyramid.

Mrs Remington sat in an expensive brown leather arm chair opposite a small antique table, complete with a reading lamp. A collection of refined oil paintings adorned the walls of the lounge, each one depicting a family member from previous generations. Mrs Remington was joined by two large imposing Bloodhounds sitting either side of her. Each one kept their gaze firmly on the detectives, suspicious to these two new strangers whom had wondered into their territory.

"Please, it's for our investigation." Jerry followed up Vincent's earlier question.

Jerry moved closer to Mrs Remington to add further urgency to his question, causing both Bloodhounds to begin growling at him. Jerry took the hint and soon backed down to his original position.

"Montague, Bertram, be quiet boys!" Mrs Remington shushed her over protective canines.

Both dogs quietened down, immediately obeying their elderly owner's command.

"Aren't Poseidon and Neptune Gods of the sea? Does this have something to do with the Figure Killer I read about in the paper?" Mrs Remington questioned.

"I'm afraid we can't discuss the details of that case," Jerry answered. "please just think hard for us. Does your husband have any connection to these words?"

Wallis the butler soon returned to the lounge carrying a well polished silver tray in his white gloved hands, so as to not tarnish the surface with his greasy fingerprints. The shiny tray was topped with the finest bone china tea set Jerry had ever laid eyes upon, with detailed blue patterning exquisitely etched down each side.

"Your tea ma'am." Wallis announced, setting down the tray beside Mrs Remington.

"Thank you Wallis, that will be all for now." she instructed.

Jerry didn't think it was possible but Wallis's upper lip was even stiffer than Mrs Remington's, as if a foul odour had gotten lodged up his cavernous nostrils many moons ago. He resembled a penguin that had been kicked through a tuxedo shop, so definitively black and white his uniform was. The immaculately clean butler soon left the room, walking as if his spine were a stiff wooden rod.

Mrs Remington began to casually pour out her tea. It seemed not even her husband's unknown whereabouts would interfere with her extravagant daily rituals. She began to stir in an addition of cream and sugar with an even shinier silver spoon than that of the accompanying tea tray.

100

After a few moments of deep thought and tea sipping Mrs Remington replied.

"Well, Harold was a member of the yacht society after all." she said.

A look of keen interest sparked in both detectives' eyes upon hearing this.

"Yacht society?" Vincent repeated her words.

Jerry wasn't the least bit surprise by this social standing.

"Sorry my memory isn't what it use to be," Mrs Remington apologised. "the ravages of time and so on."

"What else can you remember?" Vincent asked.

"I believe he purchased a new yacht a few months back in preparation for his retirement. It was suppose to be a surprise for me as well but that fell through rather haphazardly. We're moving to Cove City very soon you see. We are going to spend the rest of our days either by the sea or sailing on it." Mrs Remington smiled, picturing this near future.

She began to lovingly stroke both Montague and Bertram's furry heads and napes, confident in her husband's return. Vincent now felt a more personal connection to the case, a fellow soon to be retiree as it were.

"Cove City?" Vincent repeated.

"I believe he named his new yacht The Sea King," Mrs Remington detailed further. "might that mean anything to you?"

Vincent and Jerry as well as Mrs Remington suddenly came to realise the connection, as vague as it was.

"His yacht? The Sea King? Where is it Mrs Remington?" Jerry asked impatiently.

"It's docked in Cove City's main harbour I believe." she replied.

"Thank you Mrs Remington, we have to go now but will be in touch soon." Vincent assured her.

"Please find my Harold for me detectives." Mrs Remington pleaded between sipping her tea.

Tears began to slowly form in the corner of one eye as she continued to stroke her dogs. It almost pained her to show any real emotion towards her husband in full view of others.

Vincent and Jerry arrived into Cove City after a couple of hours of driving. The outside temperature gradually and mercifully reduced the further they got away from Hallow. Along the way the detectives passed by the famous Skull Swamps. It was hard to miss these ecological treasures, being heavily signed posted all up and down the main highway connecting the two cities together. Laying to the West and situated along the coastline, Cove City was a sister city to Hallow, but with considerably less crime. Never the less, the filth from Hallow still managed to spill over into Cove now and again. So the much smaller city still required some real policing.

After navigating their way through the far less crowded Cove City, Vincent and Jerry soon arrived outside the central harbour entrance.

"No sign of the CCPD yet." Jerry noticed as he pulled the car over to park.

"You did call them ahead of our arrival right?" Vincent asked.

"Yeah yeah don't worry. They said they'd be here to meet us. Guess they're a no show." Jerry thought.

"'Let us carry on regardless." Vincent directed.

As Jerry exited the car the warm rays of sunlight hit him instantly and the salty smell of the ocean filled his lungs. He couldn't help but close his eyes and savour this idyllic moment. Until recently it was rare to be so far away from Hallow, away from the decay, crime and choking urban sprawl. Vincent seemed to be enjoying this brief moment of peace too, removing his weighty jacket before hooking it over his strong forearm. He also took off his signature fedora, allowing the warmth of the sun to reach the top of his already balding head. With Hallow's hellish heatwave miles behind them, both detectives took this opportunity to savour the heavenly cooling coastal breeze.

"Well, we did not come all this way for nothing. Better find this boat of his." Vincent thought.

The detectives walked down the numerous jetties of the harbour in search of Dr Remington's boat, the sound of water gently lapping against the boat hulls accompanied them as they went. These gentle waves could be heard even over the noisy cries of local gulls that flew overhead. As they walked past the collection of boats, nearly all facing the jetty stern end, Jerry began to read aloud some of their names.

"Just Hooked, Anchors Away, Salty Dish, The Surly Seamen, Captain's Delight, The Stingray…" Jerry tailed off.

"The doctor's boat is suppose to be near the harbour entrance, among the much larger yachts." Vincent reminded them both.

Jerry discontinued his reading of the boat names aloud to himself, they were all too small to be Dr Remington's anyway. Being an important man of medicine in such high demand must have enabled him to purchase a fine vessel of the sea with his generous annual salary. That and marrying into Mrs Remington's wealthy family.

"I could do with one of those for my own retirement." Vincent announced.

He pointed a boney finger at a large supremely white and silver edged yacht.

"Me too. I can definitely see the appeal of a boating lifestyle." Jerry chimed into this fantasy.

The detectives had reached the section of the harbour where the wealthier members of Cove and Hallow City society anchored their luxury sea farers.

"There it is!" Jerry called out.

He directed Vincent's attention towards a large motor powered yacht with the name 'The Sea King' printed down the starboard side. Both detectives approached this impressive yacht, with

Vincent taking the lead and stepping on to it first. The gap between the jetty and the yacht was only a few feet across. Jerry nervously grabbed hold of the railing before stepping across the watery abyss below.

Now onboard the detectives moved to explore the luxury yacht, going from room to room. The interior decor reeked of wealth and financial security. Cream coloured leather seating areas, pine wood furnishings with golden trimming and even a pleasant beige carpet. A surprisingly large kitchen stored a glass fronted refrigerator, stocked full of white wines, champagne and various other spirits.

"This is certainly the life!" Jerry couldn't help but say aloud.

Briefly basking in this luxurious setting, Jerry shook himself out of his day dreaming and made for the top deck at the front of the yacht, climbing a sturdy wooden staircase to get there. A powerful fishy stench began to hit both detectives as they climbed the small staircase further up to the top deck. They came upon a large flock of gulls that had noisily crowded around what appeared to be a large fish laying motionless on the deck.

"Piss off!" Jerry yelled at the birds, clapping his hands and shouting to spook them away.

As they flew up into the cloudless sky, they unwittingly revealed what they had just been feasting upon.

There on the deck laying before the detectives was Dr Remington, dead and separated into five pieces just like the others. Vincent and Jerry were once again too late to save anyone.

"Ah fuck it! When will this psycho stop?!" Jerry cried out.

Dr Remington was unlike the other victims. In place of his waist and legs lay the headless remains of a very large fish, over a metre in length. His legs were nowhere to be seen. The fish had not been drained or gutted in any way and whilst under the intense unforgiving sunlight had begun to rot and smell. Large areas of it had been pecked apart by the greedy gulls but more gruesomely the doctor's eyes had been pecked out also, leaving behind empty fleshy sockets. The gulls had also begun pecking away at the areas where his body had been cut, despite the melted blue plastic sealant. To his left hand lay an antique three pronged trident exactly the same as the figure's from Dr Langland's corpse.

"Our killer is changing their pattern," Vincent noticed. "a male victim this time and not female as I thought."

"What kind of fish do you suppose that is?" Jerry asked.

"I have no idea. I am not much of a fishermen myself" Vincent quickly answered.

"What the fuck did the killer even do with his legs?" Jerry exclaimed.

The smell of rotting fish was proving too much for Jerry, who had begun to heave and gag at the pungent smell rising up from the dead fish. After gloving his hands Vincent took a deep breath and crouched down beside the doctor to look inside his mouth. From between his teeth he pulled out yet another plastic figure. This one was of a man dressed in a dark green t-shirt and tan coloured shorts. With him was a small tiger cub and the word 'Zoo' printed on his t-shirt.

"The killer could be targeting a zoo keeper next?" Vincent guessed.

He stood up to move away from the body, able to breathe clean air again.

A patrol car siren quickly turned the detectives's attention away from the body.

"Looks like the cavalry has finally arrived! I wonder who they've sent over to hold our hands on this? He's probably some tubby piece of crap, one too many doughnuts and not enough days of real police work. Probably sits on his fat ass all day behind a desk!" Jerry sarcastically scoffed, referring to the Cove City Police.

"I guess we will find out soon enough." Vincent replied.

"We're not far from Hallow City Zoo, we should head over there now. We might still have time to save the next victim, whoever they are. We'll leave Remington here to Dudley Do right over there!" Jerry asserted.

Jerry quickly descended the stairs of the yacht to head back to their patrol car. Vincent soon followed suit, replacing the figure beside Dr Remington's body. The detectives retraced their steps back across the jetty and back towards their vehicle, meeting the Cove City officer who had been called out to the scene half way. Jerry was immediately dumb founded by them, his earlier snide comment now rendered moot.

"Good afternoon gentlemen, I'm Officer Mana of the CCPD." introduced the young woman.

"Afternoon officer. Nice of someone to finally show up. DL Harrington and DI Wilder, HCPD." Vincent introduced in return, motioning between himself and Jerry.

The young detective didn't say a word in response, completely mesmerised by the gorgeous woman standing before him.

She was not what Jerry had envisioned earlier at all. This Polynesian beauty's long black curls were tied back by a band of sea shells bleached white by the sun, uncovering her exotic tanned face. With her dark brown eyes the officer glanced back at Jerry with an enchanting smile. The powerful scents of vanilla and coconut soon swept past his sensitive nose, originating from this Cove City enchantress. With an ample chest and toned physique, Officer Mana appeared as though she took very good care of herself to Jerry's eye.

"I understand there is a body nearby?" Officer Mana enquired downbeat.

"Yes, we discovered it over there on that yacht, named the Sea King. The victim is linked to a case we are working back in Hallow. We have to go now in order to chase up a newer, more promising lead. Our forensics team are on their way to this location now." Vincent informed.

"Understood, I'll have dispatch send out reinforcements to help secure the scene until then." Officer Mana replied.

"Mana? Like the River Mana?" Jerry couldn't help but ask.

"Haha, yes. Nice to have a river named after me." Officer Mana laughed off.

"Let us go Jerry." Vincent instructed, cutting them short.

Jerry looked back at Vincent, momentarily breaking the spell Officer Mana held over him.

"Good day Officer Mana." Jerry said, trying to sound charming as he bid her farewell.

"Bye Jerry." she smiled flirtatiously back at him.

Vincent and Jerry soon left the harbour, leaving the officer by herself. But Jerry couldn't help but take one final look back at the exquisite vision he had just encountered.

"One too many doughnuts, huh?" Vincent repeated with a bemused smile.

The detectives arrived outside the entrance gate to Hallow City Zoo and were greeted by the huge mural of wild animals painted on the walls outside. Hallow City Zoo lay to the West of the city and was only half an hour drive away from the outskirts. Vincent and Jerry immediately made their way inside and through the throbbing crowd to contact the head office.

"Police business, everybody please move aside!" Jerry called out over the crowd as they went.

At the main office Vincent demanded to speak with the zoo's CEO and heads of all the animal departments.

"DL Harrington and DI Wilder, HCPD. We urgently need to speak with whoever is in charge here!" Vincent enforced upon the mild mannered receptionist.

Both Vincent and Jerry were soon met by the zoo director. Karen Redding was a short, dumpy woman nearing her mid fifties, wearing comically large glasses and sporting an uneven haircut.

107

"Good afternoon gentlemen, what is this about?" she asked.

"My partner and I are with the HCPD," Vincent introduced hastily again. "we believe a threat has been made against one of your employees. We need you to gather together all your animal care staff immediately."

"Yes of course." Karen replied.

She ushered towards the rest of her cronies and 'yes men' that comprised the zoo's managerial team.

A message of severe urgency was soon put out over the staff radio, informing all the animal keepers to quickly report to the head office. Over several minutes the detectives watched as the majority of the animal keepers slowly trickled into a large meeting room. It was usually reserved for giving presentations on the zoo's overseas conservation work to outside investors. Various animal skins, bones and skulls were dotted around as the room also served as a place for educational talks to given to the zoo's visitors.

After twenty minutes of waiting Vincent approached Karen Redding once more.

"Is this everyone?" he asked.

"Yes I believe this is everyone working with the animals today." she replied, pushing her glasses back up her thin nose with a single finger.

"The staff members that aren't working today have all reported back to us by phone also." the head of human resources confirmed for the detectives.

Vincent stepped forward to speak aloud to the extensive collection of animal care personnel now sitting before him. All looked confused as to the situation, this meeting a considerable disruption to their daily working routine.

"Ok everyone. Please listen up," Vincent began to address the crowd. "we believe a threat has been made against one of your lives. We ask you to remain calm and wait here until police protection has arrived."

Vincent's announcement was met with mutterings and whispers being exchanged between the keepers.

Jerry surveyed the many faces staring blankly back at him and Vincent. The ratio of female to male zoo keepers was around a three to one split. None of them were particularly attractive to him, especially the women. One such zoo keeper looked like a terminally ill albino chicken, whilst another looked like the result of a bulldog having angry sex with a sow. Jerry could immediately see the ironic characteristics and features that some of the keepers shared with their chosen animals.

"Is this to do with the Figure Killer?" asked one zoo keeper.

The Figure Killer's notorious rampage of infamy was now common public knowledge throughout all of Hallow thanks to daily news reports.

"I am afraid we cannot discuss the details of that case. All you need to know is that you will be placed under police protection until the threat has been eliminated." Vincent comforted.

"We need to take down all your contact details, phone numbers, home addresses and the like in order to secure your safety." Jerry continued.

The zoo had a moderate collection of large carnivores, including wolves, bears and several big cat species.

"Would all of you who work directly with the big cats, especially the Tigers, please come with us." Vincent announced.

"The rest of you please stay here and write down your details for us, thank you." Jerry instructed.

The detectives, along with Karen Redding and her managerial team, led this handful of individuals into a separate room to question them further.

"Have any of you recently encountered someone new in your life? Someone strange or perhaps even pleasant towards you? Anyone you met at a bar or on a night out?" Vincent began to ask.

109

Nearly all the keepers replied with a no.

"Any new lovers in your life or one night stands that may now know where you live?" Jerry continued, again no one in the room admitting to any of this.

"No, nearly half of us live on site at the zoo for security reasons." one zoo keeper spoke.

"We don't get out much," the albino chicken keeper quipped. "besides the rent is much cheaper here anyway."

"Where is this staff accommodation?" Vincent uttered towards Karen.

"At the far end of the property, past the visitor car park. It's quite remote but can be accessed by a public road. So anyone could easily access the site there." she detailed.

"We'll have security set up there for a start at least." Jerry affirmed.

"This does have something to do with the Figure Killer doesn't it?" another keeper challenged.

"We are already one step ahead of the threat. You need not worry ok, the HCPD will protect you." Vincent reassured the now more distraught keepers.

Murphy and a team of uniformed officers arrived at the zoo less than an hour later. Some were there to place a police guard around the employee lodgings, whilst others escorted the potential targets that lived off site back home once the zoo had closed.

"We have got some bases covered now at least. Let us just see if it does any good." Vincent thought, yawning in the process.

The long summer day was clearly weighing heavy on the tired old man, adding even more wrinkles to his grizzled expression.

"Yeah we can only hope." Jerry sighed, falling back against their patrol car.

"I do not think Hallow has had such a manhunt in quite a few years." Vincent reminisced.

"You're gonna miss it, aren't you?" Jerry rhetorically asked.

"I will miss the satisfaction I get when I finally chase down those bastards and bring them in. But I will not miss the pain and suffering that they leave in their wake." Vincent bluntly admitted.

It had been a long day for both detectives, Vincent's stamina beginning to wain like the setting sun behind him. Jerry looked out over the horizon towards Cove City, where the ocean met the land as the sky slowly changed colour from orange to a pinkish hue. Jerry couldn't recall the last time he saw a single cloud in the sky since arriving into Hallow, nor the cooling relief of a summer rainfall.

He then thought back to Grace and the time they both got caught out in the rain. Jerry's plan in proposing to Grace had been hindered by a freak rainstorm one day, catching them off guard when out for a picnic together. By the time they had reached the relative shelter of a nearby tree they were both soaked to the bone, their damp clothes clinging uncomfortably to their skin. But they didn't care, laughing to one another over their shared misfortune. Jerry had never been so happy. He knew it right then and there. Now was the perfect opportunity to ask her the question he had nervously circling in his mind.

The solemn peace both detectives shared together as they watched the setting sun was only broken by Murphy who came shuffling over to join them.

"The CCPD got a call about an hour ago. A pair of disembodied legs were found washed ashore just outside the harbour." he announced.

"The work of our killer no doubt?" Vincent rhetorically asked.

"Yeah, the genitalia had been removed and the wound sealed with the same blue plastic. Highly likely they belonged to Remington." Murphy concluded.

111

"I don't get it. Why go to the trouble of mutilating his lower half further when it wouldn't even be left with the rest of him?" a flustered Jerry asked.

"It is a ritual to them." Vincent confidently replied.

The thought process behind the killer's macabre methods was starting to wear the detectives down, especially Vincent.

"The legs were all but down to the bone, no doubt the work of sharks." Murphy added.

"I guess the fish head met a similar toothy fate. Hide the evidence no doubt." Vincent thought.

"What kind of fish was it then?" Jerry asked.

"Some kind of Tuna. I checked with Cove City's main fish market. Hundreds of them are bought and sold in bulk on a daily basis there. We'd be hard pressed to find a suspect from that." Murphy sighed.

"Like looking for a moving needle in a moving hay stack, very clever." Jerry huffed, running his hands through his hair impatiently.

"Our killer could have simply stolen one also, when nobody was looking." Murphy theorised.

"I need a drink." Vincent gruffly announced, rubbing his tired old eyes.

"Amen to that my brother! We should get going then, if you're not wanting to miss your own shindig tonight!" Murphy hastily suggested towards Jerry.

"It is your last night of freedom after all kid." Vincent added.

In all the commotion surrounding the Figure Killer's activity, Jerry had nearly forgotten about his own stag night.

"Sure but this is more important. We're just now starting to get ahead of the killer." Jerry said.

"True, but you only get one stag night Jerry, hopefully anyway. Do not let this particular case work you too hard. Remember, you have a life outside the precinct. Never forget that." Vincent cautioned.

"I know but..." Jerry began to protest.

"Don't let this job work you to death too soon now!" Murphy joked, lightly knocking his shoulder against Jerry's.

"Fine," Jerry begrudgingly agreed. "I'll see you both later then?"

"What do you mean later? We have a perfectly decent vehicle right here" Vincent noted, looking to their patrol car.

"Vince makes a good point, what say we head over to O'Malley's now then good sir?" Murphy suggested impatiently.

"I keep telling you not to call me that!" Vincent snapped back with less distain than usual.

"Ah whatever." Murphy jokingly brushed off.

"What about Clark and Reed?" Jerry asked.

"They said they'll meet us there" Murphy replied.

The thought of Reed's gentle face staring back at him over some empty glasses made Jerry want to get going even more.

"Sure thing. You're driving though Murphy." Jerry instructed.

Vincent was glad to see his young partner was starting to see sense, that there was more to life in Hallow than just the job.

With Cove City and Hallow City Zoo now far behind them, it was back to the Arm for Vincent, Jerry and Murphy. Most of the preparation for Jerry's stag night had been planned last minute, no thanks to the work load placed upon them by the Figure Killer. So it was back to the familiar surroundings of O'Malley's for the young stag and his drinking companions. O'Malley's was the Arm's most popular Irish pub, heavily frequented by almost the entire HCPD. It was a mere stone's throw away from the precinct and situated right alongside the river's edge. This gave it a prime location and made it ideal staggering distance.

For countless decades, Hallow had been a huge melting pot for many different nationalities, creeds and cultures. After the Great Blaze of Hallow that swept throughout most of South and Central Hallow a century ago, thousands of immigrants flocked to the city, including many Irish. The abundance of job opportunities created by the fire's destruction was too good to pass up for many foreign labourers. Over the years however, it quickly became the opinion of many Hallow residents that the level of crime rose alongside these foreign workers. Tensions between people soon increased and Hallow inevitably became a breeding ground for civil unrest, leading to a further rise in crime and misdemeanours.

Among the few uniforms at O'Malley's, who weren't watching over the zoo keepers, were Clark and Reed. Reed had mentioned her partner Alex would be joining them later in the evening, so all the men were eager to meet the lucky guy who had snagged this fair maiden. Murphy took Jerry to one side and enquired as to whether or not a stripper would be arriving for Jerry's last night out as a free man.

"No nothing like that Murphy, I really don't need the extra stimulation." Jerry laughed back.

"Oh come on Jerry! We've gotta get our rocks off tonight too." Murphy complained.

If a stripper had been secretly arranged for him and had turned out to be Claudia from the Fox Glove, then Jerry knew he would not have lasted the entire night. Jerry wanted to keep his mind on Grace and Grace alone. He wanted to be as far away from Easy Street as possible tonight.

After a few rounds of drinks the stories and jokes began flowing as much as the alcohol.

"And then he says '*You stay safe now ladies!*'" Murphy laughed aloud as he recounted Jerry's first encounter with Jade and her sisters.

The small pub erupted into hysterics, Vincent also wiping away tears of laughter from his eyes as he sipped his brandy.

"You should have seen your face! You looked so terrified!" Murphy declared.

He could barely manage to formulate his words through all the laughter. Even Jerry chuckled to himself, now seeing the funny side to the situation.

"You should have got their number buddy, incase things don't work out between you and Grace!" Murphy joked further, throwing an arm around Jerry's shoulder in his fit of laughter.

"You forget Patrick. She pulled a fucking knife on me! I think I handled myself pretty well there." Jerry shrugged off.

"I'll say you handled yourself alright! Whey!" Murphy joked, moving to grab Jerry's crotch.

"Cut it out you drunken Irish goon!" Jerry laughed back at his colleague's laddish gesture.

"Hey Jerry, how do you make a whore moan?" Murphy asked.

Jerry didn't know what to say and neither did his colleagues.

"You don't pay her!" Murphy laughed.

The infectious laughter spread throughout them all like wild fire. Even Reed saw the funny side to the rather misogynistic beer soaked joke.

Jerry moved away from the commotion that Murphy was quickly riling up with their fellow colleagues to go and sit with Vincent, who sat to one side by himself.

"Hey you ok?" Jerry asked concerned.

"I am fine. Just a little tired. It is nice to see you smiling again kid." Vincent noticed.

"I thought we weren't getting close? That I'm your replacement, that you're leaving soon so what's the point?" Jerry quipped.

"What can I say? I am starting to like you son. I see a lot of my younger self in you." Vincent acknowledged.

"Don't tell me you're getting nostalgic on me all of a sudden?" Jerry jokingly taunted.

"Just don't make the same mistakes I did." Vincent cautioned.

"Like what?" Jerry quickly asked back.

115

"If we are going to get into this now, then I am going to need another brandy." Vincent subtly hinted at, shaking his empty glass in Jerry's direction.

"Fine. I'll go get you another one then," Jerry huffed. "just don't break a hip whilst I'm gone old timer!"

"Just get the damn drinks in sonny" Vincent chuckled back.

The evening was in full swing, drinks were flowing further and all were having a good time. As Jerry and Murphy waited at the bar for their next round to arrive, an unfamiliar sight entered into O'Malley's, that of a well kept attractive young woman. She appeared lost, as if coming in only to ask for directions.

"Lord have mercy!" Murphy drunkenly remarked.

Both men looked this woman up and down, as she nervously looked around the bar.

"You old dog! You did organise a stripper in the end!" Murphy exclaimed.

"No I didn't." Jerry replied, secretly fearing someone else had done so to surprise the young stag.

The young woman had a cute pixie-like hairstyle dyed an almost brilliant white blonde, instantly making her stand out even more in the predominantly male crowd. Wearing a loose fitting white lace blouse and tight fitting jeans, she didn't resemble a common stripper at all. She continued to look nervously around the pub from the doorway, anxiously clutching at her handbag, before quickly finding her target and walking over to them. She threw her arms around Reed and the two women lovingly kissed one another.

A look of surprise quickly swept throughout the men drinking in O'Malley's, as they casually observed this tame spectacle of girl on girl action. Reed removed her lips from the other woman's, only to behold a small crowd of her colleagues that had now gathered around them both. They were all staring at the two young women with slack jawed, salivating open mouths.

"Everyone, this is Alex!" Reed announced to her spectators, leaving one arm hooked around this new woman.

A moment of awkward silence fell over the entire room, only to be quickly broken by Alex.

"Sorry boys, she's all mine." Alex quickly added.

Her delicate face brimmed with a huge smile of joy and pride as she looked to Reed.

To which note the men in O'Malley's cheered in somewhat celebration, before greeting Alex one by one and enveloping her into their mutual night of drunken revelry.

"Well I'll be damned. I never figured Reed for a lady fancier!" Murphy admitted, before taking a large mouthful of his newly arrived pint of strong bitter.

"Just goes to show pal, you should never judge a person by their appearance." Jerry cautioned.

"No, you shouldn't." Murphy firmly agreed, looking only at Jerry.

Both men returned to their seats, drinks in hand and again looked to the couple standing proudly amongst the male crowd.

"Yeah she's definitely not one of those butch mannish types for a start, and neither is that Alex of her's!" Murphy exclaimed chauvinistically.

"Who's the old dog now huh?" Jerry snidely remarked back at Murphy.

"I just know what I like," Murphy replied. "what's Grace up to this evening anyway?"

"She's back at the apartment, quiet night in..." Jerry began.

"Whilst you're out getting shit faced with the boys! You two sound married already!" Murphy laughed off.

A little while later, into O'Malley's entered the Chief and with him came a hushed silence over the crowd. All eyes, now bleary from booze, turned towards him. The Chief was there more out of routine than for Jerry's stag night, egotistically sensing the attention he now held over everyone.

"Relax everyone. I'm off the clock!" he brashly announced from the bar.

He ordered himself a large whiskey on the rocks and sparked up an even larger Cuban. The Chief was soon lost in a choking cloud of acrid smelling cigar smoke, like a volcano hidden by its own towering ash column.

The arrival of the Chief caused a thought to suddenly occur in Jerry's alcohol laden mind, so he plodded over to Reed to ask her his question.

"Hey Reed, tell me something," he slurred. "how is it that you got the job here? Given the Chief's usual preference to male detectives."

"Because my girl here is just so bad ass!" Alex replied for her, one arm hooked around Reed's slender mid drift.

"I just told him why I wanted to join the HCPD. I was the right person for the job anyway, as were you. He was sympathetic to my reasons." Reed answered, taking a sip of her red wine.

"The Chief?! Sympathetic?" Jerry quietly laughed to himself.

"He's a good man Jerry. A little off now and again but I understand what he wants to do for Hallow." Reed added.

Jerry turned to Alex, this time having a far better look at Reed's woman. Her eyes were the most dazzling green and stood out like two glinting emeralds on a white sandy beach. Green it seemed was as inescapable as breathing in Jerry's world at the moment.

"So Alex what do you do then?" he impolitely asked.

"I'm a paediatrician." she answered.

"Wow, a doctor! Should I call you Doctor Alex then?" Jerry laughed.

"Alex will do just fine thanks." she laughed off awkwardly.

"So how long have you two been together?" Jerry pried further.

"A couple of months now, but it seems longer than that."
Alex smiled, looking to Reed.

"Yeah we just clicked so quickly," Reed added. "like
nothing I've ever experienced before. I didn't think I'd find
someone so quickly when I first came to Hallow. We met in
Kathy's, the coffee shop on the other side of the Arm. It was like
something out of an old movie. We picked up each other's order
by mistake, got talking and the rest as they say is history."

"That's really nice to hear." Jerry commented.
The old romantic in him steadily rose to the surface as he
remembered meeting his Grace for the first time.

"What about you and Grace? How did you two meet?"
Reed asked, as if able to read Jerry's thoughts at that very
moment.

Alex turned her attention back on to Jerry, eager to hear his
story now.

"We met through a mutual friend," Jerry replied. "we're
both orphans you see. So that was an instant connection we both
shared."

"I didn't know you were an orphan Jerry. Sorry." Reed
said.

"Hey don't apologise. It's ok. Like you said the rest is
history." Jerry smiled back.

"I'm an orphan also," Alex announced. "so I know exactly
where you're both coming from Jerry."

"Adopted or fostered?" Jerry questioned Alex.

"Adopted. My parents were super supportive," she replied.
"and you?"

"Fostered. Grace was adopted but hasn't seen her folks in a
while since moving out here." Jerry sighed.
Jerry took a long swig from his pint of ale.

"All I knew about my birth parents when growing up was
that they were filthy degenerate pieces of shit. My father
apparently went to jail for murder." Jerry brashly announced.

119

"Sorry Jerry, I really had no idea." Reed remarked sympathetically.

"That's why I became a cop, so I wouldn't end up like my father, whoever he was." Jerry affirmed.

"You don't need to become a police officer in order to be a good person though." Alex challenged.

"I know, I just wanted to give back to the people who are targeted by crime." Jerry stated back.

"So of the four of us, I'm the only one who really knew their birth parents?" Reed rhetorically joked, trying to change the subject to a more happier one.

In the process however she unintentionally conjured up painful memories from her own past. She took a long chug of her wine to wash down the sorrow quickly mounting in the pit of her churning stomach, before it could rise any higher.

As the night wore on Jerry gradually became more and more intoxicated, a fact that wasn't remedied by Murphy continuously buying him more and more drinks. Even the Chief soon came to realise the significance of the evening, ordering another pint for the drunken stag. The sight of Reed and Alex together was not helping Jerry's libido in the slightest. The old romantic in him had been quickly smothered again by his stronger inner desires of the female flesh.

Alex had knocked back a fair few pints but was still going strong, whilst Reed's tolerance to her mixture of beer and wine had begun to diminish.

"Come on you, I think it's time I took you home." Alex whispered in Reed's ear, who had slowly begun to fall asleep on the table.

Reed merely replied with a few muffled groans as Alex moved to pull her inebriated girlfriend back on to more stable footing.

"Congratulations by the way Jerry. If I don't see you again soon I hope you have a wonderful wedding day." Alex complimented the heavily influenced detective.

"Thanks Alex," Jerry slurred. "ya can be Reed's plus one if ya want?"

"That's a lovely offer, thank you." Alex replied as she hauled Reed towards the exit.

Vincent approached Jerry soon afterwards to bid him farewell also.

"I better be off too kid. Will you be alright getting home?" Vincent asked concerned, placing a comforting hand on Jerry's shoulder.

"Yeah...should be...ok." Jerry murmured.

Murphy and Clark helped each other up before staggering over to the exit, one arm hooked around the other for added support.

"And then the priest says, 'That's no crack dealer, that's my wife!'" Murphy concluded.

Both men shared a laugh from Murphy's joke, with Clark needing to rub away tears of hysterics from his eyes.

Before long Jerry was the only person left in the pub.

"I'll be closing up very soon Jerry." announced a nearby voice.

Mr O'Malley, the pub owner, stood behind the bar politely ushering the weary detective to leave.

"Yeah...sure thing, Burt." Jerry slurred, struggling to down the remainder of his pint.

Jerry soon hauled himself back on to his own two feet and staggered towards the exit.

As Jerry slumped outside into the warm sticky night air, Mr O'Malley locked the door behind him and turned off the lights. Jerry in his intoxicated state could still feel his libido growing uncontrollably. The images of Reed & Alex, Roberta & Gemma, Officer Mana and even Wu couldn't escape his mind now. His brain felt as though it was swimming in a sea of testosterone.

The moon was full and with its glow reflecting off the river's surface, Jerry began to stagger further into the city night in an attempt to find his way home. His balance was off, every step and every beat of his heart just pumped the alcohol in his system

121

further around his body. Jerry suddenly felt nauseous and preceded to puke his guts up behind a large waste bin down a darkened alley way.

"Hey pal you ok?" a concerned voice asked the detective from nearby.

Jerry turned to see the troubled face of an elderly homeless man. The rest of his body was half buried under numerous blankets and plastic sheeting.

"Yeah...just...too much..." Jerry drunkenly stuttered as he continued onwards.

"Better out than in they say!" the homeless man called out after him.

Jerry's vision began to blur as he rejoined the main road he had been walking along and in a minor panic began to quicken his pace.

After several minutes the inebriated young stag realised he was now lost and somehow further into the city centre. Jerry felt like a rat trapped within the immense walls of a complicated maze, compelling him only forwards and not backwards. The memory of Lester Fenwick, prowling Hallow's streets for new female prey, arose in Jerry's mind. The young stag could now feel very real fear creep back inside of him. He was terrified another monster was out there on the hunt, wanting him and only him for their latest kill. He began to jog, trying to run away from the worry growing inside.

Jerry eventually came to yet another narrow alleyway and collapsed against a wall he had been using to help prop himself upright. He felt breathless from his drunken speed walking, hyperventilating from the exertion. The sounds of sexual favours and propositions from numerous women were the last thing he could hear as his vision darkened completely, passing out in the process.

"Well now, look who we have here!" the familiar voices of three triplets spoke in unison.

Chapter Seven

The Clown

Jerry slowly opened his bleary eyes, the faint blue colour from a nearby fluorescent light beginning to creep back into his vision. His head throbbed from excessive alcohol consumption the night before, feeling as though it was splitting in two. Jerry looked around the unfamiliar room he now found himself to be in, soon realising he wasn't in his own bed. Soft silken sheets of the most brilliant white enveloped his weary body, his aching head and shoulders the only part of him not covered. His blurred vision slowly adjusted to the light level, helped by a few rubs to his eyes. Jerry quickly realised he wasn't alone in this strange setting.

Turning his head to the right he immediately recognised the feminine physique laying naked beside him, but it wasn't Grace's. The woman he believed to be Madame Wu was already awake, staring back at him intently through her dark sinister eyes. Her shaven head was propped up by one of her tentacle tattooed arms, and with a look of total satisfaction she uttered only a few words to him.

"I knew you couldn't resist me." she proudly announced.
Jerry felt his heart sink into the pit of his already nauseous stomach.

"And I knew you'd taste good." she added, licking her lips.
In that moment Jerry remembered the story Murphy had told him weeks ago regarding Wu's origin and rise to power. He quickly reached down between his legs to see if his precious manhood was still intact, it fortunately was. The woman let out a short burst of laughter, throwing her head back in the process. Jerry leapt out from under the covers to stand upright, away from the clutches of her bed. He realised he too was completely naked.

"You actually believe that story?" she chuckled to herself.

"Where the hell am I exactly?" a confused Jerry asked as he struggled to maintain his balance.

She slowly sat up in the bed, her naked curves proving too irresistible for Jerry to not look at now.

"Relax honey. You're safe here in my private bed chamber." she reassured.

Jerry again looked upon the unconventional bed he had been laying in. The entire piece of furniture resembled a giant clam, opened at its spinal hinge. The lower half held a scallop shaped mattress at its centre, with the upper half extending outwards over it, providing some relative cover from above. The wave-like edges of both clam halves appeared to interlock with one another if the whole structure were to close, like an underwater Venus fly trap.

"How did I get here? Jerry asked.

"Last night you rather drunkenly staggered into my parlour and then collapsed by the entrance booth. You caused quite a scene. My girls were quite shocked and weren't sure what to do. So I came down to take care of you myself, and I certainly did." the woman recounted.

"What did we do?" Jerry demanded.

"What didn't we do detective?" she flirtatiously returned.

"Oh fuck!" Jerry said grasping his face with both hands.

He realised the shit he now found himself to be stuck in.

"It wasn't that bad, you've quite the concealed weapon there." the woman teased as she looked Jerry up and down.

"Shut up!" Jerry snapped.

Wu simply laughed, as she writhed around over her silken bed sheets.

"You should feel honoured detective, not many men get to see the lair of the Black Octopus." she announced with great ego.

"So you are thee Black Octopus then?" Jerry asked the smirking woman.

"Of course I am detective." she replied.

Jerry had no energy for these mind games as he frantically began looking for his clothes. First he found his shirt, then a shoe, both socks, his trousers and then finally the other shoe. As he looked around the dimly lit windowless room, Jerry had no concept of time, unsure of even what day it was. These thoughts circled around inside his dizzying head, again and again like a swarm of angry bees.

The Black Octopus emblem was everywhere in the room. On one side of the room there was a large aquarium at least two meters wide and a metre and a half high. Inside was a large octopus, pushing itself along the sandy bottom with its eight dexterous limbs. To the side of it was a far smaller aquarium, this one containing a much smaller octopus covered in bright green rings.

"How do I know these two are safe from you?" Jerry asked, remembering the unfortunate octopus from before.

"They are my most prized possessions." Wu beamed.

She stood up from the clam bed, her naked form in the dim light captivating a cautious Jerry even now as she walked over to the aquariums. Opening the lid of the smaller tank she reached inside to gently caress the octopus, one tentacle wrapping around her fingers.

"The Green-ringed octopus is among the most venomous creatures in the sea, its venom stopping your heart dead in less than half an hour." Wu detailed, watching the octopus carefully.

"You know for someone who idolises this creature you sure do treat some of them cruelly!" Jerry snapped, referring to his last encounter with this woman.

"You're still mad about that?" Wu sniggered to herself.

Wu removed her hand from the tank, replaced the lid then walked over to a large cupboard in the corner of the room, opening one side. She took out a large glass jar similar to the one Jerry had seen on her desk before. She unscrewed the lid and took out something black from inside, before lightly throwing it

125

to Jerry. Dropping one armful of his clothing Jerry amazingly caught it, given his inebriated state.

"It's salted liquorice detective!" Wu laughed, replacing the lid on the jar and then the jar back in the cupboard.

Jerry looked down at his hands and sure enough there it was, a large piece of liquorice formed into the shape of an octopus. The liquorice even had the eyes and skin pattern moulded into it, its familiar sweet yet salty smell rising up to fill Jerry's nostrils. It looked so life-like.

"But I could have sworn..." Jerry started but stopped himself mid sentence.

Wu had played a trick on him from before. His distain for this woman began to surprisingly diminish. His gaze returned to Wu, standing there with her hands on her hips, her head cocked to one side wearing nothing but a cheeky smile.

"It's all for show honey! To put the frighteners on people. I've a reputation to uphold." Wu admitted.

She approached Jerry and took the sweet from his hand, taking a large bite out of it.

"You see, I'm not so bad." Wu coyly stated between each chew of the liquorice.

Saliva tainted black from chewing the liquorice began to stain her teeth and lips. Jerry began to anxiously drop his guard. He couldn't help but feel that standing naked before this woman, her naked also, felt so right. After swallowing the masticated liquorice, Wu casually walked over to a small mini bar to the other side of the cupboard.

From several label less bottles she swiftly made up a concoction of some kind, before returning to a still naked Jerry with glass in hand.

"Drink this tonic sweetie, it will help with the nausea and headache." Wu gently spoke.

"What happened to Hu Tan?" Jerry asked.

"Seriously? You want to get into this now?" Wu huffed.

Jerry nodded in reply.

"Fine, the old bastard had a heart attack whilst we were fucking one evening. Collapsed right on top of me! We had an arrangement you see. I got to run his massage parlour rent free but only if he had his way with me now and again. Do you have any idea how much it costs to rent around here? Anyway after his death his associates sold off his properties to dissolve any links with him due to some shady dealings. As his chief masseuse I took over the Black Octopus and that's that." Wu recounted.

Looking down at the drink, Jerry was understandably sceptical by this story and the gesture. But the promise of relieving his splitting head was too good to deny. Taking the glass from Wu he downed the drink in one, its slightly fizzy bitterness felt quite refreshing.

"Who was the old woman in your office?" Jerry asked.

"My cleaning lady!" Wu laughed back at him.

"What about the girl with the missing arm? And all the little tattoos your employees have?" Jerry continued to fire off his questions.

"Motorcycle accident and they get the tats on their own free will, usually out of loyalty to me. They even get a pay bonus for getting one." Wu laughed off again.

"What about..." Jerry began.

"Madame Wu is pure fiction detective," Wu interrupted. "an apparition, a bed time story to scare those who wish to remove me from power. My real name is Tia."
Tia took the now empty glass from his hand.

"Tia." Jerry repeated.

"Yes." she replied.

"How many other people know this?" he asked.

"I like you Detective Wilder. I wouldn't be telling you all of this if I didn't." Tia complimented, not answering his earlier question.

127

As she moved her face closer towards his, Jerry couldn't help but feel this bizarre attraction towards her return again, hopelessly trying to think of something to say.

"I'm..." Jerry stuttered, feeling his gaze return to her lips.

"You're with someone?" she guessed, looking softly upon him.

"Engaged." Jerry replied.

"Oh." Tia sighed, sounding disappointed.

In that brief moment of time Jerry couldn't help but feel sorry for her, disappointing her like that.

"Well, she is a very lucky woman indeed." Tia acknowledged.

"I'm sorry but this can never happen again, no one can ever know about this!" Jerry affirmed.

"I understand detective, discretion comes with my line of work." Tia smiled.

She returned his glass to the mini bar, giving Jerry another chance to admire the very detailed octopus tattoo on her back. It almost looked like it was slowly coming to life right there on her skin.

A sudden knock at the door caught both their attentions. A young woman spoke briefly in Thai, causing Tia to reply in Thai also.

"A taxi is here for you, it will take you wherever you want to go. No charge, compliments of the house." Tia offered as she walked back to Jerry.

"Thank you." Jerry replied, gathering up the rest of his clothes.

"Perhaps you'll come back for an actual massage sometime, my treat?" Tia propositioned with hope in her voice. She looked longingly at him once more.

"It has been so long since I've been with a man." Wu admitted.

"I think it's best I don't, sorry." Jerry replied, shooting down her advances.

128

The young scantily clad Chinese girl Jerry had met before opened the door and walked into the room, wearing the familiar blue tank top and matching mini skirt. She moved to the side of Tia and whispered something into her ear, a smile quickly growing on Tia's face as they looked each other over

Jerry suddenly felt very invigorated, as if the tonic had just kicked in. He felt energised, as if his blood was on fire, completely forgetting his fragile state. He began to dress himself but his hands were stayed, his attention quickly redirected elsewhere. Tia had began to undress the now giggling girl, starting with her tank top before pulling down her revealing mini skirt. Now naked Tia grabbed the girl firmly before kissing her repeatedly, groping her buttock and upper back. The girl's hands began to explore Tia's body in return.

Jerry shook his head as if unable to believe what was happening, becoming far more alert and less nauseous in the process. He felt like he had received a shot of adrenaline. Tia stopped kissing the girl, turning to Jerry and locking eye contact with him. Jerry could almost feel Tia peering into his very soul.

"There isn't a taxi is there?" Jerry asked, already knowing there wasn't.

"What do you think?" Tia mused.

She moved to sit down on the end of her bed, half laying back in the process and spreading her legs.

"Has anything you've ever said been true?" Jerry questioned, confused by the mixed signals this naked woman was giving him.

"An octopus can change its colours and form to hide itself from both predators and prey." the young girl cryptically proposed.

She got down on her knees and moved to bury her face between Tia's legs. Jerry couldn't look away, Tia beginning to groan whilst arching her back upwards, softly thrusting forwards and grabbing the girl's head with one hand. She opened her eyes again to look at the young bewildered detective.

"Come to me!" Tia commanded, holding out a tattooed hand for him to take.

At that moment Jerry thought he heard a muffled voice coming from somewhere in the room, as if crying out for help. He thought that he was hearing things, mistaking the young girl's mumbled cries for someone else.

Jerry struggled to keep his mind on Grace, not answering this temptress in the process as her lustful moans began to grow louder. He turned away and moved to leave the room, the conflict welling up inside him as he grabbed the door handle. He didn't want to give in to his inner desires but the temptation was too overpowering. He was engaged to be married to the love of his life. But the images of Reed & Alex, Officer Mana and the arousal he felt for Wu when he first met her powerfully resurfaced in his mind.

Jerry closed the door, sighing to himself and casting all doubt aside in his decision. Only he was still inside the room. The temptation had proved too great to simply ignore. He turned around again and dropped his clothes to the floor. Slowly he approached the grinning Madame Wu and her young play thing. The Black Octopus's hold over him was now complete.

It was much later in the morning, when Jerry stumbled back into work at the precinct. Back at his desk all Jerry could think about was Wu, the line between profession and personal desire having become heavily entangled like knotted tentacles. The image of her body cavorting with her young employee had deeply imbedded itself in his mind. Jerry had to forget his involvement in this meeting, as hard as he would try. He had cheated on Grace, the one and only good thing in his life.

"What time do you call this then? I will let it slide just this once as it was your stag night." Vincent cautioned as he entered their office.

He looked Jerry over, seeing the sickly and exhausted look plastered all across his sweaty face. The hot summer day outside was already sweltering. Hallow's merciless streets had felt like an oven to Jerry during his walk of shame back to the precinct. Jerry could feel large beads of sweat collecting on his forehead, before tricky down his brow and cheeks. A couple stopping along the way to sting the corners of his dry eyes.

"You look like death warmed up." Vincent noticed.

"Please...not so loud." a hung over Jerry softly begged, covering his ears.

"Where did you disappear to last night then matey? You get home alright?" came another voice.

Murphy entered their office soon afterwards, slapping his hand down hard on Jerry's shoulder.

"I don't know exactly but somehow I managed to walk my way home." Jerry lied, paranoia beginning to take hold.

"You look like how I feel." Murphy quietly uttered, feeling just as fragile as Jerry.

"So here is the young stud of a stag!" a familiar voice announced.

Into Vincent and Jerry's office came Reed, looking the most awake and sober of them all.

"How is it that you're so cheerful this morning?" Jerry snidely questioned.

"Well maybe because I sobered up before I went to bed," Reed admitted. "or should I say because Alex sobered me up. Plenty of water, coffee and bacon always does the trick. Thanks again for last night Jerry, we all had fun!"

"Yeah that was one hell of a shindig!" Clark added as he walked in also, sipping an antacid.

"Well get over yourselves, we have got work to do." Vincent commanded unsympathetically.

A stickler for the rules and for getting on with the job at hand, Vincent approached their evidence board.

"We have some new murders to look into now so grab your gear and get ready to move." he ordered.

"More? What is it?" Jerry moaned.

131

"Multiple homicide. Three new victims all together in the same location. Sounds like it could be our Figure Killer." Vincent summarised.

"We better get going too." Clark motioned to Reed.

Jerry finally looked to his phone, seeing several unopened and unanswered messages from Grace. He quickly typed in where he was and what had happened last night, immediately feeling the guilt with every syllable as he spelt out his lies.

"Jerry come on!" Vincent firmly ushered him out.

All three detectives arrived into a housing district in South West Hallow. They pulled up outside the address and approached the crime scene. Edward was already onsite. He rushed out of the house, removing his mouth mask in the process and proceeded to vomit violently.

"Who could do...?!" he asked himself.

Edward continued to lurch forth the remainder of his lunch on to the well mowed lawn. Vincent kept walking towards the front door of the house, undeterred by Edward's noticeable repulsion. Jerry followed closely behind Vincent, who upon viewing Edward's own struggle to keep down his lunch had to keep his own stomach from turning inside out also. The young detective could still feel the alcohol seeping out of his skin, creating a booze laden cloud of stink around him. As they walked through the front door and into the large living room their eyes beheld a truly gruesome sight.

Three bodies, a man, woman and younger woman, lay parallel to one another, each one divided into the familiar five sections of the Figure Killer, but this wasn't their work. The bodies were still clothed, their genitals most likely still attached and they had all been severed ferociously. It was if they had been hacked to pieces in a frantic violent rush. The carpet was so saturated with blood from the victims that the forensics team struggled to carefully tip toe around all three of the deceased.

Extra shoe covers were needed as wherever they walked blood squelched upwards under each foot step. Extensive blood splatter coated the surrounding walls, ceiling and furniture also, so violent the attack must have been. Some droplets of blood were still dripping down from above them.

"Oh my lord." Vincent uttered, removing his hat in the process.

Photographs of the bodies were being taken from every angle, so wide spread was the slaughter.

"Who are they?" Murphy asked one of the officer's already on scene.

"Gwendoline, Barry and Jill Waller. They're the family that live at this address." he replied.

"Mother, father & daughter?" Murphy guessed.

"Yeah. Neighbours reported hearing screaming and the sound of a chainsaw this morning." the officer reported.

"Any witnesses?" Jerry asked.

"Only one. A neighbour reported seeing a male figure of unknown description fleeing the scene in the early hours of the morning, covered in blood." the officer continued.

Something about the older woman looked strangely familiar to Jerry, her ample chest perhaps.

"Wait a minute." Jerry spoke aloud to everyone as he peered closer at the older woman.

"It is Mrs Waller, from Roberta's college." Vincent concluded as Jerry came to realise this himself.

Laying there before the detectives was Mrs Gwendoline Waller, her body so mutilated and her blonde curly locks so tainted with red it was no wonder the detectives hadn't recognised her sooner.

"Why do you think she was targeted?" Murphy asked.

"Who knows? But this isn't our killer," Jerry admitted. "there's so much blood."

"What is that over there?" Vincent asked, pointing a finger towards the left hand side of Jill.

Jerry stepped closer to have a look, placing shoe covers on his feet beforehand. From a distance it appeared to be some of Jill's entrails but as Jerry got closer he realised what it really was, to his horror.

"It's...it's a child!" Jerry loudly cried.

Vincent and Murphy stepped closer to look for themselves. Laying to the left hand side of Jill was her unborn foetus. Looking again at Jill's body, Jerry realised she must have been in her third trimester. Her swollen abdomen still showed the signs of heavy pregnancy, despite having been almost completely eviscerated. Unlike like their mother's body, the infant had been divided into three sections and not five.

"Sick bastard!" Jerry angrily snarled.

"This looks like the work of a copycat killer." Vincent said, turning to Jerry.

"Not much of a copycat though." Murphy said, noticing the inaccuracies.

"Now we have two maniacs to find, shit!" Jerry exclaimed, running a hand through his greasy hair.

"We found what we believe to be the murder weapon in the kitchen." Edward announced to the detectives.

Upon his return to the crime scene, Edward wiped away the vomit from the corners of his mouth.

"This way." he gestured.

As Edward led them all into the kitchen, Jerry noticed several trails of bloody footprints leading away from the bodies and into the kitchen as they followed. Sitting on one of the kitchen work surfaces was a gas powered chainsaw, bloodied and caked in the Waller's entrails. The back door of the house, located in the far right hand corner of the kitchen, was wide open.

"Was the door open when you arrived?" Vincent asked Edward.

"Yeah it was. Looks like the killer broke into the house through the front, murdered all three victims and then fled the scene via the back door." he replied.

"Why did they leave the murder weapon?" Murphy wondered aloud.

"Maybe they were in a rush, too heavy to carry. My guess is this was a crime of impulse, not planned or thought through carefully enough beforehand." Vincent theorised.

"This wasn't our killer. This must have been someone else trying to steal the Figure Killer's spotlight." Jerry reiterated.

"Crazy tends to attract more crazy." Murphy remarked.

"We'll dust for prints and check for DNA." Edward assured the detectives.

"You might want to start with the chainsaw. There are prints here on the handle." Vincent pointed out to Edward.

"Also the back door has bloodied hand prints on the handle and frame." Jerry noticed also.

"Good, looks like we might be able to catch this psycho quicker then." Edward said with cautious optimism.

"Hey Jerry, what's funnier than a dead baby?" Murphy giggled to himself.

"Seriously Murphy, now is not the time for..." Jerry began.

"A dead baby in a clown costume." Murphy proudly concluded.

His wickedly dark sense of humour was still heavily prevalent, even in the grimmest of settings.

All three detectives were back at the precinct after yet another eventful day of murder and mayhem. Jerry had managed to pop back some heart burn tablets throughout the day in between his usual multiple coffees. This time they were laced with double lashings of sugar. Vincent stared blankly out of their office window. The fading afternoon sunlight over the river and in between the surrounding buildings further highlighted the stern worried expression on his face.

He sat with one hand under his angular chin, supporting his burdened head. The day's events appeared to be weighing heavy on his mind. Jerry couldn't help but wonder what was going through his partner's head and why he was so deep in thought.

"Hey you alright?" Jerry asked concerned.

He garnered no response from his partner.

"Vincent?" he asked aloud.

"Bloody Belle." Vincent muttered to himself in response, continuing his gaze out the window.

"What?" Jerry replied, thinking he had misheard him.

"Lullabelle Blair, aka. Bloody Belle, The Demon Midwife." Vincent filled in further, turning his line of sight back on to Jerry.

"I'm sorry you've lost me." Jerry admitted.

"You do not know this case?" he asked.

"No, should I? What case?" a puzzled Jerry asked.

"The worst in Hallow's history." Vincent replied.

"Even worse than Lester Fenwick?" Jerry challenged.

"For me at least." Vincent sighed.

The old detective turned back to peer out through their office window.

"Just over thirty years ago I was a rookie in this city," Vincent began. "just out of uniform like you are now. A wave of murders swept through the city over several months. It was something no one had ever seen before, and nothing like it since. All the victims were heavily pregnant women, twenty seven in total and all in their third trimester. They were all strangled to death, most within a few blocks of their own homes. All of them had their baby cut out of them and taken. None of the infants were ever found, complete anyway."

Jerry shuddered at this thought, as Vincent paused his story to breathe in deeply.

"I was assigned to the case from the very beginning, it was my very first. Some of the victims were teenage girls from the South. We interviewed friends, family, distraught husbands, boyfriends, girlfriends and even some of their older children. Our investigation soon took us over to Hallow City General. We questioned doctors, nurses and midwives about the victims, hoping to find some sort of lead. One of the midwives I questioned was a young woman named Lullabelle Blair, a real country bumpkin. I will remember meeting her until the day I die." Vincent sighed.

"Go on." Jerry encouraged.

"She was nearly your height, early thirties, fairly easy on the eye, I thought nothing of it. I asked her about the women whom had been murdered. Around a third of the victims had previously seen her for consultations and were due to be her patients on the day they went into labour. She cried her crocodile tears, sobbed her eyes out, even asking God above how anyone could do such a monstrous thing, and I foolishly bought it. I got too close, even comforting her in my arms in my rookie ignorance. I was so young and stupid!" Vincent said through gritted teeth.

A look of anger at himself began to grow on his weary face.

"We had nothing to go on, no witnesses, no prints and no DNA. Whoever this was planned each attack very carefully, nearly always attacking the women at night. Fear spread throughout the city like a sickness. All remaining pregnant women were advised to not go out unaccompanied and to stay indoors after dark. Then one early morning the precinct received a call from a woman saying she had been attacked by a crazed woman who had broken into her home. The intruder had tried to strangle the woman but she somehow miraculously fought her off. She even managed to knock the woman out and gaffer taped her hands and feet together before calling for help. We drove to that address as fast as we could, and when we arrived I found the perpetrator to be none other than the midwife I had interviewed only a few weeks before, Lullabelle. We took her in for questioning and found her to be the killer." Vincent recounted.

Jerry continued to listen on intently.

"The next day I joined the raid on her home address. What we found in that apartment still haunts me to this day. Blair had

137

taken the babies home with her after carving them out of their mothers, where she proceeded to cook and eat the vast majority of the bodies. We found tiny femur, rib, arm and finger bones in the trash bin. Blair had been cannibalising the infants, preserving the uneaten heads in individual jars which she then kept on a mantle piece above her bed. She told me that she felt safe knowing her children were watching over her whilst she slept." Vincent continued.

"Are you serious?" Jerry uttered.

"We later found out that Lullabelle was infertile, unable to successfully conceive children of her own. To this day I do not know why she killed all those women and ate their children. Maybe she was jealous of them being able to create life and she could not. Maybe she thought eating other infants would help her conceive. Maybe she was just born crazy or maybe she was literally the Devil himself. All I know for certain is that that woman was pure evil incarnate. Lullabelle walked, talked and even acted like a human. But underneath her mask she was a monstrous thing, plain and simple. She knew exactly what she was doing and the fact that she hid it from so many people, including me, for so long proves just how wicked and cunning she really was. Of the twenty seven infants she ate over half were girls. When I questioned her again later about her crimes, she told me that the girls tasted the best." Vincent finished.

"What the fuck?!" Jerry uttered to himself.

He collapsed back into his desk chair in shock, folding his arms over his forehead.

"The press got wind of her arrest and during her trial coined her Bloody Belle, the Demon Midwife. A few years later I met Martha and we were married soon after. Martha so wanted us to start a family. I thought I wanted the same but I could not bear the idea of raising a child in this world anymore, not if people like Lullabelle Blair or Lester Fenwick were out there. Martha tried for years to convince me otherwise but I never yielded. That is why she filed for divorce in the end, she wanted a family and had had enough of trying to change my mind." Vincent concluded.

"So that's why your marriage ended. I'm so sorry to hear that Vincent." Jerry sympathised.

"Seeing that mutilated infant today brought back so many memories I thought I had buried away long ago, but evil seems to always resurface in Hallow somehow." Vincent sighed.

"Where is Blair now?" Jerry asked.

"She should have taken a trip across the Narrow and have been hanged for her crimes. The Hallow City Government even considered reinstating the death penalty just for her. But it fell through, not enough political support. Instead she got life without parole and as far as I know she is alive today, still behind bars. Apparently she became a vegetarian but I do not believe that for one second. A rumour circulated for a while that she fell pregnant after being assaulted by one of her prison guards, but again I do not believe that." Vincent concluded.

"What if she did? Imagine being that child, born from the womb of that creature." Jerry shuddered at the thought.

Seeing the pain in Vincent's eyes Jerry got up, deciding it best to leave him alone.

"You know what really keeps me awake at night now and again?" Vincent asked himself.

Jerry turned back to ask him but Vincent soon answered his own question.

"What if that woman had not managed to fight Lullabelle off? What if Lullabelle had made her victim number twenty eight? How many more women would there have been afterwards?" Vincent wondered.

"I know it's too late to say this but try not to dwell on it. At least she was caught! Our Figure Killer is still out there somewhere, try and focus on that." Jerry consolidated.

"Thanks for the thought kid. You run along home now to Grace. It is too late for an old fossil like me to find love again but not for you." Vincent replied.

Jerry took his advice and stepped out of the office. He left a grizzled Vincent behind to stew in his own ghosts of the past.

Back home at his apartment Jerry cautiously opened the front door and slowly entered, his hangover even now still lingered in his aching bones and splitting head. In a flash, Grace appeared down the hallway and sprinted into the weary detective, throwing her arms around him.

"Where the hell have you been?!" Grace demanded to know.

She released her hold on Jerry and slapped him hard across the chest in frustrated annoyance.

"Not so loud." Jerry uttered in response, covering one ear with his hand.

"You didn't come home last night! You didn't call me all day! I was so worried Jerry!" Grace exclaimed.

"I sent you a message." Jerry pleaded.

"That isn't good enough! What happened to you last night?" Grace continued to demand.

Jerry felt a sinking feeling in the pit of his stomach again, causing his legs to turn to jelly and nearly collapse in the hallway. For the briefest of moments he had forgotten all about his night and morning with Wu, so distracted he was by the Waller's bloody end and Vincent's even bloodier past. Grace saw the exhaustion in her fiancées eyes and posture.

"Here, come sit down Jerry." Grace ordered.

Jerry took off his jacket and walked into their living room, collapsing on to the couch in an almighty thump. Grace squatted down in front of the detective, looking deep into his eyes.

"So what happened?" she pried.

"I had too much to drink with the guys, went for a walk, got lost and woke up in a skip this morning. I was late for work so I went straight to the office and then headed out to another homicide. That's all I can remember Grace, honestly." Jerry lied.

"Did you hurt yourself Jerry? You slept in a skip! You could have fallen on broken glass or a used hypodermic needle! You know what this city is like!" Grace exclaimed.

She grabbed Jerry's arms and began to frantically looking him over for any cuts or scratches.

"No I'm ok, just still really hungover. I need a stiff drink and a long soak in the tub. I'm sorry I didn't call." Jerry said.

He moved to stand up from the couch but was immediately accosted by Grace.

"I need to tell you something Jerry and it can't wait any longer." Grace hastened.

Jerry listened on, curious to her insistence.

"After I went to see the doctor today I took an at home test. It confirmed what I already suspected. I'm pregnant Jerry." Grace announced.

Jerry felt the blood drain out of his face upon hearing this news.

"That's why I didn't want us to do anything until our wedding night, or until I knew for absolute certain." Grace further admitted.

The young detective felt like such a huge fool, a stupid adulterous clown. Jerry's mind was suddenly awash with a collection of images ranging from Wu's shaven head in his lap, to the mutilated baby at the Waller crime scene, to Bloody Belle gnawing on the bones of murdered infants, to her collection of jarred heads and finally to the octopus ink squirting out of Wu's mouth. All these images swirled around in Jerry's head like a violent tornado, spiralling all the way down into the pit of his already queasy stomach. Jerry now felt like he had a live octopus squirming around in his own belly.

That was the final thought that went through Jerry's mind as he sprinted over to the bathroom, where he proceeded to spew and heave violently into the toilet. The sound of him retching and the splash back echoed back at him like some sort of horrific porcelain choir.

"That wasn't exactly the reaction I was hoping for." Grace calmly responded.

She came into the bathroom and propped herself up against the doorframe.

"I'm sorry, that's wonderful news! I just still feel like shit Grace." Jerry replied, wiping his mouth clean of vomit.

"You must really have one mother of a hangover. I suggest a Bloody Mary. I'll just go make you one yeah?" Grace asked.

A drink with the word bloody in it didn't exactly make Jerry feeling any better, but he knew of its healing capabilities.

"Yes please. I love you Grace, you know that right?" Jerry pathetically whimpered into the toilet bowl, before turning to look at his fiancée.

Grace looked back at the mess of a man slumped on the ground before her, softly smiling at his foolish antics before moving to the kitchen.

A wave of panic soon rippled throughout Jerry's entire body from head to toe. No one could ever find out about his involvement with Wu, especially Grace. He had to do something. As Jerry pondered over his fate the image of Wu's slender alien-like body sliding up and down his own crept back into his head, causing him to retch further. His stomach was virtually empty even before he arrived home. The only thing he was spewing forth was foul bitter tasting bile which now coated the inside of his throat, burning it further.

A little later Jerry had run himself a hot bath to soothe his exhausted body. The water was deep enough for him to completely submerge himself, holding his breath as he did. The silence underwater was intoxicating, allowing him to quieten the internal storm of worry and deceit brewing in his mind. Every now and again he slowly exhaled, watching the tiny air bubbles quickly rise up to the shimmering surface of the water before bursting on impact.

The hard unfiltered water clung uncomfortably to the outside surface of his eyes, but he didn't mind. So briefly at peace Jerry was that he felt like he could stay below forever. But all good things come to an end eventually and as the concentration of oxygen began to deplete in his blood and the pressure in his lungs built further Jerry had to resurface, inhaling loudly. He sat up and rubbed away the remaining water from his vision.

With that Grace entered the bathroom with his precious Bloody Mary.

"Here you are you drunken fool." Grace smirked, handing him his drink.

"Thanks." he replied, taking a good long sip.

Grace moved to sit down on the rim of the bath.

"I'm pregnant Jerry," she repeated. "and I know we didn't plan this right away but I had hoped we would eventually. I want to keep this new life growing inside me and I hope you do too."

"Of course I do Grace," Jerry assured his worried fiancée. "this really is wonderful news."

"I can't help but imagine the day when we tell baby the story of how daddy was skunk drunk when mommy told him the good news." she innocently joked to herself.

"Hey not drunk, hungover. It was my stag night." Jerry tried to justify.

Jerry fell silent as he looked up at his fiancée and wondered again how he had gotten so lucky in finding her.

"What?" Grace asked, clearly seeing this hopeless romantic twinkle in his eye.

"Nothing, I was just thinking about our first date." Jerry reminisced.

"I remember it very well. We went to the zoo. You were so nervous. You called the Tigers Zebras by mistake. You freaking idiot." Grace smiled.

She innocently poked fun at Jerry's past slip of the tongue.

"Tigers are slightly different to zebras Jerry." Grace chuckled to herself.

"Hey they both have stripes right?! I was just nervous because you looked so incredible. I wasn't sure you would even turn up, that you would come to your senses and leave me waiting there all day." Jerry moaned.

"But I didn't. Instead I had the most amazing day with a man I didn't know at the time would become my future husband." Grace reminisced.

"You smiled nearly the whole day. I couldn't take my eyes off of you because of it." Jerry remembered.

After a moment of pause Grace suddenly remembered something.

"Hey there is another zoo near to Hallow right?! We should go this weekend, for old times sake!" Grace suggested.

With the Figure Killer's next target potentially a zoo keeper, Jerry was at first hesitant to Grace being anywhere near Hallow City Zoo. But he saw sense in maybe surveying the zoo further. Perhaps he might just bump into the killer and stop them before they could commit their next atrocity.

"That sounds like a great idea my love. Hey, you wanna join me in the tub?" Jerry kindly offered.

"I've already washed Jerry." Grace replied.

"Let me rephrase that. Join me in the tub right now!" Jerry softly yelled.

He grabbed his fiancée around the waist and pulled her fully clothed form into the bath.

"Jerry! No!" Grace laughed out loudly as she was pulled in.

Grace could feel her blue dress becoming quickly saturated by water the deeper she fell into the bath.

With his naked form wrapping itself around her's, Jerry proceeded to kiss and playfully tickle bite Grace's neck, causing her to laugh harder. Water splashed and sloshed out of the tub and onto the bathroom's tiled floor as the young lovers continued to thrash and frolic together. Grace's long black hair, now wet from the bath water, clung desperately to Jerry's face like clumps of seaweed amidst the bath time foolery. Once their playful antics had slowly died down, Jerry and Grace looked deep into each others eyes, her head resting on his shoulder.

"You've ruined my new dress you dumb ape!" Grace complained girlishly.

"I'll buy you another one. Call it an early wedding gift," Jerry assured her. "something new and something blue."

"You big goon." Grace smiled, stroking the back of his head.

"I love you Grace and I'll do anything to keep you safe, to keep you both safe." he promised, now gently stroking Grace's abdomen.

"I know you will daddy." she replied.

She looked down at his hand now caressing her future baby bump, interlocking her fingers with his own.

It was nearly three in the morning, according to the crude green pixelated numbers on his alarm clock, and Jerry was still wide awake. He looked over at his Vietnamese goddess, sleeping soundly next to him on her front whilst purring softly to herself. He already had to protect his growing family from the horrors of Hallow but now he also had to protect them from his own mistakes.

No matter how he looked at it, Jerry had cheated on the woman he loved. Any other woman would be bad enough but he had to go and choose Madame Wu, the Black Octopus of Hallow. Grace would never venture over to Easy Street but Jerry knew his guilt would be too unbearable to keep just to himself. Something had to be done.

Chapter Eight

The Zoo Keeper

It was late morning again and back in the precinct's morgue Edward was detailing his further findings from the chainsaw massacre to the detectives. News of the Waller's triple homicide had become public knowledge, with Hallow City's media ever hungry for further news surrounding the Figure Killer's quickly mounting notoriety and body count.

"Well I found no figures anywhere on the bodies," Edward admitted. "all three victims did not have their genitals removed either."

"Four, you mean four victims Edward." Vincent reminded him.

The thought of Jill's infant being savagely brought into the world far too soon was not an easy thing for Vincent to get over. But this was a cold hard fact to the case and so he had to acknowledge it.

"Yes, sorry four victims. None had their wounds sealed with plastic as I'm sure you'll remember, given the extensive blood loss. Need I go on?" Edward asked.

"This was not the work of our Figure Killer gentlemen." Vincent confidently stated.

"So we do have a copycat killer?" Jerry asked Vincent.

"It definitely seems that way kid." he replied.

"Again where the hell is the Figure Killer even getting these figures from? They must be making them surely." Jerry pondered.

"What about the baby?" Murphy questioned Edward.

"No nothing peculiar with him," Edward sighed. "all four victims had nothing removed or replaced."

"So she had a son." Jerry summarised to himself, wondering if he would have a son himself.

"Yes but more importantly this new killer was stupid enough to leave their prints all over the place. We have a match for the prints on the murder weapon and the door frame. Suspect's name is Walter Sinclair. He worked as a janitor at the same city college Roberta Woods attended a few years ago, but he apparently struggled with mental health issues. He forced himself upon a female student there and was subsequently fired from his position by..." Edward detailed.

"Mrs Waller." Vincent guessed expectedly, cutting Edward short.

"Exactly. He was diagnosed a paranoid schizophrenic last year and sentenced to two years in prison. It says he was released early some weeks ago now due to good behaviour and newer medication." Edward continued.

"They released him?!" Murphy exclaimed.

"The system fails yet again," Vincent replied downbeat. "now we have an entire family destroyed because someone screwed up on the paperwork."

"You have an address we can find him at?" Jerry asked Edward.

"Yes but it's from before he went to prison. The property might have already been sold off to new owners." Edward explained.

"We'll still check it out. Crazy bastard might still think of it as home. What's the address?" Jerry asked.

"Fourteen Maple Drive, it's in the South East housing district." Edward replied.

He handed Jerry the address, as well as Walter's mugshot from his first arrest.

Walter was in his late forties, wrinkled face and balding, with a ridiculous comb over. With puffy eyelids, fat lips and a stubbly face he was by no means a looker.

"Ugly cunt." Jerry remarked, grimacing at the photo.

"Murphy you stay here and see if you can find anything more on these figures. Jerry you come with me to the address." Vincent instructed.

Joining the detectives once more on their hunt for Walter Sinclair was Commander Briers and his elite SWAT team. Arriving into the house district, the SWAT van came to a screeching halt just outside Walter's address, with the detectives pulling over just behind it. Located in a slightly more remote part of the city's outskirts, Maple Drive was a quiet street, with few vehicles parked up outside the houses. A *'For Sale'* sign had been erected on Walter's front lawn, which was now over grown and full of insects pollinating wild flowers around its edges. Commander Briers led the charge again, exiting the SWAT van first and followed shortly after by several members of his team.

"You reckon he's even still here?" Jerry asked Vincent quietly.

"Let us hope so kid." Vincent replied just as quietly.

The SWAT team immediately dispersed and surrounded the house in complete silence. Once all the entrances and exits were covered, Commander Briers gave the order to storm the premises. One member of the team again caved in the front door with a miniature battering ram before entering inside.

"You decks follow me!" Briers instructed both Vincent and Jerry.

After entering into the house Vincent and Jerry were greeted by the sight of blood droplets on the floor, along with the shouting calls from Brier's team.

"Walter Sinclair! Come out with your hands up!" one member called out.

"Where are ya hidin' ya sick twisted fuck?" the Commander couldn't help but let slip out.

Vincent and Jerry proceeded further into the small house, passing through a living room and past a kitchen that had not been cleaned in a long time. Both detectives held guns in their sweaty hands, ready for Walter if he chose to not come quietly. Soon after sweeping the entire house it was clear their suspect was not home.

"Shit where is he?" Jerry called out frustrated.

"Fuchs, any luck upstairs?" Briers called up the staircase.

"No sir, all rooms up here are clear!" Fuchs called back down.

"Sir we've got something here!" another SWAT personnel called out to Briers.

Vincent, Jerry and Briers's attentions were instantly drawn over to a closed door leading down into the basement. On the ground before it were several small pools of dried blood. Commander Briers silently signalled for two of his team to stand either side of him as he moved to open the door and descend down the rickety wooden staircase. Nothing but silence filtered up the staircase, until Briers called out for assistance.

"Decks, get down here!" Briers ominously commanded up to them.

Vincent and Jerry descended down into the basement also, unsure of what they would find. The air surrounding them all smelled dead, dampened by poor insulation and mould. Before them stood Commander Briers with a look of minor annoyance on his face, his gun now hanging down by his side in a relaxed stance.

"This is becoming all too familiar decks." he sarcastically remarked.

Laying beside him only a few feet away was the naked body of Walter Sinclair. He had been divided into the Figure Killer's signature five pieces, his wounds sealed with melted green plastic and his genitals cut away and removed. Floating over his body was a large green balloon, the end of its string tied around his left wrist.

"Ah shit!" Jerry spat out.

"Remind me not to tag along with you decks again next time." Briers remarked.

149

He glanced again at Walter's mutilated corpse.

"What's with the balloon anyway?" he asked.

Vincent stepped forward to take a better look at Walter's remains, only slightly illuminated by the sunlight coming in through the narrow basement windows.

"How is he the zoo keeper?" Jerry asked Vincent.

"I do not think he is." Vincent replied.

He crouched down to inspect the inside of Walter's mouth further. Gently prising it open with gloved hands, Vincent soon produced the small figure of a clown. It had bright green hair in the style of an Afro, white face paint with red lipstick, a bright blue jacket with a large pink bow tie, yellow trousers with red suspenders and a small green balloon accessory.

"Walter isn't the zoo keeper. He's a clown?" Jerry asked.

"Looks like the real killer did not take kindly to Walter copying their work. I think this was a retaliation kill of punishment." Vincent guessed.

"A clown for trying to be like the real Figure Killer?" Jerry guessed.

"Precisely." Vincent replied.

"They must have known about Sinclair even before we did, but how?" Jerry thought.

"Beat you to the punch eh decks!" Briers scoffed.

Vincent pondered over Walter's barbaric end, worried that the killer was much closer than they all thought. Jerry could clearly see the cogs turning in Vincent's mind.

"What are you thinking?" Jerry asked.

"Maybe our killer had planned on doing something with the Waller's, only to be beaten by Sinclair somehow. They then kept tabs on him, waiting for their moment to strike." Vincent replied.

"That's an awfully big coincidence ya got there deck." Briers noticed.

"But none of the Waller's had any connection to Hallow City Zoo or a zoo keeper." Jerry replied.

"Not that we know of. Something is a miss here." Vincent thought, rubbing his chin in contemplation.

A day out with Grace was just what Jerry needed. After the mistake of his stag night and the Figure Killer's unrelenting work throughout Hallow, the young detective was beginning to feel run down. Grace skipped girlishly as the two of them walked through the zoo entrance, holding one another's hand. Jerry thought back to the first time he visited the zoo and the very different circumstances surrounding that particular visit. He wondered whether he would run into the keeper who looked like an albino chicken again, or even the bulldog sow one.

"Yay we're here! Can we go see the Penguins first? Can we huh? Can we?" Grace beamed, tightening her grip on Jerry's hand.

Jerry smiled in amusement at his fiancées quick transformation back into the charming girl he first fell in love with.

"Yeah sure thing." Jerry agreed.

This day was just like their first date together, full of playful flirting and totally undivided attention on one another. Jerry cast aside all the self loathing and worry growing deep within him, instead trying to focus all his attention on the gorgeous woman before him and not the heinous wench he had betrayed her trust with. Gone were the detective's heavy work clothes and gun, replaced by loose fitting shorts and a t-shirt. The summer's warmth still clung to the detective, even outside of Hallow City.

As the two young lovers passed by the expansive children's play area, Grace stopped dead on the spot and began watching the many children. They resembled a miniature tornado composed of tiny screaming faces and grabby hands, sticky from candy. The many children spiralled around the climbing frames, causing yet more mayhem and concern for their own parents. Grace smiled and began rubbing her mid drift, where her own new life was slowly developing. Jerry saw this and moved his hand to stroke her abdomen also. The two of them looked deep

151

into one another's eyes as an unspoken knowledge of the journey they would be embarking on together passed between them.

Jerry's attention was soon taken away from his future wife by the iridescent yellow hair of a nearby clown, inflating balloons with a helium tank just outside the children's play area. The detective's work had managed to find him even on his day off. He knew immediately that he'd need to know who this clown was. Even though Walter was dead and the target victim for the clown figure, doubt had crept into Jerry's mind. He had to be sure this clown was not in fact the Figure Killer's next victim.

"I'll be right back." Jerry spoke in Grace's ear.

He let go of her firm grip and speedily made his way over to the clown.

"Excuse me, hey buddy!" Jerry hastened.

"If you want a balloon you're gonna have to get in line like everyone else." the clown brashly replied to Jerry, looking up from the child he was tending to.

Jerry took better notice of the long line of children and their parents waiting patiently behind this first child.

"No I don't want a balloon. I'm a homicide detective for Hallow City Precinct and I need your details please." Jerry instructed.

He reached for his badge, only then realising it was back at his apartment.

"Hey look pal, I'm no threat to the children here ok! I've no priors or criminal record alright!" the clown replied back defensively.

"No it's nothing like that. I need your name for your own safety. Your life may be in danger!" Jerry hastened with urgency.

"Danger? What danger?" the now worried clown asked back.

Suddenly a piercing scream from the nearby tropical house cut across the whole vicinity. It was quickly joined by the screams of other visitors, the sound rising up like a cacophony of terror. The tropical house was essentially one giant greenhouse. Its semi permeable walls and roof were made from thick sheets of bubble wrap plastic, allowing enough sound to pass through it with relative ease.

"Wait here, don't you move from this spot! I mean it! I'll be right back!" Jerry instructed the clown.

The clown didn't reply, distracted by the nearby screaming.

Jerry sprinted into the tropical house, making his way through the crowd of adults and children that began to spill out of the exit. Long heavy ropes hanging down from the doorway guarded one half of the entrance, opening up into a small partition. Jerry then pushed his way through a set of large plastic curtains that hung down from the ceiling. Evidently these two barriers were designed to keep the winged inhabitants of the tropical house from escaping outside. As Jerry entered into the tropical house he was instantly enveloped by its warm humid environment.

All around him flew several species of brightly coloured butterflies, each one in search of a sweet sugary boost of energy from the many plates of ripe fruit scattered about. Amongst the dense green foliage of the tropical house stood numerous species of brightly coloured flowers. Jerry had no time to stop and admire this pleasant sight as the screaming continued from further down the damp wood chipped pathway. The young detective soon arrived at the source of all the noisy commotion. The only visitors left appeared to have been stunned on the spot. One visitor was even beginning to take photographs of the scene before them all. Jerry followed their line of sight and soon beheld what had frightened so many away. His relaxing day off with Grace had now come to an abrupt end.

"Everyone step outside now." he firmly instructed the remaining witnesses.

Poking out from amongst the lush green foliage of the tropical house was a human foot. Jerry carefully climbed over the flimsy rope barrier that guarded the richly dark brown soil the dense green undergrowth sprouted up from. Jerry carefully rummaged

153

through the vegetation around the foot, peeling back layer after layer until his eyes fell upon what he feared he would find.

Laying on the moist tropical soil was another body from the Figure Killer. It was of an Hispanic woman roughly in her early forties. The woman's long dark brown hair had been tied back in a ponytail and lay to one side, camouflaging well with the rich brown soil. Her decapitated head was separated from the torso, her torso separated from her waist and legs, her arms cut away from just above the elbow and her nipples removed.

Like the artist and the snake charmer before her, the woman's feminine region had been sealed shut with melted orange plastic, as were all her severing wounds. Sitting beside her right hand, slightly dampened by the humidity, was a plush soft toy Tiger. Its bright orange colouration stood out amongst the greenery as much as the orange plastic. The zoo keeper figure found with the merman Dr Remington had been for this unfortunate woman all along.

Jerry sighed heavily as he moved away from the crime scene, not wanting to contaminate it any further. Thinking back to the discovery of Walter's body, it was now even clearer to Jerry that his murder was definitely a standalone killing, away from the Figure Killer's real work. Jerry climbed back over the rope barrier and took out his phone to call in his murderous discovery to Vincent.

"Vincent, we've got another figure kill here at Hallow City Zoo," he informed. "inside the tropical house."

"I am on my way. I will bring Edward and forensics with me." Vincent confirmed.

"See you soon" Jerry replied before hanging up.

He then remembered Grace, putting away his phone and quickly running back outside to find her. But Grace wasn't to be seen.

"Grace!" Jerry called out in a panic.

Jerry began to run through the crowd of zoo patrons, some embracing their own family members over the fear of losing them to the Figure Killer also.

"GRACE!" Jerry yelled across the sea of faces.

The now on duty detective began to feel very real fear creep back inside him, terrified over the lose of his pregnant fiancee. His fears were soon smothered as Jerry came to see Grace over by the clown, talking with him and getting a balloon for herself.

"Hi Jerry." she greeted innocently enough.

"Grace! Are you alright?" Jerry worried.

He grabbed her firmly by the shoulders, as if Grace were to float away somehow like the balloon she now held.

"Yeah I'm fine, why? What's wrong? What was that screaming about?" Grace casually asked.

The large green balloon, now tied around her slender wrist, mirrored that of Walter's. The resemblance was frightfully similar in Jerry's eyes.

"There has been another murder in the tropical house. I've already called it in." Jerry whispered in her ear.

A look of concern quickly spread across Grace's angelic face.

"Oh that's horrible! Is everyone else ok?" she said.

"Yeah they're fine but I'll have to cut our day together short." Jerry sighed.

"Back to work for daddy then?" Grace sighed in return, rubbing her abdomen with her balloon hand.

"I'll see what I can do my love." Jerry promised.

The tropical house had been cordoned off for forensic investigation and Vincent was busy questioning the zoo director Karen Redding about the victim. Jerry sat with Grace on a nearby play area bench, waiting for Vincent to be finished. He sat with both arms wrapped around her nimble frame, protecting her from the harsh reality taking place before them. Vincent soon finished his questioning and came over to them both.

155

"Our latest victim was Eliza Santiago. She was the curator of living collections here at the zoo until a few weeks ago. She had previously worked as a zoo keeper with large carnivores, including Tigers, at several other collections." Vincent informed Jerry.

"The killer knew we wouldn't have protected her," Jerry realised. "because they knew she wouldn't have been apart of our initial focus group of potential targets."

"It would seem so. According to Mrs Redding, Miss Santiago wasn't a well liked member of staff so we could have a number of suspects close to her." Vincent informed.

"Why is that?" Jerry asked.

"Apparently she gave the order for a number of healthy animals here to be culled for breeding purposes. That did not exactly sit well with a lot of the animal loving staff here. According to Mrs Redding, some were very vocal about her hopefully leaving the position one day. But murder seems a bit of an extreme measure for that." Vincent thought.

"Just slightly." said Murphy as he walked over to join them all.

"Hi Murphy." Grace greeted.

"Hey Grace." he greeted back.

"Do you think our killer has been one of the zoo keepers all this time?" Jerry asked.

"Who knows? We will check all the zoo staff for an alibi just to be sure." Vincent suggested.

"Miss Santiago's partner, a Miss Katherine Driver, is the section head of primates here at the zoo. Apparently the pair of them weren't well liked either. According to several other zoo staff members Miss Driver only secured the position as section head due to her existing relationship with Miss Santiago. Between them they apparently managed to drive away numerous staff members." Murphy detailed.

"People politics, they never change no matter where you go." Vincent remarked.

"It's not what you know, it's who you know." Jerry added.

"More like who you're sleeping with you mean!" Murphy laughed.

"We should look into the zoo's records of past and present employees. See if any of them have a motive to target Santiago." Vincent suggested.

"I'll get right on it." Murphy volunteered.

"What about the clown you met here at the zoo?" Vincent asked Jerry.

"Jeffrey King, white caucasian male in his mid twenties. It's probably nothing but we should look into him as well, see if he has any prior convictions." Jerry recommended to both Vincent and Murphy.

Vincent stopped talking and turned his attention to the gentle smile of Grace, for the two of them had yet to properly meet in person.

"And you must be the fabled Grace I have heard so much about." Vincent smiled.

Taking off his hat with one hand, Vincent offered the other to Grace in greeting.

"And you must be Vincent, the other man in Jerry's life, besides Murphy here." she quipped, shaking Vincent's hand in return.

"I am so sorry your day had to be tarnished by this awful business my dear." Vincent apologised, replacing his hat atop his head.

"It's ok. I'm unfortunately getting use to all this death and misery. I guess it comes with the territory of being the wife of a Hallow City detective." Grace joked with an air of sadness to her words.

"Fiancee." Jerry corrected with a smile.

Edward exited the tropical house shortly afterwards, removing his gloves and peeling back the protective hood of his overalls. He headed over to the three detectives and Grace, bringing with him more information on Eliza's body.

"And I thought it was hot out here!" a very sweaty Edward remarked.

"What did you find for us Ed?" Jerry asked.

"There was another figure in her mouth, a little man with a miniature camera. The killer could strike a photographer next." Edward assumed.

"Start looking up all professional photographers in the city." Vincent instructed Murphy.

"They could even just target a random tourist Vincent. It's gonna be hard to narrow down a search using 'man with camera' as the vague criteria." Jerry suggested.

"Do not start thinking like that Jerry," Vincent cautioned. "there is still time to save this person and stop this maniac."

"They're playing with us Vincent! Making it all one big game to them!" Jerry protested.

"What about the toy tiger?" Vincent asked.

"If it was purchased here from the zoo gift shop then we could have potential witnesses to the killer's appearance." Murphy thought.

"Good thinking, check into that for us also." Vincent instructed Murphy.

"Sure thing." he replied.

Over the zoo's harsh sounding tannoy system came an announcement, informing all visitors that the zoo would be closing early due to the recent traumatic discovery. An audible groan of complaint erupted from the crowd of spectators that lined the perimeter of the crime scene, morbidly hoping to catch a glimpse of Eliza's body. Vincent stepped closer to Jerry and Grace with purpose.

"Do not worry about this now. You two go and enjoy what remains of your day together. The weather is still nice, why not pay the Skull Swamps a visit? Lots of wildlife to see there." Vincent recommended.

"That's not a bad idea actually. You sure you don't need my help anymore today?" Jerry asked.

"I'm sure, you kids go have fun." Vincent gushed.

"Bye Vincent." said Grace.

"Goodbye my dear. See you after the weekend Jerry." Vincent replied.

The senior detective headed back over to the tropical house, whilst Murphy made his way towards the zoo's head office to question human resources.

"Come on, let's get outta here." Jerry motioned towards Grace.

He took his fiancee by the hand and lead her away.

Jerry and Grace ducked under the police line tape that cordoned off the tropical house and play area. They then slowly made their way through the crowd of spectators that outlined the crime scene.

"Detective Wilder." one uniformed officer standing guard acknowledged.

He tipped his hand at Jerry in a vague salute of professional courtesy.

"Officer Pace," Jerry replied. "got you stuck on perimeter duty again have they?"

"You know it! Is it definitely the Figure Killer again?" Pace asked.

Jerry nodded in response.

"Will they ever stop?" Pace continued to question.

"I certainly hope so Kenneth." Jerry replied back.

Fresh out of the academy, Officer Kenneth Pace was as new to Hallow as Jerry was, only differing in their age and title. He had joined the force to become an officer like his father before him. Jerry had liked him immediately. Baby faced and with a voice still breaking, Jerry feared Officer Pace was just too naive to survive the dangers lurking throughout Hallow. He wondered how long it would be before Hallow took him down. Looking more like a frightened school boy, Jerry worried the criminal underworld would simply eat Pace alive, shoe laces and everything.

Jerry was still learning all the names and faces of his colleagues back at the precinct and it appeared the other officers had failed to make a lasting impression in his mind. Clark and Reed were pretty much the only other people he really knew well enough at the building besides Vincent, Murphy, Edward and the Chief. If he was going to make a long term career out of Hallow City, Jerry figured he should really start paying more attention to the other people around him.

"This is Ray Sanders, reporting for Hallow City News." introduced one news reporter.

By the time Jerry and Grace had left Hallow City Zoo, a swarm of news reporters and press officials had already descended upon the zoo's exit. Most were busy interviewing some of the hapless visitors. One such visitor was giving an in depth look into how they came across Eliza's body.

"I'm joined now by one eye witness to the Figure Killer's latest crime here at Hallow City Zoo. Sir what more can you tell us?" Ray Saunders asked.

"The Figure Killer was here!" one male visitor announced before the reporter and their cameraman.

This was all happening just within earshot of Jerry.

"What did you actually see then?" Ray urgently asked the man.

They thrust their black microphone back into the face of the interviewee.

"A man's body cut into pieces, blood everywhere! It was horrible!" they lied.

"Blood? Really? But I thought the Figure Killer drained their victims?" Ray challenged, confused by this account.

Jerry quietly laughed at this man's inaccurate details. He clearly hadn't seen Eliza's body but thought claiming he had would have gotten him his five minutes of fame on Hallow's late night news report. In the meantime Jerry and Grace had managed to slip past the vulture-like press, narrowly avoiding their barrage of questions.

"Why are some people so fascinated by death and destruction?" Grace innocently asked herself.

She tightened her grip on Jerry's hand, resting her head on his shoulder as they kept walking.

Jerry thought to himself as to how good natured Grace really was to ask such a question. She really was the one good thing in his life. A guiding light, a pure spirit to keep him on the straight and narrow. But then he remembered Wu and how his new darkness threatened Grace. He felt dirty and tarnished by deceit. His lies were cutting deep into his mind like shards of broken glass, lacerating every emotion he had towards Grace. Jerry had to tell her, but how and when he hadn't figured out yet. Until then there was only one solution he could think of. Wu had to go away somehow.

Chapter Nine

The Photographer

The very next day Vincent, Jerry and Murphy were called over to a photography studio a few blocks away from Easy Street named Captured Perfection. They were greeted by an all too familiar sight. Only a day after the discovery of Eliza and the Figure Killer had struck again. The killer was accelerating their rate of killing and the detectives were once more too late to save anyone.

The body of a man in his early thirties lay in front of a large white backdrop which almost filled the entire room. His body was divided into the expected five sections, his genitals removed and all the wounds sealed by melted plastic black in colour. To his right hand lay an old film roll camera. Surrounding his body was a small collection of camera tripod, each one facing him. Extensive harsh lighting illuminated his divided form from above, casting hardly a single shadow around him.

The whole scene was pristinely clean, devoid of any blood splatter or any other escaped bodily secretions, yet another one of the Figure Killer's staple trademarks. The photographer's grim end immediately cast Jerry's mind back to the discovery of Joshua Langland. Both crime scenes were remarkably similar.

"We weren't quick enough again." Murphy sighed.

"How are we suppose to stop this psycho?!" Jerry almost yelled.

Vincent removed his hat to rub away the beads of sweat slowly trickling down his brow, stopping them from stinging the corners of his eyes.

"There are less than twenty professional photographers in this fucking city! We had time to check them all but the killer is still always one step ahead of us! They're laughing at us Vincent! Got us chasing our own bloody tails!" Jerry asserted frustratingly.

Jerry very nearly kicked over one of the tripods in anger, instead choosing to slam his fists against the wall. Vincent could see his frustrated young partner was starting to take things very personally.

"Why an old film roll camera anyway? Why not one of these new fangled digital ones?" Murphy asked.

"Too expensive maybe," Vincent guessed. "technology is advancing so quickly these days. I cannot keep up with it myself."

"We should examine his camera back at the precinct. If there is a roll of film inside it, then we might have some photographic evidence." Murphy suggested.

A member of Edward's forensic team continued to take photos of the crime scene, including the camera laying beside the man's body. The irony of a camera having to take the photo of another camera instantly leapt out at Jerry.

"What do we know about him?" Vincent asked, motioning towards the dead man.

"Victim's name is Alexi Kovalev. He only recently moved here from Siberian a month ago. Captured Perfection is his own business, yet opened thanks largely in part to a helpful donation from his wealthy father. So the studio wasn't particularly well known yet." Murphy detailed.

"It will be now. But for all the wrong reasons." Jerry added.

"Alexi's studio still didn't have much in the way of advertisement," Murphy continued. "he wouldn't have been on our radar soon enough."

"Who found him?" Vincent asked.

Jerry looked Alexi's body over once more, noticing his thick black hair and the beginnings of his five o'clock shadow.

"His first client of the day, a Claudia van de Vries. She came here for a photo shoot this morning, before discovering the body and then calling us." Murphy filled in.

"Where is she now?" Vincent asked.

"Downstairs, in the waiting room with a couple of uniforms. She is quite the looker I must say. I still need to take her full statement." Murphy admitted to them.

"Ok Jerry, you go and take care of that." Vincent instructed.

Jerry left the studio to go and find the witness, heading back down to the small waiting room. To Jerry's surprise the woman was the very same Claudia he had seen working at the Fox Glove.

"Hello Miss, I'm DI Wilder of the HCPD. I need to ask you some more questions please." Jerry began.

"I already answered the other officer's questions." she began to protest.

Jerry could still remember his irresistible attraction to this young women from before and now tried desperately to hide it.

"Hey wait, I recognise you! You've been to the Fox Glove a couple of times yes?" Claudia challenged in her thick European accent.

"Yes I have. That was to investigate the murder of your colleague Becky Childs." Jerry reminded her.

"Do you think the same person who killed Becky also killed Alexi? This Figure Killer?" she asked concerned.

"That's what I'm here to find out," Jerry returned. "why did you come to Alexi's studio today?"

"He is my newest photographer. He takes my photo to help with my portfolio. You see I want to get into the professional adult entertainment industry, to get away from Easy Street." Claudia admitted.

Jerry's frustration had been momentarily slain by his night and morning with Wu. But to now hear that Claudia wanted to become a professional porn star instantly reignited the fire of his desire for her. Beforehand Claudia had always been a good distance away from Jerry. Now she was standing right in front of him and he could barely take his eyes off her.

Claudia had the most brilliantly blue eyes, which took centre stage in her round face. Natural blond hair, almost golden in colour, fell loosely around her shoulders. She had a cute slightly upturned nose and a quite angular chin. Claudia was all natural, no surgical enhancements, no discerning tattoos and no scars. She was pristine in Jerry's eyes. Draped in an exquisite fur coat and wearing tight leather trousers, Claudia's earnings from the Fox Glove were clear to see. She stood atop an impressive pair of heels, making her even taller than Jerry.

"Did you see or hear anything before and after you arrived into the building?" Jerry questioned.

"No nothing. I always meet Alexi in his studio. The front door was already unlocked so I climbed up the stairs. That's when I found him." Claudia recounted.

She moved to wipe her nose with a tissue, upset by the death of her friend.

"Were you two close?" Jerry questioned.

"A little yes. He was nice to me, a real decent guy, something I rarely meet these days." she replied.
Claudia began to tear up further.

"van de Vries. Is that Dutch?" Jerry bluntly asked this towering Amazonian.
He had hoped this personal question would distract her from the grief she was starting to feel again.

"Yes it is," she smiled, impressed by his intuition. "you've been to my homeland?"

"No but I'd like to visit there sometime in the future." he replied.

"I go back home to see family every few weeks. If you're ever over at the same time as me then I'd make an excellent tour guide for you." Claudia kindly offered.
Claudia softly bit her lower lip flirtatiously at Jerry upon her very generous offer. The young detective could feel his adulterous desires surging inside him once more as this siren looked him up and down.

165

"I don't think my fiancée would..." Jerry began to say but cut himself short.

At that moment Jerry came to realise that it wasn't just Wu who he had faulted for. It seemed he didn't want Claudia to know he was with someone either. The mere mention of the word fiancée caused Claudia's cherub like smile to instantly vanish. This young woman appeared to be rather taken with him but now that Claudia knew he was engaged to be married she knew he would not be her's.

"I'm sorry, I didn't realise you were with someone. I'm so embarrassed." Claudia apologised, covering her blushing face with both hands.

Claudia tried to hide her foolish proposal again with a masking smile, but deep down she was hurting.

"Jerry!" Vincent suddenly called down from the studio.

"You're an incredibly beautiful woman Claudia and if I wasn't engaged then I would definitely like to pursue this." Jerry quickly admitted.

"Well, she doesn't have to know." Claudia coyly replied.

"I'm sorry but I love her too much to do that again." Jerry admitted.

"Again?" Claudia asked.

"Jerry!" Vincent yelled out once more.

"Excuse me." Jerry hastened to Claudia before sprinting back upstairs.

Jerry had resisted an overwhelming temptation but Claudia had reminded him again of his betrayal towards Grace. As he approached Alexi's body Edward, who had been squatting down beside him, stood up and presented Jerry with his finding. In his gloved hand Edward held out another small plastic figure and Jerry could immediately see the look of worry in Vincent's eye.

Her body and legs were predominantly white with an eloquent lace printing on them, a tiara atop her blond hair and a bouquet of yellow flowers in one hand. A wide happy smile was printed across her face. She looked just like a blushing bride. Gone completely was his desire for the stripper named Claudia. At that moment Jerry could think of only one person in the whole universe.

"Grace." he uttered.

The roll of film from Alexi's camera was later developed back at the precinct. The old photography red room, now slowly being rendered obsolete due to the encroaching digital age, had been posthumously brought out of retirement. Vincent couldn't help but feel like a relic himself, still floating around the precinct from the days of old school detective work.

From the roll of film found at the crime scene several photos of Claudia were soon developed. Each one was of her posing half naked in an array of different positions.

"Bloody Nora!" Murphy exclaimed as he thumbed through the photos.

Jerry looked over this collection of photos as well, thumbing through them quickly so as to not linger on any for too long. This he hoped would help hide his interest in Claudia. But Jerry had to study the next few photos very carefully, for they were of Alexi.

They showed him hanging upside down from his ankles, naked and appearing to be unconscious. The next few photos showed blood pouring down over his face after the killer had stabbed his neck. He wasn't gagged in any way, still appearing to be unconscious or at the very least sedated. The last few photos showed his body being cut into the signature five pieces, the killer's gloved hands operating a workshop band saw to slice through the neck and torso. All these photos gave the detectives a small window into the Figure Killer's mind and their methods.

"Our killer definitely took these," Vincent confidently stated. "they want us to see how they do their work."

After shuffling through each photo he handed them back to Jerry once again.

"But why now?" Jerry asked.

"They could be nearing the end of their work, hidden secrets too good to hold on to just themselves now. They're showing off." Murphy thought.

"Could the killer have an accomplice?" Jerry asked.

"Unlikely, our killer does what they want. They are methodical, having someone else around would just hinder their work and slow them down." Vincent guessed.

"The camera was dusted for prints, only Alexi's were found on it according to Ed." Murphy informed his colleagues.

"The killer is taunting us with these!" Jerry hastened to say.

He held the photos up in one hand, all of them facing Vincent picture side.

"We're getting closer and they know it, but they keep staying just out of reach." Jerry said.

"The killer is getting cocky, and in their over confidence they could slip up. Then we might finally nab the bastard!" Murphy wished.

"Look closer at these photos. There has to be something that will trip them up, something they have missed or some small detail they have overlooked. Why would the killer now be giving us help almost?" Vincent questioned.

"The background to all these photos is just a brick wall, but the brick wall of what?" Murphy asked himself.

If the killer was indeed getting that much closer to them then Jerry feared for Grace's safety more than ever.

Out of the corner of one eye, Jerry saw the Chief briskly walking over to them all with some interesting new developments.

"Gentlemen I just received word from narcotics saying that they're conducting a raid over at the Black Octopus. Apparently they got an anonymous tip off, saying Algae is exchanging hands there." the Chief informed.

"What does that have to do with our case?" Vincent challenged.

"Well the owner, this Madame Wu, wants to talk to you about it Wilder." the Chief replied, looking to Jerry.

Jerry felt his heart stop dead, before leaping up into his throat upon hearing this news. Paranoia was hitting him hard, worried over what Wu wanted with him and what she might say in front of Vincent.

"What would she want to talk to you about then Jerry?" Vincent asked suspiciously.

"Beats me." Jerry lied, trying to act dumb.

"Nevertheless you two head over there now and find out what." the Chief ordered.

The raid on the Black Octopus was well under way by the time Vincent and Jerry arrived outside the entrance to Bang'd Kok. The thick sickly air of Easy Street felt even more choking than ever. What little sunlight that reached the city street from above felt searing to the touch. Jerry felt like a small insect being cooked alive under a magnifying glass. A few flaps with his jacket in no way helped him cool down.

Whilst the law had no control over the legal prostitution in Hallow, Category One drugs such as Algae were definitely illegal and worthy of such raids and subsequent confiscation. Vincent and Jerry arrived in time to see the Black Octopus's numerous female employees being escorted away in handcuffs. After them came their clients, barely clothed and mostly male but with a few women sprinkled between them. It seemed that in the sudden frenzy of the raid that all they had time to do was to put on their customary white dressing gowns.

The next few individuals to be led away were Wu's bodyguards Jerry had seen on his first visit. Both men were just as large as he remembered. Narcotics had needed to use two sets of interlocked handcuffs to restrain their arms behind their backs due to the broadness of their shoulders. Jade and her sisters were still no where to be seen.

Finally Madame Wu emerged from the entrance, her hands also handcuffed behind her back, being led away by one imposing narcotics agent. Her slender alien-like form was now covered by a simple black tank top and a pair of ugly sweat pants. Jerry had never seen her during daylight hours before so was immediately struck by the oddity of the situation. Her skin was even more ghostly pale out in the unforgiving summer sunlight, nearly blinding Jerry upon viewing. Only in darkness had he seen this woman. Wu soon spotted Jerry, her piercing eyes now transfixed on him alone.

"Detective help me please! What's going on?" Wu began to plead.

"Narcotics got a tip off saying that you have Algae on your premises." Jerry informed her.

"That's a lie! I've never dealt with drugs!" Wu quickly answered back.

"Why did you ask for me to be here Wu?" Jerry bluntly asked.

"Help me detective, please! Get me off the hook. For old time's sake." Wu pleaded, her eyes beginning to mist up with tears.

Jerry ignored her plea for help. He wasn't fooled by her suspicious crocodile tears for one moment, remembering Vincent's past mistake with Bloody Belle.

"Detective Wilder?" Wu cried again.

"I'm sorry Madame. I really don't know what you're talking about." Jerry lied.

In a matter of seconds a look of pure rage welled up on her face, replacing Wu's earlier desperate expression.

"Bastard! This was your doing wasn't it?! Didn't want your dirty little secret getting out did you?! Thought you could get me locked away!" Wu screamed at Jerry.

Vincent looked to Jerry, puzzled by Wu's loud wailings.

"I'll fucking get you for this you piece of shit cop!" she screamed further.

Her voice became so high and shrill it was almost like a banshee's wail.

"I'll fucking get you for this!" Wu continued to threaten.

Wu lashed out at Jerry, trying to savagely bite at his face, the officer restraining her only barely managing to control this rabid creature. Jerry winced as Wu got tantalisingly close.

"My girls! My girls!" she screamed as she was quickly led away.

Wu was escorted over to Easy Street and shoved into the back of a haphazardly parked narcotics van.

Jerry looked over at Wu's female employees, wondering why she was so distraught even though they were right there. He thought she must have been referring to the octopi in her bedroom, her 'prized possessions' he remembered her addressing them as. From inside the van Jerry could still hear Wu struggling to get loose, still screaming his name.

"What the hell was that all about?" Vincent demanded.

"Beats me! That bitch is crazy!" Jerry exclaimed, denying any involvement with Wu.

"What did she mean by 'her girls'?" Vincent asked.

"Wu can be tricky, eager to mislead and disguise certain things as something else. I reckon there is Algae here, she's just hiding it very well. And I think I know where it is." Jerry claimed to know.

The young detective egotistically thought that finding a large haul of Algae would help boost his career and reputation back at the HCPD. It would also put Wu behind bars, keeping her and Jerry's secret locked away for good.

"This is not our job Jerry, leave it to narcotics." Vincent reminded him.

The old man was still very much a stickler for the rules. But his words fell on deaf ears as Jerry quickly made his way back inside the Black Octopus. With a flash of his badge Jerry easily made it past the entrance guard.

"Jerry get back here!" Vincent demanded after his eager partner.

Once inside the all too familiar surroundings of the Black Octopus, Jerry briskly walked down the narrow corridor towards Wu's office, Vincent trailing behind him. There was no one armed girl in the booth this time. She was standing outside with the other employees, handcuffed rather ingeniously to one of her ankles. The massage rooms were all open now, allowing Jerry to briefly take a peek inside. They were all very uniform, each one containing the same style massage bed and dim lighting from candles. A copious assortment of oils and lotions lined all the shelves in each room, complete with boxes of tissues for messy endings.

Narcotics had ransacked the entirety of Wu's office, turning over furniture and emptying all the draws of her desk in a bid to find the drugs. Sniffer dogs accompanied some of the team as they continued to raid the whole premises, heading up a stair case that led away from the central corridor. Jerry moved into the room on the right hand side of Wu's office after Narcotics had finished their search inside, knowing full well that it was Wu's personal bed chamber. Jerry looked again upon a familiar sight.

The clam bed in which his adulterous ways had gotten the best of him lay before him once more. The bedding was unkept, as if Wu had been napping before the raid began. Jerry moved to the octopus tanks and peered under the lids, thinking some drugs were stuck underneath. But there wasn't.

"There you are." Vincent called out as he entered the room.

Jerry moved to the foot of the irregular bed frame, thinking something lay underneath. He got down on to the floor for a better look.

"We should not be here Jerry." Vincent asserted.

Jerry was now too engrossed in his one man search for Algae, selfishly thinking about his own glory. He soon spied upon a small rug under the bed. With one hand he pulled it away, thinking something may lay hidden under it. To his surprise, instead of drugs, he uncovered a secret hatchway built into the floor.

"We are leaving now Jerry!" Vincent instructed.

"There's something under here." Jerry replied as he climbed back on to his feet.

"I don't care. This is not our case to solve." Vincent firmly put.

Jerry tried pushing the bed frame away to one side but it was heavier than he imagined.

"Help me move this." he asked.

Vincent didn't reply, instead choosing to stand there like a statue and glare at his young impulsive partner.

"Look I'm not leaving until I know what's under here!" Jerry asserted.

In all the excitement and commotion Jerry had gotten completely carried away with his own escapade.

"Call it intuition but I know something is here. Surely you must have felt something like that in your time?" Jerry asked.

Vincent could see his much younger, reckless self reflecting back at him through Jerry's excitable expression. Nostalgia for his earlier cases crept back into Vincent's mind, knowing he wasn't going to be doing anything like this ever again after his retirement. He knew his headstrong partner would be in much safer hands with his guidance.

"I am going to regret this." Vincent sighed.

Yielding to his young partner's assistance, Vincent moved to help push the bed to one side. With their combined strength they pushed it away, exposing the secret hatchway. Jerry crouched down next to the door and pulled the metal handle to open it. All that was revealed was the top of a small ladder, leading down into a dark abyssal basement.

"I knew it! I bet you the drugs are down there." Jerry softly cried out.

"Only one way to find out kid." Vincent replied back.

He crouched down next to Jerry, getting ready to climb down the ladder ahead of him.

"I will go first, just in case something goes wrong and one of us gets fired over it. Might as well be me." Vincent offered.

Jerry was surprised by Vincent's sudden cavalier attitude to the situation, the younger more excitable man within him steadily rising to the surface once more. He watched as his surprisingly spry partner slowly disappeared into the darkness below. Jerry followed soon afterwards. Having climbed down roughly three metres the detectives now stood together in total darkness. The only source of light around came from Wu's bedroom above them. Vincent suddenly motioned for Jerry to be silent, stopping dead himself.

"Shh, you hear that?" Vincent whispered to Jerry.

The sound of several muffled cries began to fill the empty darkness around the detectives. Using the light from above Vincent struck upon the outline of a light switch on the wall next to him. He flipped the switch on. The small dank basement they were standing in was immediately lit up by a single lightbulb hanging from the centre of the ceiling. Down in the basement both Vincent and Jerry beheld a truly horrifying sight.

"Oh my lord." Vincent uttered.

On the wall before them, sitting side by side, were six young women. They were gagged and chained up by their necks and wrists. Their shackles allowed them only enough give to sit down on the ground. All of them were naked and dirty, having been previously stripped of their clothing and modesty. None of them appeared to have been washed in many days. What was most shocking however was that the women were incomplete, all of them missing at least one limb.

The first girl had most of her left arm and right leg missing, whilst the second had both her legs missing above the knee. The third girl had both her forearms missing and so was only chained by the neck. The fourth girl had her left arm and both legs

174

missing. The fifth girl was the most fortunate of them all, having only her right leg missing. All of the women had the same little black ink tattoo of an octopus on their limb stumps, exactly the same as the girl from the booth now handcuffed outside. All their stumps were very neatly sown up and despite the filthy setting looked surprisingly clean of infection. The work of a meticulous professional no doubt.

The final girl sadly had it worse, having had both arms and both legs removed. However this girl was different to the others. What remained of her upper legs were propped up and spread apart by a bizarre birthing holster. On a small wooden table in front of her was a range of sinister and stomach churning medical instruments, several looking more gynaecological than the rest. In the corner of the room was an empty tank of water with a filtration system quietly humming away.

Vincent rushed to the side of this limbless girl and removed her gag.

"Help me," she desperately pleaded to him. "it's inside me."

She sounded like she had no energy left in her what so ever.

"What is? What's inside you?" Vincent replied with urgency.

"IT'S INSIDE ME!!" she suddenly screamed again in response.

Having not answered Vincent's question the girl soon burst into tears of very real pain and sorrow.

"It's ok. We're with the HCPD. We're here to help." Vincent informed all the girls.

"Who did this to you?" Jerry asked.

The girl with no limbs only continued to scream further in agony, sounding like she was almost in birthing pain. Both Vincent and Jerry's attention was immediately drawn down to between her legs as a long black tentacle began to snake its way out from between her labia. The girl continued to scream, a painful orgasm to Jerry's ears now. Before the stunned detectives

175

more tentacles began to slowly emerge, one by one from inside her.

They blindly reached out to grab hold of anything, wrapping around her upper thighs for better anchorage. The moist body of an octopus, the size of a cantaloupe, began to slowly erupt from her loins in one final push. The creature clumsily fell to the ground before squirming away in a desperate search for life preserving water.

The girl let out one final deafening blood curdling scream of terror that chilled both Vincent and Jerry to the bone. As her scream echoed around her grim prison she beheld the slimy animal now struggling to crawl away from her.

"Oh fuck!" Jerry cried out, moving one hand to cover his mouth in repulse.

"Get an ambulance here! Get these women medical attention now!" Vincent almost yelled at Jerry.

Without a hint of hesitation Jerry leapt over to the ladder as Vincent continued to comfort the young woman.

"You are safe now, you are all safe now." he hopelessly tried to reassure them.

Vincent removed the gags from the women and began to desperately pry open the lock around the limbless girl's neck with his bare fingers. Jerry stopped his ascent up the ladder as he noticed a set of keys hanging on the wall away from the light switch. He quickly unhooked them.

"Vincent I found the keys." he said urgently, tossing them over to his partner.

Vincent thumbed through the small set before unlocking the girl's restraint around her neck, causing her to collapse into his arms, still sobbing hysterically. Vincent took off his jacket and wrapped it around the traumatised girl, rubbing her shoulders and what remained of her upper arms in an attempt to warm her up. Jerry grabbed the keys from Vincent's side and unlocked the rest of the women, their cries of desperation and thanks echoed back at him.

Jerry again noticed the octopus on the ground, hopelessly struggling to crawl across the cold dusty floor. As horrific as the situation was Jerry couldn't help but feel sorry for the poor animal, it too an innocent victim in all this misery. Jerry awkwardly grabbed the squirming cephalopod and quickly moved to drop it into the tank of water in the corner of the room. With its soft fragile body now supported by the weight of the water, the octopus quickly recovered from its ordeal and regained some of its strength.

Jerry frantically rubbed the mixture of slimy juices now coating his palms on to his trousers to remove as much as possible.

"What are you still doing here? Get help now!" Vincent ordered.

Jerry moved to climb the ladder again but stopped to look at the girls once more. His discovery was monumental.

"Vincent. They're the women from Joshua's tapes!" Jerry suddenly realised aloud.

Vincent's eyes darted between the faces of all the women, before settling on the limbless girl he was comforting. In the shock of the moment Vincent hadn't realised either, now recognising the familiar features of each of the women.

"Rosie?" he asked the girl in his arms.

The limbless girl looked at him as if she hadn't heard her name in years, before bursting into tears again and pressing her face against his shoulder.

Jerry immediately felt a stronger connection he now held with Vincent. Both detectives shared a kinship in their first case. Vincent's monster was Bloody Belle and now Madame Wu was Jerry's. Jerry pushed this thought to the back of his mind as he quickly climbed the ladder back into Wu's bedroom. She must have been referring to these poor creatures when she cried out for her girls earlier, suffering down there in the dark. But then Jerry remembered hearing that muffled voice on the morning he awoke in Wu's bedroom, mistaking it for Wu's young employee. If only he had known its real source at the time.

Back at the precinct, Jerry filled Murphy in on their accidental yet fortunate discovery of Wu's basement girls during the raid of the Black Octopus.

"What?!" Murphy exclaimed upon hearing the news.

"So the rumours you heard were true all along. She really did have a dungeon and right under our noses no less." Jerry pointed out.

Murphy shuddered at the thought as Vincent entered with the full report on Wu's arrest.

"The dismembering of the women. It must have been Wu or someone she knows. We need to question the girls." Jerry hastily asked his approaching colleague.

"Yes, but later Jerry." Vincent answered.

"What do you mean 'later'?" Jerry challenged.

"I'm grateful for your intuition in finding those girls Jerry but right now they need time to recover from this. I am sure they are going to need a great deal of therapy, both physical and mental, before they are in any shape to help us. You really want them to relive that nightmare again right now? They could retreat further into their psychosis and may never be able to completely recover from this ordeal." Vincent justified.

"Then we have only Wu to question then," Murphy noted "seeing as all her employees are keeping a tight lip on this."

Jerry could sense what was to come, and he dreaded it.

The anonymous tip off called into the precinct had now karmically embedded Jerry's adulterous mistake with Wu even deeper into his life.

"When then? When do we question her?" Jerry asked, trying to act like he had nothing to hide.

"As soon as possible, while it is still fresh in her mind. She may have other girls locked away somewhere." Vincent thought.

Over to their conversation came the Chief with further news on the raid.

"Well detectives, Narcotics informed me that they didn't find a single trace of Algae in or around the Black Octopus building." he announced.

"The tip off must have been fake then, or she's hiding it very well." Murphy thought.

"What the hell is this Algae anyway?" Jerry asked.

"It's new in Hallow and is starting to spring up in more districts across the city." answered the Chief.

"So why is it making all of the junkies out there cream in their proverbial pants?" Murphy crudely asked.

"Algae is similar to Crystal Meth, crossed with crack cocaine in its effects on the system. Only much stronger and in some cases proving deadlier." the Chief began to list.

"What more do we know about it?" Vincent asked.

"It appears as fluorescent green crystals and leeches vitamins from the body after use, particularly Vitamin C. Hence its street name Algae." the Chief continued.

"What about its manufacture and distribution? Any news on that front?" Vincent wondered.

"We think it's coming from further up North, possibly from Garden Ridge City. But addicts found with it all show the same symptoms." the Chief replied.

"Like what?" Murphy asked.

"Severe scurvy." the Chief simply put.

"Argh, scurvy matey!" Murphy joked in a piratical accent.

The Chief was understandably unamused by Murphy's sea faring impression. With a blank expression plastered across his old beaten face he continued to detail.

"So far all the crackheads found to be using it had bleeding gums, little to no teeth, severe joint pain and breathing difficulties. Some Algae dens already raided in Hallow were found to have piles of empty juice cartons everywhere. In a vain attempt to counteract the scurvy, the addicts drink excessive amounts of fruit juice, particularly orange. But since they keep using, the juice has no affect on the Algae." the Chief concluded.

"Sounds problematic." Murphy quipped.

"It will be Murphy, if we don't stamp it out now before it establishes further. If we're not careful this Algae could spread further, flood the streets and become an epidemic across the whole of Hallow." the Chief cautioned.

"We'll keep our eyes open for it Sir." Jerry reassured his superior.

Vincent, Jerry and Murphy all stood behind the one way glass silently observing the heinous creature that had been caught in their net. Wu sat at the only table in the interview room, her wrists handcuffed to the table and her ankles handcuffed to a metal hoop on the floor. The interview room was wired to the back teeth with video surveillance and hidden microphones. A single guard stood in the corner of the room, by the only door in or out. Armed with an impressive shotgun, Wu was not intimidated by him in the slightest, even making sexual offers and jokes at the guard. He didn't reply to a single one of her offers or taunts.

"Ah man, MacReady in there is one stone cold SOB. I couldn't last five minutes alone in that room with her." Murphy remarked.

"Well you are going to have to alright. I am going in there with you and Jerry." Vincent returned.

Jerry could feel his pulse racing ahead of him and his own heart beat. It felt like his mind was hopelessly treading water in a sea of panic.

"I can't go in there Vincent, I just can't." Jerry blurted out.

Vincent and Murphy both looked to Jerry, confused by his outburst. Jerry's secrets were beginning to quickly unravel in front of them.

"Why not?" Vincent challenged.

"I just can't, trust me on this." Jerry replied.

"We do not have time for your delays Jerry. We will talk about this later." Vincent cautioned the young detective.

"You pansy!" Murphy lightly jabbed at Jerry.

"Come on Patrick." Vincent directed.

In they went, the sound of their metal chairs squeaking over the microphones as the men pulled them out from under the table to sit down. Wu just sat there in her new inmate onesie, not saying a single word.

"Let the record know that conducting this interview today is Detective Lieutenant Vincent Harrington. I am joined by Detective Inspector Patrick Murphy and we are..." Vincent stated aloud before being interrupted by Wu.

"Where is he?" Wu blurted out.

"Who?" Vincent replied.

"The other one, Wilder." Wu responded.

She looked up at the security camera in the corner of the room filming her every move. On the monitor in front of him, it looked as though Wu was staring right at Jerry, cowering on the other side of the one way glass. Wu then looked again at the one way mirror in the room, knowing that there would be more officers on the other side.

"You in there detective?" she asked aloud.

At that moment the Chief entered into the room with Jerry. Things were going from bad to worse for him.

"Chief, what are you doing here?" Jerry questioned, launching a preemptive strike.

"What am I doing here? What are you doing in here Wilder? Get in there rookie! This is your case now!" the Chief ordered him.

"Not enough seats in there sir." Jerry joked, hoping it would fly.

"Very funny Wilder. Close but no cigar. You need the practise. You gotta get use to making the perps sweat and give up information. That's how you save lives rookie. That's what it's all about! Now get in there!" the Chief ordered again.

181

There was no hiding from this now. Jerry found himself to be in a compromising situation. The detective sighed before composing himself for what was to come. Jerry opened the door and walked in.

"There he is!" Wu spat out as Jerry entered.

"It's ok Murphy, I got this." Jerry motioned to his colleague.

"Oh thank you Lord in heaven!" Murphy replied.

He immediately leapt to his feet and rushed out of the room, slamming the door closed behind him.

Jerry gingerly sat down in the now vacant seat to the right of Vincent. His pulse was racing as Wu glared back at him, not even acknowledging Vincent anymore, her gaze boring right through Jerry. The young detective was visibly nervous and Wu could smell his fear in the air, like a shark closing in on a bleeding fish.

"What's the matter detective? You look like you've seen a ghost." Wu softly asked.

With that Wu suddenly lunged forward, throwing her full weight as far as possible in Jerry's direction. The sound of her chained handcuffs rattled loudly on the metal table in front of the detectives, adding further impact to her attack. So sudden was her move she even frightened Vincent and the trigger eager MacReady in the corner. Jerry flinched amazingly but Wu hadn't tried to bite at his face this time. It was all for show and mocked the detective's resolve. MacReady ran forward with his shotgun already aimed at Wu's head.

"Easy there handsome. I wouldn't want your big gun to go off in my face, just yet." Wu teased him, looking down to his crotch.

Wu recoiled back into her seat, a large smile on her face proving she had successfully rattled all in the room.

"So where are my girls?" Wu casually asked.

"Somewhere safe, somewhere you can never get your hands on them ever again." Vincent assured her.

"No matter, I'll still find them again," Wu assured the detectives. "I always do."

"What's your connection with this man?" Jerry began.

He pushed a photo of Dr Joshua Langland across the table to her.

Wu looked down at this photo, Langland's mugshot from his earlier arrest.

"Oh my dear Dr Langland, my plastic surgeon." Wu admitted, to the surprise of the detectives.

"You knew this man? You knew what he was doing with those girls?" Vincent followed up.

"Of course, how else do you think we met? I went to see him for a consultation about having my tits enlarged. You see I've never been a big girl up front." Wu oddly confessed.

With that Wu motioned to cup her chest, only to further highlight the restraints now binding her to the table.

"But the good doctor assured me that I didn't need any alterations, that I was beautiful enough already. How odd for him to turn away business I thought. He was such a charmer I couldn't resist inviting him back to the Black Octopus for a courtesy 'hand shake', no charge." Wu continued, shuffling on her seat to readjust her sitting position.

"You two 'dated' then?" Vincent enquired.

"I guess a puny vanilla worm like you could describe it like that. You might say that we shared similar tastes, darker appetites as it were." Wu answered.

Vincent wasn't sure whether or not to be offended by the term vanilla. Casting her flimsy insult to one side, he chose to continue listening on. Wu leaned back in her seat as if to make an announcement, speaking much louder in order for all the microphones to register her words.

"I must say, for the record, it is so much nicer to be fucked by a real man and not by some boy!" she declared.

Wu's gaze returned to Jerry directly after this bold statement, Jerry in turn looking away with embarrassment, clearing his throat in the process.

"Things got far more physical between us, the doctor's rather violent fantasies heavily colliding with my own. He loved it when I bit down on him, asking me harder each time." Wu detailed.

Jerry's mind cast back to the discovery of Joshua's body. The mysterious bite marks across his shoulders, arms and chest were now explained.

"We found a deep connection in our affinity for pain." Wu purred.

"How did the girls become involved then?" Vincent hastened to ask.

"He rather impulsively presented me with the first, after he'd had his way with her. He then showed me his video, and oh how I wanted to punish her like he did." Wu unnervingly admitted.

Wu looked away from the detectives before closing her eyes, deep in thought over her past sinister and abusive misdeeds.

"But now he's dead! Who will provide me with my new play things now?" Wu cried.

"You freely admit to being an accessory to this rapist and torturer?" Jerry asked, amazed by her confession.
Wu simply hissed loudly in response.

"He was a real man! Something you'll never know how to be Jerry!" Wu lashed out.

"So Dr Langland brought you these girls after he was done with them for your own sick pleasure?" Vincent asked, trying to make sense out of this sadistic relationship.

"Yes. Can I go now?" Wu asked.

"No, no you cannot!" Vincent replied.
He was stunned by this woman's apparent naivety to the situation she now found herself to be in.

"I loved watching him hurt those girls, knocking them out long enough to amputate their arms and legs, one...by...one. Oh how they screamed when they came around and saw his handy work." Wu remembered.

She closed her eyes to savour the memory of those screams echoing back in her mind.

"Dr Langland performed these 'surgeries' on the girls?" Vincent questioned further.

"Of course, I'm no surgeon you fucking moron! How else do you think they survived? The doctor was good." Wu praised.

"So Langland was the Figure Killer all along, before you killed him and took over his work right?" Vincent challenged, hoping Wu would slip up and confess.

"What? No, neither of us are your true target detectives." Wu denied.

"I find that hard to believe, given the mounting evidence against you both." Vincent acknowledged.

"So what did you do with the girl's limbs?" Jerry hated to asked.

"I had them locked up for months detectives. My girls eventually needed something to eat." Wu smiled.
Her evil words chilled the very air around them.

"You're seriously sick in the head Tia! You know that right?" Jerry snapped, unable to restrain his severe distain for this woman.

To which result Wu spat in his face with impressive aim.

"Don't you call me that you pathetic fuck! You lost that privilege the moment you ratted me out!" Wu lashed back.

"But I didn't." Jerry assured her.
He removed a tissue from inside his jacket pocket to wipe away Wu's noxious saliva from his face.

"Must have been someone else you've screwed over in the past bitch." Jerry spat back.

"Are there anymore girls locked away?" Vincent asked.

"No, you took them all." Wu complained, her continued confession surprising.

"I think we have got enough to go on." Vincent said turning to Jerry.

"Yes I think that's enough for today." Jerry replied, standing up with Vincent to leave.

"I'll get out of here, I can assure you of that detectives. An octopus always finds a way to escape." Wu guaranteed.

"Do not count on it. You are going away for a long time for this." Vincent assured her in return.

Both men moved to leave the room via the only door, passing MacReady as they did.

"Oh detectives. Rosie was my favourite screamer. Please tell her from me that Madame will miss her precious parts tonight. She loved it really, what we did together down there in the dark." Wu smiled evilly again.

Both men exited the interrogation room, as questions about her relationship with Jerry continued to grow in Vincent's mind. Murphy joined them again as Wu was led back to her holding cell.

"What did she mean about you and her?" Vincent asked.

"I have no idea." Jerry lied, trying to act innocent.

"She was certainly quite taken with Jerry on our first visit to the Black Octopus." Murphy remembered.

"No, it was like she knew you more than that." Vincent pried further.

"The hell should I know! That crazy bitch was keeping young women chained up in her basement, whilst periodically having their limbs removed and forcing an octopus inside them." Jerry summarised.

He desperately tried to hide his deeper connection with Wu behind the cold hard facts of her evil misdeeds.

"The night of your stag do, where did you go afterwards?" Murphy enquired.

"What is this twenty questions? Why the third degree all of a sudden?" Jerry cried.

He frantically tried to move the discussion away from him.

"You went to see her again didn't you?" Murphy guessed, sensing Jerry's unease.

Jerry didn't reply, failing to hide the guilty expression on his face. Even Vincent began to see the truth slowly emerge through the cracks.

"You didn't?" Murphy gawked.

"I don't exactly know how I got there. I was drunk and..." Jerry tried to justify.

"That's right, blame it on the drink!" Murphy joked sarcastically.

"What about Grace? Did you not stop to think about her?" Vincent rather angrily challenged.

"Of course I did. But Wu must have put something in my drink and..." Jerry started.

"I told you to not get involved Jerry. I did not want you to make the same mistakes as me son and now look what has happened." Vincent stated.

There was an air of sadness to his words, sounding severely disappointed in his young partner's actions.

"What's going on?!" the Chief burst into their discussion. His sudden appearance caught all three detectives off guard.

"Well Glenn, Jerry has something to tell you about Wu, in private." Vincent replied.

He ushered the Chief's attention on to Jerry.

"I see. Wilder, my office." he calmly ordered Jerry.

As the Chief stormed off Jerry looked again at Vincent, annoyed that the old man had ratted him out so easily. Jerry begrudgingly followed the Chief over to his office. Once both men were inside and the door closed behind them the Chief began his questioning.

"So, what do you have to tell me then Wilder?" the Chief demanded to know.

Jerry hesitated for a moment, frantically trying to assemble his words in his mind awash with panic.

"Well?" the Chief asked impatiently.

187

"Just that my involvement in this case has taken a more personal turn Sir." Jerry admitted.

"Go on." the Chief instructed, brushing his thick grey moustache with one finger.

"Well Sir on the evening of my stag night I...I...somehow got over to Easy Street and spent the night at the Black Octopus. I didn't want this to get out and that is why I didn't want to interview Wu earlier with Vincent in the room also, incase he found out." Jerry detailed.

"Did you know about those girls in her basement?" the Chief asked.

"No, of course not Sir," Jerry admitted. "if I did I would have arrested her then and there!"

"I see." the Chief replied.

"I'll understand if you take me off the case Sir," Jerry said. "I'm ashamed of my actions."

The Chief stood up and turned to face out of his one office window.

"I still see a lot of potential in you. This city needs new blood and this precinct needs risk takers like you. We'll chalk this little indiscretion down to a simple mistake. We all make them. All you can do is learn from this." the Chief said.

"Believe me Sir it won't happen again!" Jerry assured his superior.

Jerry was relieved by the Chief's understanding nature on the matter.

"Besides the only real crime I see here is adultery against your fine young wife to be. I think you'll be punished enough by her." the Chief pointed out.

"I know." Jerry uttered, still surprised by how easy the Chief was being on him.

"And in any case you've saved the lives of six young women and put a stop to the torturous ways of that creature. You followed your intuition. That's the mark of a great detective.

188

Your actions today have probably saved the lives of more women." the Chief praised.

"Thank you Sir." Jerry uttered, not wanting to push his luck on the matter any further.

The Chief turned to look out of his window again, peering out over the river and across the city skyline.

"I swear Hallow is just one giant petri dish. It grows and cultivates psychos, murderers and rapists like bacteria. It throws new monsters at us with each passing day. With every one we cut down, another one just rises up and takes their place. This city needs another Great Blaze, another sterilisation of fire and flame." the Chief poignantly proposed.

He crossed his arms in front of him in a poise of complete certainty.

The Chief's impassioned words on Hallow City's future made Jerry realise more than ever how much good his superior wanted to do for the city.

"Go home Wilder. Make sure you come in tomorrow with your head firmly back in the game." the Chief instructed the faltering detective.

"Yes Sir." Jerry whimpered.

Jerry exited the Chief's office and made his way back over to his and Vincent's office, passing by the rest of his colleagues answering calls and chasing up leads for other cases. He was greeted by the sight of Vincent surveying their evidence board on the Figure Killer's work. Jerry slumped down into his chair, drawing Vincent's attention away from the board.

"How did it go with the Chief?" Vincent asked.

"Fine, he says I'll be punished enough by Grace for this." Jerry informed.

"That you will. She is a lovely girl Jerry. How could you?" Vincent asked.

Jerry didn't reply, instead sitting and stewing in silence before a thought occurred in his head.

"Wait, what mistakes did you make?" Jerry asked, referencing Vincent's earlier words.

Vincent didn't answer, instead looking to the pile of paperwork on his desk.

"You got involved with her didn't you? You got involved with Lullabelle?" Jerry deduced.

This time Vincent stopped what he was doing and turned to look at Jerry again. Vincent simply sighed and moved to sit down in his own chair opposite Jerry.

"One of Lullabelle's earliest victims was a colleague and close friend of her's. When I questioned Lullabelle about her disappearance she fell into my arms in floods of tears. All I could do was comfort her and hold her close until she calmed down. We went for coffee later and got talking. There was some chemistry there so we continued to see each other after that." Vincent confessed.

"Wouldn't that be against regulations?" Jerry challenged.

"No, she fooled me into excluding her from the investigation," Vincent admitted. "but little did I know that it was all an act. We saw each other after that a few more times, spending a few nights together. I remember one evening I invited her over to my apartment. I offered to cook for her but she said that she had already eaten."

Vincent's voice trembled in memory over these words. Jerry could easily guess as to what she had already eaten.

"When I went over to her final victim's house and found her to be the killer I was so angry at her for fooling me like that. I was so angry at myself for letting this woman kill so many innocent women and for becoming so embedded in my life. I hit a real low after that and was off work for some months. I saw a shrink to help me get past it and eventually went back to work with a new perspective on life. The guys at the precinct were really good about the whole thing and I never once got any hassle from them. I could not be close to another woman for quite some time after that." Vincent sighed.

190

"I don't blame you" Jerry sympathised.

"When I questioned Lullabelle again in custody she told me that she did not just eat their bodies, she also ate their souls. I could not help but feel like she had taken a piece of mine also." Vincent recounted.

"She really sounds like a complete monster." Jerry sneered.

"But then one day I met Martha. The most beautiful and charming woman I had ever seen. I soon felt my soul whole again." Vincent reminisced with a smile.

"Why didn't you tell me this? I thought we were sharing our shit! We're partners" Jerry reminded.

"Because it is in the past son. If you dwell in the past for too long you miss out on the present." Vincent spoke wisely.

"Well from now on we don't keep secrets from each other ok?" Jerry said, offering his hand to shake on it.

"Deal." Vincent agreed, shaking Jerry's hand.

Jerry stood up to go and make himself some more coffee before being stopped by Vincent.

"You have to tell Grace, you know right? Otherwise the lies will slowly poison your mind and turn you rotten inside." Vincent advised.

"I know. I just need to think about how I'm going to tell her. She'll probably leave me and end our engagement." Jerry sighed.

He could easily picture the love of his life leaving him for good over this.

Jerry arrived home to the welcoming sight of Grace cooking him dinner again, her beaming smile partially helping him to forget the horrors of Wu's basement. Their apartment was awash with the fragrant smells of her native cooking.

"Hey!" she called out lovingly.

Grace almost ran over to Jerry and threw her arms around him.

"How's my big strong future husband today?" she gushed.

191

"Fine, just tired." Jerry replied.

"Wanna talk about it?" Grace asked, offering a sympathetic ear.

"I can't sweetie sorry, confidentiality of the case and everything." Jerry said.

"Ok no worries, I'm here for you regardless." Grace smiled.

She kissed him firmly on the cheek before skipping back to the kitchen.

Jerry slumped down on to their couch, spying the large green balloon still floating in the corner of the room. It loomed over him as much as the Figure Killer's unknown whereabouts.

"I made your favourite! I hope you don't mind." Grace beamed from the kitchen.

"That's fine honey." Jerry called back.

He was going to tell her tonight, somehow someway Jerry was going to tell Grace but he didn't know how to start. He had to though, the truth was eating him up inside.

With that Grace came over and sat down beside the weary detective, before burying her face lovingly into his neck.

"Grace I...I need to tell you something." Jerry started, his voice trembling slightly.

Grace moved to bring her face closer to his.

"What is it? Jerry you look terrible. You look like you've seen a ghost" Grace said.

Her words eerily echoing back Wu's own from earlier.

"It's...it's this case I'm working." Jerry admitted, failing on telling her the real truth.

"What about it? Can you even tell me?" she asked concerned.

"We have reason to believe the killer will target a bride next." Jerry informed her.

"Well we're not married yet are we!" Grace laughed off.

"Grace this is serious! I can't lose you ok! I just want you to be safe!" Jerry asserted.

"I am safe, with you Jerry." Grace confirmed, kissing him again on the cheek.

"But I'm just one man Grace. I can't be everywhere at once." Jerry sighed.

"You're all that I need." she smiled, burying her face deeper into his neck again.

Jerry didn't know what to say, instead choosing to sit in comfortable loving silence.

"Hey, I was thinking about names for the baby today. Scarlett, Violet or Daisy if it's a girl and Max, Tommy or Zack if it's a boy. What do you think?" she asked.

"They all sound good to me Grace, I just want both you and the baby to remain safe and healthy." Jerry replied.

"Ok. Hey can we go to Hallow Aquarium on your next day off?" Grace asked.

"Yeah sure sounds like fun," Jerry replied. "it will make up for our failed trip out to the zoo."

"Cool." Grace simply put.

In that moment Jerry decided that he was never going to tell Grace the truth about him and Wu, that he was to carry around the shame of his betrayal until his very last days. He couldn't bear the idea of hurting her so deeply and crushing her spirit. The truth would remain locked inside him forever.

Chapter Ten

The Bride

The next morning Jerry went over to Murphy's place to meet him before work. Jerry knocked on his apartment door and after a few moments of waiting it was answered.

"Oh, hi Jerry." greeted Jenny.

She peered round from behind the partially opened door. Her pale scared face and brightly dyed red hair were easily recognisable.

"Jenny? Morning...is Murphy in?" Jerry clumsily asked, surprised to see Jenny there.

"Yeah he's just in the shower, come in" Jenny offered, opening the door further for him to enter.

Jerry entered into the small modest apartment and was quickly greeted by the early morning mess of pillows and blankets sprawled across Murphy's couch. Jenny appeared to have only recently woken up, managing to quickly dress herself in another one of her suggestive street outfits.

"Did somebody sleep on the couch last night?" Jerry pried. His gaze returned again to the mess of bedding before them both.

"Yeah Murphy did. I'll let him know you're here." Jenny admitted.

She made for the bathroom and soon entered inside. Jerry could just make out faint murmured voices coming from the other side of the bathroom door shortly afterwards.

"You answered the door?! Jenny!" Jerry could hear Murphy exclaim from inside.

A still damp Murphy exited the bathroom with only a towel round his waist.

"What are you doing here?" he asked Jerry, as water dripped onto the carpet.

Jenny stood in silence whilst nervously picking her nails, sensing tension in the awkward moment.

194

"Jenny go finish packing. I need to speak with Jerry alone." Murphy instructed.

Jenny moved to enter Murphy's bedroom, closing the door behind her.

"So what's Jenny doing here then?" Jerry asked.

"The anonymous tip about Algae at Wu's place, I think Jenny had something to do with it. If Wu finds out she'll have her killed somehow, or worse." Murphy said.

He shuddered at the thought of Jenny being chained up down in Wu's basement of horrors.

"Why would she call it in?" Jerry asked.

"I don't know and she won't say why." Murphy mused.

"So you got her out of there before the shit really hits the fan?" Jerry guessed.

"Exactly, we both now have more reason to fear that woman. Jenny is a good kid and doesn't deserve to be caught up in Easy Street's sludge anymore!" Murphy firmly put.

Jerry could see the real worry and care Murphy held for Jenny in his eyes, a glimmer of adoration it seemed.

"You love her don't you?" Jerry asked.

Murphy sighed as he sat down on the couch.

"So what if I do? She's a lovely girl regardless of her profession." he admitted.

"Hooker with a heart of gold, how cliché!" Jerry smirked.

"Don't cheapen her like that! She's much more than that to me." Murphy retorted.

"Now I see why you never talk about your love life. It's always been about her hasn't it?" Jerry assumed.

"I just have a lot of sympathy for the poor girl," Murphy admitted, reflecting on her scarred face. "besides women and I have never quite clicked together on a romantic level. Treat em' mean never keeps em' keen."

Murphy tried to brush the seriousness of the situation off with his trademark humour.

"What about her pimp, boss or colleagues?" Jerry asked.

195

"They don't know. That's why she needs to leave the city today. Before they find out and drag her back in." Murphy said concerned.

"How did you even get her out of there?" Jerry asked.

"I offered them a stupid amount of credits to take her back to mine. They couldn't refuse." Murphy admitted.

"Good thinking." Jerry thought.

"No one can know about Jenny being here Jerry, OK? I mean it!" Murphy warned.

"You can trust me. My lips are sealed." Jerry promised.

He compared his own love for Grace to that of Murphy's for Jenny, understanding the worry and anxiety Murphy was feeling.

"Anyway get dressed, we still have a killer to find." Jerry reminded.

"We do indeed." Murphy returned with a wry smile.

Jerry and Murphy entered into the precinct. The entire building was now a feverish hive of frantic activity, even more than usual. Uniformed officers were busy running around whilst a couple of paramedics tended to some injured guards. Their fluorescent yellow jackets with bright green stripes were easily visible amongst the murky stream of blue and grey clothing. Jerry spotted Vincent standing idly by whilst speaking to the Chief. He made is way through the crowd over to them both.

"What's going on?" Jerry asked.

"Wu escaped last night." the Chief informed.

Both Jerry and Murphy could sense one another's unease upon hearing this terrifying news.

"What? How?" Jerry asked straight away.

"She somehow managed to pick the lock to her holding cell." the Chief announced.

"What could she have used? We performed a cavity search on her right?" Murphy double checked.

"Could it have been an inside job?" Jerry asked.

"Who knows what she used. But she managed to grab keys off the guard on patrol, before snapping his neck." the Chief sighed.

"Wu then took Higgins hostage with his own gun, before shooting two more officers dead as she escaped the building." Vincent concluded.

"She jumped into the river and fled downstream afterwards." the Chief added.

Jerry and Murphy looked over at Higgins wallowing in self pity, still being looked over by a paramedic for shock. His younger partner Pace was also there providing a comforting hand on his shoulder.

"It all happened so fast." Higgins uttered to himself.

"Three good men now dead." Vincent sighed.

"I've put out an order for her to be shot on sight. This won't end with her going to trial, it will end with her being put down like a dog in the street. A single bullet right between the eyes." the Chief unlawfully asserted.

"Where was this bitch last seen heading then?" thundered a familiar voice behind Jerry.

Over to their conversation with the Chief came the swaggering towering form of Commander Randall Briers. He was flanked on either side by two members of his team. All of them were heavily armed, armoured up and not to be messed with. Briers held an impressive, well maintained sighted rifle in his hands, with two trusty handguns at either side.

"She fled the precinct around three this morning. Wu swam down the river so she could be anywhere now. She will probably go back to Easy Street." Vincent guessed.

"Too predictable deck. She's somewhere in this city, probably crawled back down another shit hole of her's I'm sure but we'll find her!" Briers confidently theorised.
He turned to face his small accompanying team.

"Looks like calamari is on the menu tonight boys!" Briers yelled aloud to them as they stormed off in pursuit.

197

"Let's just hope he finds her. That someone, anyone finds her before she does something!" Murphy added.

There was very real worry in his voice, for Jenny's safety. Jerry felt exactly the same for Grace as an officer came running over to the detectives and the Chief.

"Sir, we've got another Figure Killer victim! Just called in now, like the others!" he puffed and panted.

"Where?" demanded Vincent.

"Hallow City Cathedral." the officer replied.

"That is just across the river. This could be our bride." Vincent thought.

Jerry went pale, picturing Grace dead and hacked into pieces. She had already been placed under police protection by the Chief but that still didn't feel safe enough for Jerry.

"Get over there now and find out." instructed the Chief.

"Hang on a minute. Another body and with Wu's escape. What if she really was the killer all this time?" Murphy asked Vincent.

"We know she is certainly capable of committing such horrors." Jerry added.

"She could very well be. Her relationship with Dr Langland may have played more of a part in all this than we originally thought." Vincent theorised.

"But with her recent escape that doesn't leave much time for her to kill and prepare a victim." Jerry thought.

"That's why I need you all down there now!" the Chief repeated.

Jerry reached for his phone to call Grace, but there was no reply. Again and again he tried but still received no answer.

"Jerry! Come on we need to move!" Murphy hastened.

"I can't get through to Grace." Jerry replied.

"Keep trying on our way there. Maybe the signal is busy." Murphy suggested.

"Come on Grace. Pick up!" Jerry demanded down the line.

Vincent, Jerry, Murphy and Edward arrived outside the cathedral. Jerry's heart was beating fast enough for him to feel the arteries and veins throbbing in his neck. He feared what they may find inside the old building. The detective still had not received any word from his fiancee, causing his heart to ache with worry. News of the Figure Killer striking again had already gotten out to the press. The detectives and Edward were all quickly ushered inside through the large crowd of press reporters and television cameras that had descended upon the cathedral.

Jerry was relieved to finally get inside, not only to get away from the throbbing mass of noisy individuals outside but also the rapidly rising morning heat. Outside it was starting to swelter but inside the cathedral the air was cool and refreshing. The cathedral had been constructed centuries ago, its ancient walls and foundations built from solid stone taken from the mountains in the North. A thin layer of dust and dirt coated the floors and furniture throughout the cathedral, even after years of regular upkeep.

The detectives were all led further into the building by the already onsite uniforms, directing them towards the cathedral's central altar where wedding ceremonies and baptisms were held. Vincent stopping for a moment to admire the colourful stained glass windows above the altar. Jerry too was momentarily distracted by the sunlight shining through the windows, casting a beautiful rainbow mosaic down on to the ground at the foot of the altar. The altar itself was draped in an expansive and supremely white cotton sheet. This too had some of the stained glass patterning cast upon it. But then all their eyes fell to the body of a young woman laying only a few feet away. Jerry feared the worse and cautiously stepped towards her.

Jerry nervously stepped down the aisle towards the body, almost tiptoeing due to each footstep echoing around the hollow inside of the cathedral. He pictured Grace in a vision of white walking down her own aisle towards him on their upcoming wedding day. Jerry passed by rows upon rows of empty pews, picturing the people who would fill them on the day. Vincent, Murphy, Clark, Reed and even Edward would all most likely be in attendance. Grace's parents would be making the trip over to Hallow for the big day also.

Finally arriving beside the body Jerry looked down at the woman's short blond hair and curvy figure, breathing a sigh of relief that she wasn't Grace. A young woman had still been killed and mutilated though, Jerry now feeling a sense of guilt in relief over her tragic death. The young woman had all the trademarks of the Figure Killer. Her body cut into the signature five sections, her nipples cut off and her vagina sealed shut with melted yellow plastic. All her severing wounds were sealed with the same melted yellow plastic. Beside the young woman's right hand lay a bouquet of already wilting yellow roses, doomed to dehydrate further if exposed to the heat outside.

Either side of the altar table were two large flower stands, each one filled with brilliantly vivid pink and purple flowers, contrasting with the bride's own yellow and white colouration.

"We do have our bride then." Murphy stated aloud.

Murphy's jarring words cut through the soothing silence like a bullet and echoed back at them all from the spacious void above.

"Do we have an ID of the victim?" Jerry asked.

"No not yet but I'm on it." Edward replied.

"Who will be next then?" Vincent sighed.

Edward took the hint and knelt down beside the woman's body. He carefully pried open her mouth, reached inside and removed yet another figure.

This time it was a man in a smart black suit and tie, holding a rolled up certificate of some sort. Atop his head was perhaps the most vital clue of all, an academic mortarboard hat.

"They're going to kill a graduate next. College students are all finishing soon for their summer break." Jerry remarked aloud.

"Hundreds of students will be graduating soon." Vincent remembered.

"How on earth can we protect them all? We couldn't even protect all the women who were getting married soon." a flustered Murphy cried out.

He desperately ran his hands through his thick head of brownish red hair in sheer frustration.

"Wait, I've got something else here!" Edward remarked aloud.

He peered closer at the figure and this new clue through his thick glasses.

"It's a hair, a single strand of hair stuck between the two halves of the figure." Edward announced.

He held it up for Vincent to have a closer look. Between the figure's two main halves was a hair strand, bright red in colour. Fearing it to be one of Jenny's hairs, Murphy got ready to run for the exit but was stayed my Jerry's hand.

"Murphy wait! It's not dyed red. It's natural red, long and curly!" Jerry called out after him.

"I'm not taking any chances!" Murphy called back, taking out his phone to call Jenny.

"What is he up to?" Vincent asked.

"No idea." Jerry lied.

"The killer is slipping up, to leave hard DNA evidence like this now." Edward said to them both.

"Or maybe they are telling us even more about their next victim." Vincent thought.

"I'll get this back to the lab and run it through the system right away to see if there are any matches." Edward assured them.

The curly red hair caused an image to arise within Jerry's lucid mind, a familiar and angelic face.

"Gemma! Roberta's friend from the college!" Jerry suddenly remembered.

Vincent looked to Jerry upon hearing this.

"She had curly red hair just like this. The killer could be finishing their work right back where they started." Jerry theorised.

"At the college." Vincent added.

"Mrs Waller as well. Some of your other victims are connected to the college." Edward realised.

"Yes but that was Walter Sinclair's doing." Vincent replied.

"It's still something though." Jerry thought.

"Call the college now. Tell them to keep Gemma safe and wait for police protection to arrive." Vincent instructed Murphy.

Murphy hung up his phone after speaking to Jenny, making sure she was safe. Jerry had also finally gotten through to Grace, her sweet voice upon replying to his call filling him with calming reassurance. Both he and Vincent soon drove over to the college in hopes of getting to Gemma before the killer could.

Back at the precinct Edward conducted a DNA test on the hair sample found with the graduate figure and a sample of Gemma's hair. The results were conclusive. The hair sample was a positive match with Gemma's. She was now the main focus of the investigation and police protection.

"I also discovered something more about this particular figure." Edward informed the detectives.

Jerry, Vincent and Murphy had gone to see him again in the precinct's morgue.

"This particular figure has a logo printed inside it, see." Edward said, handing Vincent the figure and a magnifying glass. The detectives took it in turn to inspect the tiny graduate. Printed inside its torso was a logo that read 'DPH'.

"DPH?" Murphy recited aloud.

"Doyle's Plastic Heroes," Edward replied proudly. "I checked the system for any leads and came across a Jack Doyle. He was a former toy maker from right here in Hallow. Had his own business called Doyle's Toy Chest."

"We have our killer then!" Jerry excitedly stated, hoping this would all be soon at an end.

"Well no not exactly," Edward replied, cutting short the detective's hopeful new lead. "Jack Doyle died, many years ago now. He was murdered along with his wife by thieves who broke into his store one evening. He was found stabbed to death in the basement along with his wife. There were three assailants at the scene, also found badly wounded, along with the Doyle's two children. They saw the whole thing."

"Shit," Murphy remarked. "what happened to them?"

"They were sent to an orphanage in Garden Ridge City but there are no records about them after that. Seems they just vanished." Edward detailed further.

"Do we have an address for this Doyle's Toy Chest?" Vincent asked.

"Yes right here." Edward said, handing him a copy of the address.

"What about the other figures? Did they not have the same logo printed inside them as well?" Jerry asked.

"No, I cross checked them all but the graduate is the only one to have it so far." Edward replied.

"The killer is slipping up again, to leave such a clue as this behind for us!" Jerry noted.

"Let's check this address then." Murphy suggested.

"We will need a warrant before we can search the premises." Vincent reminded.

"I'm on it." Murphy offered.

"No, you go to Garden Ridge City and chase up this lead at the orphanage. Jerry and I will look into this address." Vincent instructed.

"Good luck detectives, I hope you find something from this." Edward added as they left.

Vincent and Jerry travelled undeterred over to the Doyle's address, which was located near a small derelict area in East

203

Hallow. Several abandoned buildings lined the dirty, unkept street, most of which were tagged by either drably coloured graffiti or '*For Sale*' property signs.

"Where is this building then?" Jerry enquired as he looked out the window.

"It should be around here somewhere." Vincent replied.

The street was indeed dirty, littered throughout with trash blowing in the wind. Several homeless took shelter under some of the building stoops, whilst others pushed their trolleys of plastic bottles and metallic cans along the sidewalks. Even the trees outside the buildings appeared dead and lifeless, as if tainted by decay deep beneath the soil. They should have all been fully leafed in extensive green foliage, typical of the summer month. Instead they were heavily gnarled brown stumps, devoid of any earthy character.

After finally arriving at the address they had come to investigate, both men quickly exited their vehicle. Vincent and Jerry now beheld the outside of this building. Most of the windows had been previously broken by unknown vandals. The only remaining windows left completely intact were coated in a thick layer of grime, acquired from the many years of exposure to Hallow's city air. The building looked abandoned, showing no signs of current ownership. Above the doorway entrance and front windows was a heavily weather beaten wooden sign. Although it was partially bleached by sunlight and rotten from many damp winters, Jerry could just about make out the faded letters that comprised the store name.

The only tree that stood proud and alone in front of Doyle's Toy Chest was unlike any of the others. It was awash with colour, with leaf after leaf of tough, brilliant greenery adorning its grizzled and hardened branches.

"This is the place." Vincent said, removing his fedora hat to mop his forehead.

"Where the killer's figures could be potentially coming from?" Jerry rhetorically asked.

He turned to Vincent, keeping the suspicious looking green tree within his peripheral.

"I hope so. Looks like this building has been abandoned for many years Jerry. Who knows what we'll find inside." Vincent replied.

Jerry approached the front door and grabbed its handle. He tried turning it open but it wouldn't budge an inch, firmly held in place by large areas of rust. Jerry removed his hand, only to find it now coated in a thin layer of orange and green powder. He could smell its metallic stench lingering on his sweaty palm.

"So how do we get inside then?" Jerry asked, brushing away the rust down one pant leg.

"Let us try round back." Vincent suggested, replacing his fedora back atop his head.

Both detectives entered the secluded alleyway running down one side of the building, looking for another entrance as they went. They soon came upon an old back doorway. Jerry firmly grabbed hold of this door handle. Unlike the one from earlier, it moved much more easily, having some give. But the door was still locked.

"Argh!" an impatient Jerry cried out.

He took a step back and then slammed into the door with his shoulder.

"Take it easy kid. Do not go injuring yourself on my account." Vincent cautioned.

He watched on as his determined partner took another step back, before kicking the door hard.

"Hey!" Vincent cried out to no reply.

Jerry continued to kick in the door several more times, before it eventually buckled at the handle and flew open. Vincent held a disapproving look on his wrinkly face.

"What?" Jerry puffed from the exertion.

Vincent didn't answer, instead moving to step inside the old building with Jerry following suit.

The detectives made their way through the back and slowly edged towards the front of the store. The building had no power connected to it. Vincent tried a couple of light switches by the doorway but to no luck. It was dark inside, the few windows still intact were so caked in dirt that sunlight could barely pass through. Jerry took out a small flashlight and shone it towards Vincent.

"Here." Jerry motioned, passing Vincent the light.

He took hold of it in his old wrinkled hands and carried on forwards.

As they approached the front of the store the service desk came into focus. Dust and grime was everywhere, a thick layer covering everything inside. Multiple spider webs hung precariously throughout the store, some larger than the rest. Jerry spied upon a couple of dead mice in an enormous web in one corner of the room. Almost completely decomposed down to their fur and bare bone skeleton, each rodent was strung up like some disturbing marionette. Either they had gotten stuck in the sticky web and died of natural causes, or there was a truly monstrous arachnid laying in wait at the end of a nearby hole in the wall. Never the less Jerry moved onwards, feeling a shudder run down his spine as his face brushed against a low hanging web.

Multiple empty shelves where toys would have proudly sat were just as dusty as one another.

"It does not look like anyone has been here in years." Vincent softly repeated.

He shone the light down onto the ground to reveal the areas of dirt and dust he and Jerry had kicked up by their intrusion. Vincent made for what looked like the basement door and stopped.

"Look over here." he motioned to Jerry.

His flashlight illuminated the oddly dust free handle, before moving the light down to the base of the doorway. On the floor was a much thinner layer of dirt and dust, appearing to have been more recently disturbed than the rest of the store.

"The basement again." Jerry moaned.

Vincent took out his gun, fearing the worse case scenario. Jerry wrapped his sleeve over the door handle to guard against fingerprints and turned the door open.

The creaky doorway leading down into the basement slowly opened. Vincent shone his light further down the stairwell whilst Jerry tried another nearby light switch with his sleeved hand. There was still no power connected to it.

"Hello? HCPD, anyone down there?" Vincent called down.

There was no reply. Jerry pulled out his gun and took the safety off, before starting his descent down the staircase. Once both detectives reached the basement floor they beheld a monumental discovery.

"Get Edward over here now." Vincent instructed his young partner.

Before the detectives was a small work station, complete with a portable generator hooked up to a large electrical band saw. The work station had been recently cleaned but traces of blood splatter could still be seen across its surface and adjacent walls. In one corner of the windowless basement, hanging from a hook above a surprisingly clean drain cover, was a link of well polished chains. Attached to a wall magnet beside it were a couple of long sharpened knives. On the other side of the room was a large heated melting pot, with liquifying plastic slowly bubbling away inside. Multiple sheets of acrylic lay close by, ready to be melted. Sculpting tools hung neatly together above another work bench that paralleled the melting pot. Vincent and Jerry had discovered the Figure Killer's killing and preparation lair.

"We gotcha now you bastard!" Jerry announced with glee.

Doyle's Toy Chest, once abandoned and left to the mercy of the elements, was suddenly no longer derelict and lifeless. Discovery of the Figure Killer's lair had caused a fevered frenzy of forensic officials to descend upon the whole area. Even the lone tree standing outside the building's front served as a rooted anchor for the usual police line tape to be wrapped around. Edward's team were busy taking photos of the entire basement, even plucking a couple of hair samples from both the band saw and drain cover.

"I feel like a kid in a candy store!" Edward squealed. He excitedly dusted for prints with a wide beaming smile spread across his peculiar mug.

"This has to be the pinnacle find of my career!" he continued to squeal.

"Just see what more you can find for us Edward." the Chief instructed.

"Yes Sir!" Edward replied with sincere excitement.

The Chief appeared uneasy in his new surroundings, as if the ghosts from the killer's victims still haunted the basement around him. He shrugged off this peculiar feeling as if it were a troublesome spider web from upstairs. He turned his attention back to the discoverers of this break through.

"Good work detectives. We're that much closer to nabbing this psycho." the Chief praised at Vincent and Jerry.

"Thank you Sir. This should put a stop to the killer's cycle, for now at least." Vincent thought.

"It could be weeks before they do anything else. We've got them on the run now." Jerry added.

"What more do we know about Jack Doyle?" the Chief asked.

"Well he was a carpenter by trade. Doyle started out designing and manufacturing wooden toys, before turning his hand to plastics to keep up with the booming market. His murder put a stop to further manufacture and future distribution." Edward informed.

"Doyle must have only made a select number of these figures prior to his death." Vincent thought.

"So if Jack Doyle is dead already, then who has been doing all this killing?" the Chief asked.

"That we don't know yet Sir, but we're certainly closer than we've ever been before." Jerry replied.

"This building has not been owned by anyone for nearly three decades now." Vincent added.

"Unsurprising. The Doyle's murders hit the local area pretty hard. No one has wanted to live in or go near this building since." Edward divulged.

"What about Doyle's missing children?" the Chief asked.

"Murphy is checking with the orphanage in Garden Ridge City as we speak Sir. Perhaps they will have something more on these missing children." Vincent proposed.

"And what of the figures? Do we have any idea how many Doyle originally designed and made?" the Chief continued.

"No Sir. But my team and I are going over the whole building with a fine comb and brush." Edward assured.

"Well detectives stay on it. Don't let this new trail go cold on you now." the Chief advised, before walking back up stairs.

"So I guess my kicking in the back door proved useful after all." Jerry smugly commented.

"Well, it was not my way of doing things. But you have certainly proved yourself throughout all this mess kid. Well done." Vincent replied, offering his hand.

"Thanks Vince." Jerry replied, taking his hand and shaking it in return.

"Do not call me that." Vincent replied.

His distain for that nickname aside, Vincent couldn't help but let slip a wavering smile of proud amusement.

Later that day, Vincent and Jerry ventured over to West Hallow to begin the first watch at Gemma's home address. Jerry knocked

209

on the front door and to his surprise Commander Briers answered, gun in hand.

"What the hell are you decks doing here?" he challenged.

He was ready to shoot, his firearm expertly aimed at their heads.

"Easy Randall." Vincent answered.

Both he and Jerry raised their hands up in defence to show the confused man they were no threat. Now off duty, gone was Brier's familiar kevlar body armour and more intimidating appearance. All he wore now was a t-shirt and jeans.

"What are you doing here?" Jerry asked.

"Gotta keep my little girl safe." Briers answered.

Stepping out from behind his hulking form appeared a visibly nervous Gemma.

"Daddy, who is it?" she asked.

"Baby I told ya to stay away from the doors and windows now ya hear!" he firmly instructed, keeping his eyesight on the two men before him.

Jerry remembered his initial attraction to Gemma when he first met her all those weeks ago and how good she had smelled. Whether is was the immediate threat of now knowing her father was the hulking Commander, or his newly rekindled desire for Grace and Grace alone but Jerry now felt absolutely nothing towards this girl.

"Randall, Jerry and I are here as an extra precaution. Just incase the killer comes for Gemma tonight." Vincent told him.

"Waste of time decks if ya ask me. I've already got some of my boys heading over here as we speak. And besides no one is going to keep my little girl more safe but me. Let this bastard come! And if it is this Wu, then she'll regret ever stepping one foot on my property!" Briers threatened aloud.

"Ok Randall. Well if you need us then we are just outside in the car." Vincent reassured.

Without thanking them Briers closed the door on them both.

"You're welcome!" Jerry sarcastically called out.

Vincent and Jerry returned to their patrol car, making themselves comfortable for the long night ahead.

"How did Grace take the news about you and Wu then?" Vincent asked.

"I haven't told her yet. And I'm not going to. Especially after the raid at the Black Octopus." Jerry replied.

Vincent looked disappointed by his partner's decision.

"I still think you should kid. Better she hears it from you than from someone else." he advised.

Vincent's phone rang out, cutting short their conversation. It was from Edward back at the precinct.

"Did you find out anything else on our bride?" Vincent asked him.

"Victim's name is Kristen Scott. She was due to be married next week in the same cathedral we found her body in." Edward replied.

"What about the other potential targets for the graduate kill?" Jerry called out.

"Security has been arranged for them. There were only six other red haired students graduating this summer at the college." Edward said.

"I can only hope we get it right this time." Vincent said.

"Do any of them have a connection to Roberta, Gemma or Wu?" Jerry asked.

"Apart from the college, no. Also none of them have ever been to Easy Street before so I doubt they'd have any prior knowledge of Wu." Edward added.

"Well thanks for the update." Vincent said before hanging up.

Vincent replaced his phone back inside his jacket pocket before turning to Jerry.

"You can head off back home now Jerry." Vincent instructed, yawning in the process.

"What about the first watch?" Jerry asked his weary partner.

"They will not need us both here. Besides, Randall said he already has some of his men coming over." Vincent repeated.

"You going to be ok by yourself then?" Jerry asked.

"This is not my first stake out sonny, but it could very well be my last. In any case, another officer will cover my shift later on." Vincent mused.

"Ok, well if you're sure then take care of yourself alright." Jerry advised. bidding his senior partner goodnight.

"Are you going to be ok getting home?" Vincent asked after him.

"Yeah I'll catch a cab, no big deal." Jerry replied.

It had been a long, eventful and stressful day. Jerry returned home to his apartment late evening, his keys already to hand in order to enter quickly. News of Wu's escape from the precinct had shaken Jerry to his very core. The fact that Brier's crack squadron of sharp shooters hadn't even found her yet made Jerry even more apprehensive. He knew she would come for him at some point, for thinking he had sabotaged her business, uncovered her sickening reputation and for taking away her girls.

Jerry entered inside and speedily closed the door behind him. The lights were already on in the apartment. Grace was evidently home already, having been released from police protection. Jerry walked into the lounge, tossing aside his jacket.

"Grace?" he called out for his fiancee.

"Welcome home darling, you certainly took your time." came the reply, but not from Grace.

From behind one corner leading into the kitchen appeared the sinister alien-like form of Madame Wu, holding Grace hostage in her arms. Wu glared devilishly at Jerry from over Grace's right shoulder, using her nubile body as a human shield. She held a long silver knife to Grace's vulnerable throat. Completely taken aback by Wu's sudden appearance in his home, Jerry could think of only one question to ask her.

"What the hell are you doing here?!" he asked with dread.

"You have good taste detective, she really is quite a rare beauty." Wu mentioned.

She looked Grace's body up and down, smelling her thick black hair in the process.

"Let her go!" Jerry demanded.

"If you were mine, there would be no other." Wu whispered into Grace's ear.

Wu sadistically licked Grace's cheek with a serpentine tongue, leaving behind a trail of saliva and causing Grace to grimace from the experience.

"Let her go Wu, now! This is between you and I! Leave her out of this!" Jerry demanded.

"Oh no detective, this involves all of us." Wu hissed.

She pressed the knife firmer and closer to Grace's throat.

"Put your gun down on the floor and kick it over here!" Wu ordered.

Jerry begrudgingly complied, unclipping his gun from its holster. He slowly placed it down on the floor, before kicking it over to Wu.

"Let her go please, I beg of you." Jerry pleaded again.

He stepped back further away from his grounded weapon, real fear now filling his voice.

"That's right you snivelling worm, grovel before me!" Wu chuckled evilly.

"Please don't hurt me," Grace begged over Wu's taunts. "please don't hurt my baby!"

"Grace don't!" Jerry pleaded, causing Wu to stop her threats.

"Oh! Well isn't this a coincidence. That's another reason I came here tonight." Wu smiled.

Wu momentarily flexed her grip around the knife's handle. Her other slender hand began to stroke Grace's abdomen, where the young couple's future family was slowly developing inside.

"You see I have some news to share with you both. I've been blessed with child also…" Wu began to announce.

213

Jerry felt faint as all his blood rushed out of his head and straight down to his feet, fearing the end of her sentence.

"...and Detective Wilder here is the father." Wu uttered into Grace's ear, looking to Jerry in the process.

"What?" Grace asked.

"That's right darling. Your sweet husband to be here, your knight in shimmering armour and I fucked! We screwed hard and it was good!" Wu beamed.

"Jerry, what's she talking about?" Grace asked aloud, tears beginning to form in her eyes.

"Oh, you didn't tell her! How sweet!" Wu taunted Jerry further.

She was like a cat playing with a struggling mouse that had no hope of escape.

"Well here's your chance Jerry. Tell her, tell your fiancée why I'm now with child." Wu instructed.

Grace looked to Jerry, hoping he wouldn't say what she was now suspecting.

"Tell me it isn't true Jerry. Tell me it isn't true!" Grace pleaded further, tears now rolling down her cheeks.

"I'm sorry Grace, I'm so sorry. It happened on my stag night," Jerry began to confess. "I spent the night with her."

Upon hearing her fiancée's words of betrayal, Grace broke down crying. Her heart had been horribly split in two by the one man she truly trusted.

"Well detective, in the spirit of being honest with one another, we actually didn't do anything until you woke up the next morning. Sorry did I forget to tell you that part?" Wu added, savouring the pain she continued to dish out.

Jerry glared back at Wu, feeling the burning rage build up inside him.

"Why are you doing this you evil cunt? I hate you so much!" Jerry spat back.

"Well that's a shame. But don't you feel better now Jerry, like a huge weight has been lifted off your shoulders. I find

214

confession is always good for the soul." Wu responded, revelling in his misery.

"What the hell do you know about having a soul you monstrous witch?!" Jerry angrily lashed back.

"Tell her again detective or I'll slice her pretty little throat." Wu threatened.

She pushed the blade harder against Grace's neck, causing her to yell out in pain.

Jerry hesitated as if hearing his own words of betrayal again would be the death of him also.

"I fucking mean it!" Wu yelled out.

She jabbed the tip of the long blade into Grace's throat, enough to draw a small droplet of blood which rapidly pooled on the surface of her skin.

"Alright! I cheated on you Grace...with her!" Jerry sobbingly admitted.

Grace continued her sorrowful crying, her face now stained by the tears she was shedding.

"Your honesty is commendable detective. Too bad it'll be the last thing Grace will ever hear." Wu mused.

She moved the knife away from Grace's throat, only to then swiftly stab her hard in the side of her abdomen.

"NO!!!" Jerry yelled.

Wu plunged the knife deep into Grace's side once more, before withdrawing it to use against Jerry. As she tossed Grace to one side, Jerry sprang towards Wu with the knife still in her hand, ready for Jerry's assault.

"I'LL FUCKING KILL YOU!!" Jerry screamed as he and Wu wrestled each other to the ground.

Wu slashed Jerry across his arm and chest as he struggled to take the knife from her. Jerry managed to knock the knife out of Wu's hand and it slid all the way to the other side of the room. The two of them fell to the floor again with Wu now on top of Jerry. She started violently slashing at him with her nails. Jerry

215

had to cover his face with one arm whilst he kept Wu at bay with his other.

Wu screamed and snarled at him like a wild animal, possessed by an unquenchable blood lust. Amidst the thrashing attack, Jerry managed to punch Wu hard in the centre of her chest, winding her. This caused Wu to fall backwards, coughing and spluttering from the shock. As she struggled for breath, Jerry quickly scrambled over to where his gun lay. He seized it in one hand and took the safety off.

Jerry turned to take aim at Wu and fired. But she had already recovered and sprung at him once more, knocking his firearm away in time. The lone bullet fired off to one side, missing Wu and hitting the lounge wall instead. Wu was upon Jerry again like a ferocious beast. She moved to bite at his face, Jerry only managing to block her attack with his right forearm, his gun still held tightly in his hand. Wu clamped down hard on his arm with her powerful teeth. Even through his thick shirt she bit hard, drawing enough blood to stain his sleeve a crimson red.

"ARGH!" Jerry cried out agony.

Wu bit down harder, shaking her head from side to side like a rabid dog to add more pressure to her bite.

Jerry quickly reached over with his left hand to gouge her eyes with his fingers. This caused Wu to release her hold on his arm and fell back clutching her face. The pair now stood opposite each other, Jerry's gun now aimed precariously at Wu's head. His right forearm was now wounded badly by her earlier assault. Jerry struggled to hold his weapon straight as blood dripped down on to the carpet.

"Go on! Do it you fucking coward! You'll be a murderer, just like me!" Wu hissed, baring her teeth stained red with Jerry's blood.

Jerry hesitated in shooting, wincing from the pain running up and down his arm.

"You took my girls away!" Wu reminded him.

"Those girls will never be the same again thanks to you!" Jerry replied angrily.

"They were only whores, but they were my whores!" Wu fired back.

"Are you the Figure Killer?" Jerry challenged her.

The only response Wu gave the detective was another sinister smile.

"Are you? ANSWER ME!" Jerry yelled.

Again, Wu gave no reply.

"What about Roberta, Becky, Kristin or even Joshua?" Jerry followed up.

"Hallow is my playground," Wu proudly announced. "and you're all my playthings!"

"You're crazy! You're fucking crazy you know that?!" Jerry shouted.

"Go on! Kill me detective and you'll be just like me!" Wu threatened.

"I'm nothing like you!" Jerry retorted.

Wu let out one final blood curdling scream as she lunged at the detective again, her face now twisted into the most horrific expression of pure hate and rage. She raised up her hands like sharpened talons ready for the kill and leapt at him.

"You go straight to hell, bitch!" Jerry cried out.

Barely able to hold his gun upright with his badly lacerated arm, Jerry took precarious aim.

This time the bullet hit Wu square in the chest and she fell to the floor hard on one side. She starting coughing up thick globules of blood as she hopelessly crawled across the floor towards the knife, wincing from the pain with every movement. Turning over on to her back she looked up at Jerry who towered over her.

"You...loved it really...didn't you?" she laughed, coughing up more blood in the process.

"No, I really didn't." Jerry calmly replied.

Taking aim once again and with a small tug by his trigger finger, Jerry fired a third shot. This time the bullet found its way between Wu's eyes and buried itself deep within her brain. Her body slumped dead at Jerry's feet. A great and terrible Kraken had finally been slain, the Black Octopus of Easy Street was dead.

Wu's cold lifeless eyes now stared blankly up at the triumphant detective, her blood beginning to trickle out of the bullet wound and on to the floor. Jerry dropped his gun and rushed over to Grace, picking her up in his bloodied and heavily lacerated arms.

"I'm so sorry Grace, I love you so much." he began to weep.

Grace was barely conscious, having lost a lot of blood during Jerry's struggle with the murderess. Jerry grabbed his phone from his pocket and called for an ambulance. As he waited for help to arrive he kept pressure on the wound, gently rocking his dying bride to be in his arms. Seconds felt like minutes, minutes felt like hours, until the paramedics finally arrived and Grace was stretchered away.

Chapter Eleven

The Graduate

Jerry sat slouched in the chair beside Grace's hospital bed, both of his hands clasped tightly around one of her own. His forearms were now heavily bandaged up, with surgical stitching underneath holding together the wounds inflicted upon him by Wu's assault. The sounds from all the medical machinery filled the deafly quiet room. Grace's heart monitor beeped away continuously as Jerry sat there in complete silence, contemplating the grief he had brought down upon her. Jerry looked to Grace's IV drip, watching every hypnotic droplet of fluid filling the small tube, one by one. The peace was suddenly broken by an entering doctor.

"Mr Wilder, I'm Dr Sachs. Your girlfriend sustained a large amount of blood loss and internal bleeding but I managed to stop it in surgery." the doctor informed Jerry.
Jerry continued to stare blankly at Grace.

"However, given the shock her body has been through it's highly likely she will lose the baby." Dr Sachs informed him.

"She's my fiancée," Jerry corrected him. "will she be ok doctor?"

"Your fiancée should be just fine. She just needs plenty of rest now. We got to her just in time but we very nearly lost her Mr Wilder." Dr Sachs said.

"Thank you doctor." Jerry thanked.

"I'll be just outside if you need anything." the doctor offered, before leaving the room.

Grace began to slowly come around from the anaesthesia, her eyes slowly adjusting to the new surroundings she now found herself to be in.

"Jerry?" she asked softly, looking to the distraught man sitting next to her.

"I'm here Grace. You're in the hospital. You were in surgery but you're ok now." Jerry comforted.

"I hurt Jerry." she said painfully.

"You were stabbed Grace. It will take some time for you to heal completely." Jerry replied.

"Not the knife Jerry, you." Grace simply put.

Jerry looked to the floor in shame.

"How could you Jerry?" Grace began to cry.

"Please don't think about that now Grace. Focus on healing and getting better. I love you Grace. I love you so much." Jerry comforted.

"The baby?" Grace asked.

Jerry didn't answer her, his silence cutting her deeper than Wu did. Grace pulled her hand away from Jerry's hold and turned her head away from him, spending the next several minutes in icy cold silence. Jerry continued to sit by her side, with only her mournful crying for comfort.

A few weeks had passed. Vincent came to visit Grace once again at the hospital to see how she was doing. Grace had miscarried in the end, adding further injury to her already damaged mental state. She had regained much of her physical strength but still struggled to walk completely upright without any pain. Whilst she practised walking again in physiotherapy. Vincent talked with Jerry in private.

"How are you doing son?" Vincent asked.

"Don't worry about me. I'm not the one who got stabbed," Jerry responded. "worry about Grace"

"You were lucky kid. You both were." Vincent replied.

"I know, but I don't get it. If Wu was so angry with me then why didn't she just kill Grace outright?" Jerry pondered.

"Because she enjoyed watching others suffer Jerry. There would not have been anything in it for her if she just outright killed Grace and be done with it. She wanted you to suffer." Vincent thought.

"I don't know whether she was pregnant or not Vincent" Jerry sighed.

Vincent looked to Jerry and the sad expression on his face.

"Maybe she was lying, maybe she wasn't? If she wasn't then I murdered my own child!" Jerry cried.

"Do not think about that son. Wu liked to torture people, physically and mentally. She played mind games and then some." Vincent said.

"Any more Figure victims?" Jerry suddenly asked, trying to change the subject.

"No, our killer has not struck again since we discovered their killing lair and since Wu's death also. It is looking likely that in some way Wu was the Figure Killer all along." Vincent thought.

"I don't get it though. What would be her connection with Doyle's Toy Chest?" Jerry wondered.

"I do not know yet." Vincent admitted.

"Did Edward find anything else in the basement?" Jerry asked.

"He found a couple of hair samples that matched with Becky, Alexi and Kristen." Vincent replied.

"Anything matching to Wu though?" Jerry followed up.

"No, sadly nothing solid there." Vincent admitted.

"Dammit!" Jerry remarked.

"Even if she did not outright confess to it, you still stopped her Jerry. I will let you know if anything else happens" Vincent reassured.

"I shouldn't have shot her Vincent. I should have kept her alive, so she could pay for all her crimes." Jerry admitted.

"The woman broke into your home and tried to kill both you and Grace. If I were you I would have done exactly the same." Vincent consoled his young partner.

"Really?" Jerry asked back.

"Really." Vincent assured.

"Thanks." Jerry said.

"I have squared things with the Chief. You take as many days off as you need until Grace is completely well again." Vincent informed.

"Thanks." Jerry repeated.

With that a frail Grace slowly staggered into the room, accompanied by her physiotherapist.

"Hello Grace," Vincent greeted. "how are you my dear?"

"I'm getting there, I don't need crutches to walk anymore and I've had my morphine reduced." Grace replied with a small smile.

Jerry moved to hold on to Grace's arm but she shrugged him away. Vincent sensed the understandable tension between them.

"Well I'm so happy to see you up and about my dear. I shall leave you to it." Vincent said as he gently hugged Grace goodbye.

Vincent replaced his fedora back atop his head and motioned to leave the room.

"Remember what I said." he reminded Jerry as he walked out.

"I will." Jerry called out after him.

"I'll see you tomorrow ok?" Grace's physiotherapist asked.

"Yes and thank you again for all your help Sarah." Grace returned as the physiotherapist left the room also.

Grace moved to her bedside to begin packing her belongings.

"What did Vincent mean earlier? Remember what?" Grace asked Jerry while she packed.

"That I can take as many days off as I want until you're completely recovered, within reason." he said.

"Oh no, I'm ok now Jerry. And besides you'll need the money to pay for my half of the rent." Grace informed.

"What do you mean?" Jerry questioned.

"I'm leaving you Jerry," Grace declared. "for the next month or so. I need more time to forgive you for what you did, and for that I need to be away from you."

222

"What about our wedding Grace?" Jerry asked.

"I've cancelled all the arrangements Jerry." Grace replied.

"But Grace?" he moved to ask her further.

"Don't Jerry. Just don't! You betrayed my trust and slept with another woman who then nearly killed us both!" Grace softly yelled at him, wincing in pain and clutching her right side.

"Grace I love you." Jerry began to beg.

"And I still love you too, as crazy as it sounds. I just need time to properly forgive you." Grace sighed.

"I understand." Jerry uttered, tears forming in his eyes.

"I'm going to be staying at a friend's place for a while ok. I'll be in touch later." Grace informed.

She moved to kiss Jerry on the cheek.

"Goodbye." Grace bid farewell.

"Grace?" Jerry quietly called after her but to no reply.

The young detective's fiancée picked up her bag and walked out of the room, and out of his life for the foreseeable future.

Weeks later Jerry paid Murphy a visit at his apartment. Jerry's own apartment felt very empty since Grace had moved out, taking most of her belongings in the process. In truth he couldn't bear the silence that awaited him upon his return home from work. He just wanted someone to talk with. Jerry felt it logical to seek out Murphy's company on a more regular basis outside of working hours.

"So how is Jenny?" Jerry asked Murphy.

"Yeah she's ok," Murphy replied. "I managed to get her out of the city in time."

"Where is she now?" Jerry followed up.

"Somewhere safe and that's all I want to say Jerry. Sorry no offence but I want as few people to know where she is, just incase they find her again and drag her back to Easy Street." he said.

Murphy took an anxious sip of his whiskey, his hands almost shaking in the process.

"These people, they don't let their property go easily." he huffed.

"I understand completely Murphy. I know how it feels to want to keep those that you love safe." Jerry sympathised.

"Thanks pal." Murphy responded.

"Will you go and see her soon?" Jerry enquired.

"I said to her that I will leave it a few more weeks. Wait until the heat has died down a bit more. What will you do now?" he asked.

"I'm not sure really," Jerry admitted. "just try and carry on as normal. Maybe Grace will come home soon, I can only hope."

"Any word from her?" Murphy asked between sipping his whiskey.

"Yeah we still talk now and again over the phone but I haven't seen her in person since she left the hospital." Jerry answered.

"I guess she still needs more time then huh?" Murphy rhetorically asked.

"Maybe. At least she's completely healed now, her physical wounds anyway." Jerry replied downbeat.

"Will you two try again for another child?" Murphy asked.

"I don't even know if she'll come back to me yet." Jerry sighed.

"I'm so sorry to hear that." Murphy replied sympathetically.

"It's alright. It's kinda funny actually when you think about it. Wu not only took Grace from me but also my child." Jerry joked.

Upon hearing his own words of pain, lightly masked in humour, Jerry quickly clasped his hands over his face and began to ball his eyes out. Murphy moved to sit closer to Jerry, putting a tentative comforting arm around his partner's shoulders.

"Hey, come on Jerry! It will be ok." Murphy said, attempting to consolidate his friend.

Jerry simply continued to weep like the new born baby he would now never hold in his arms. The young detective had never been so physically and emotionally vulnerable with anyone before, not even with Grace.

"I just miss her so much Murphy." Jerry managed to formulate between his sorrowful cries.

"Hey pal I'm here for you. Have some of this. You need it more than I do." Murphy said, offering Jerry his glass of whiskey.

After taking a few sips Jerry managed to compose himself and stood up from the couch.

"Sorry to be such a wreck Murphy. I should probably head off now." Jerry announced, embarrassed by his emotional meltdown.

"No further news on our Figure Killer then?" Murphy asked rhetorically.

"It has been weeks since they last struck. We must have really hit them hard by discovering their lair." Jerry replied, wiping snot from his nose.

"Certainly seems that way, for now." Murphy noted.

The loud ringing and vibrating of Jerry's phone suddenly cut short their conversation. After composing himself and wiping away another trail of teary mucous running down over his lips, Jerry answered the caller.

"Hello Grace." he spoke.

"Hey Jerry." she answered.

"Everything ok?" Jerry asked, looking to Murphy with a smile.

"Yeah I'm fine. I just wanted to ask you if it would be ok to come back to the apartment tomorrow afternoon?" Grace asked.

"Sure, that's fine. Did you forget something else?" Jerry asked back.

"Well no, I just wanted to come back home," she admitted. "I mean I'm ready to come home now."

Jerry felt truly elated upon hearing this news.

"Really? You mean it?" he asked hopefully.

"Yes. I miss you Jerry and I want to come home." Grace admitted.

"That's so good to hear Grace." he replied.

"I want us to try again Jerry. I want us to be a family again." Grace asserted.

"So do I Grace. I want nothing more in the world but you." Jerry said.

"What's done is done. It's all in the past now," she replied. "I want a future with you again"

"I'll see you back at the apartment tomorrow then, after work." Jerry said.

"Bye my love." Grace said before hanging up.

"Bye Grace." Jerry replied back to a dead phone line.

Jerry breathed a huge sigh of contempt as Murphy guessed the obvious.

"Grace coming home then?" he asked.

"Yeah tomorrow." Jerry replied.

"That's great news pal!" Murphy comforted, patting him on the back.

"I should head off anyway, get the apartment back to looking more presentable for Grace's return." Jerry proposed to himself.

"No worries Jerry. Come round whenever you want to talk ok?" Murphy offered.

Jerry exited his colleague's apartment, replacing his jacket as he stepped outside and closed the door behind him. Now back out in the floor's narrow corridor, Jerry made for the elevator. He pushed the large green button indicating the ground floor. Jerry breathed another sigh of relief as the elevator arrived back down on the ground floor. He almost skipped out of it in pure glee.

Weeks of intense heat had finally culminated in a massive thunderstorm over Hallow. A torrential down pour of rain began to fall all across the city and soon the streets were flooded, creating miniature rivers which flowed along the sidewalks. A far reaching cloud of steam sprung upwards throughout Hallow as rainwater collided with the searing hot surfaces of concrete, asphalt and roofing tiles. The cooling yet heavy rainfall was a welcome relief however and paid Jerry no ill mind. He didn't mind the monsoon conditions for one second, the thunderstorm even harkening back to his day of proposal. All day long he could think of nothing else but Grace's return.

Jerry had stopped off at their favourite restaurant on his way home to surprise Grace with their usual takeaway, having to leap frog his way over the scores of lake-like puddles now obstructing his path. Jerry had arrived back home to their apartment later than he had hoped. Too much last minute paperwork on the Figure killings had delayed his return home. It was late evening now as Jerry awkwardly fumbled through his keys with his free hand to open the front door. A fork of lighting cracked outside, startling him enough to drop his keys in the process.

"Stupid!" Jerry exclaimed to himself.

After retrieving them from the welcome mat beneath his sodden feet, Jerry slid the front door key deep inside the lock to open it. But the door was already unlocked. Jerry reassured himself again that he had definitely locked up the apartment on his way out this morning.

Now feeling understandably hesitant, Jerry replaced the keys into his pocket and pulled his gun out ready. The memory of Wu infiltrating his home was still fresh in his mind. Jerry slowly opened the front door and entered, quickly turning on the hallway light. Sitting there in his hallway was a very welcome sight. It was Grace's bags, she had already arrived home before him. She still had their spare key. Jerry's quickening pulse soon slowed as he replaced his gun back into its holster.

"Grace? Grace are you home?" Jerry called out but to no answer.

Jerry placed the take away boxes down on the kitchen work surface and walked into the lounge, turning on the lights there also. He received no reply from Grace so continued further into the apartment, confused as to why the lights were off. Jerry walked over to the bathroom and opened the door, thinking she might have been taking a bath or shower. The room was barren and empty, devoid of any moisture. He then entered into their bedroom, thinking she was possibly taking a nap there. To his relief Grace was there, laying under the covers with only her beautiful face poking out from underneath, gently nestled on a pillow.

"Grace, are you awake?" Jerry softly asked to no reply.

He turned their bedroom light on but Grace didn't stir. Jerry thought to himself that maybe she had taken some sleeping pills to help her sleep. He softly sat down by her side, carefully as to not disturb her too suddenly. But Grace still didn't stir awake, her eyes remained closed.

"Grace?" Jerry softly asked again.

He gently shook her pillow in an attempt to wake her. Her head merely rolled to one side, now facing him. Jerry reached over to feel her forehead with the back of his hand, just in case she was running a fever of some kind. But her forehead was ice cold.

"Grace?" he asked again nervously.

Jerry then felt the sharp stench of recently melted plastic leap up into his nostrils. He immediately leapt to his feet, his heart in his throat as he threw back the duvet cover. Grace was dead, laying there divided into five sections. Jerry felt the heart in his throat stop dead as he beheld her naked mutilated body. He fell back against the wall before collapsing to his knees, the blinding grief welling up inside him. The Figure Killer was back.

"GRACE!!!" Jerry screamed in agony.

His fiancée, his one true love, his guiding light was no more. Jerry burst into hysterics, collapsing further to the floor and pounding his fist into the carpet in a bitter rage. The stab wound scars she had sustained from Wu were now barely visible, hidden by the main severing of her torso from her waist. Her womanly temple that momentarily bore his child was now sealed shut by melted black plastic, as were all her severing wounds. Breasts that would have nourished his child were now grossly cut up and rendered useless. By her sides lay a mortarboard graduate hat and her framed diploma that had previously been hanging on their bedroom wall.

"Grace!!! I'm so sorry!" he violently sobbed again.

Jerry knew full well his actions had caused this. Just as she was about to be back in his life for good, Grace had now been taken away from him again, only this time forever.

So loud and painful were his wailing cries, Jerry failed to hear the footsteps behind him, nor the heavy panting of the figure now looming over him. Jerry didn't even realise there was anyone there until the chloroform soaked rag reached round his face to smother him. Jerry kicked and lashed out in defence, but the figure behind him was too strong and the chloroform too overpowering. As Jerry's eyes began to blur and darken the last thing he saw was Grace, before his eyes went black forever.

Chapter Twelve

The Policeman

News of the grim early morning discovery, mere days after Jerry's disappearance, had filled Vincent with considerable dread. He had gone to investigate the scene along with Murphy. Yellow police line tape had already been strung up across the alleyway, cordoning off the entire alleyway that ran behind the precinct building. As both detectives turned one corner of the building they beheld the Chief, standing over what Vincent feared they would find.

Laying on the heavily sodden dirty city ground, surrounded by numerous foul smelling garbage bags and bins, was Detective Jerry Wilder. His naked body was divided into the Figure Killer's signature five sections. Just like the other male victims before him, Jerry's adulterous appendage had been cut away and replaced by a layer of melted yellow plastic, exactly the same on his severing wounds.

"Ah Jesus no!" Murphy cried, running his hands through his thick auburn hair in disbelief.

Vincent didn't utter a single word. He just stood there in complete silence, quietly contemplating the horrific fate that had befallen his young partner. He moved to kneel down beside the body. Jerry's boyish yet manly good looks were now cold and lifeless. His spiky blond hair, normally well kept with styling product, now flattened and greased by death. His baby blue eyes were now concealed by closed pale eyelids. To his right hand side was Jerry's badge, to his left lay a set of handcuffs.

"I am truly sorry kid. I am sorry I could not protect you from this city." Vincent whimpered towards Jerry, forcing back tears of sorrow.

"So Wu wasn't the killer, at least this time." the Chief thought, coldly pushing aside the more pressing matter of Jerry's death.

230

"It certainly looks that way Sir." Vincent exhaled loudly. He wiped away a single tear that had managed to squeeze its way out of one duct. Edward came to stand beside the two surviving detectives, news of Jerry's murder only having just reached him.

"So it's true!" Edward exclaimed, looking to Jerry's divided form.

Vincent thought back to the day when both he and Murphy visited Jerry and Grace's apartment. After not appearing at work for a few days and not even answering his phone, Vincent had begun to worry about the fate of his young partner. The shocking discovery of Grace's body coupled with Jerry's disappearance caused a thought, as crazy as it was, to momentarily arise in the old detective's weary mind. That Jerry had been the Figure Killer all along. But to murder Grace would have been grossly out of character for Jerry, so Vincent never formulated his outlandish theory into spoken or written words.

When Edward had arrived and the next figure was removed from Grace's mouth, Vincent had feared the worse. The small figure of a policeman had emerged from her decapitated head, complete with handcuffs and a police badge.

"The Figure Killer is still not done then." Murphy stated.

"Or maybe Wu was the killer and these last two murders were done by an accomplice. To punish Jerry in Wu's absence." Vincent guessed.

"Either way we still need to find who did this Vincent!" Murphy desperately pleaded.

"Indeed." affirmed the Chief.

"What was Grace a graduate in again?" Murphy asked.

"Teaching and child behavioural studies," Vincent remembered. "she had been looking for work as a kindergarten teacher for some weeks before all this."

"Grace had always wanted children in her life then?" Murphy guessed with an air of sadness.

"Shall I check him for a figure Sir?" Edward interrupted.

The Chief nodded in response. Edward crouched down beside Jerry and slowly moved to open his mouth, inserting his gloved fingers between Jerry's upper and lower jaw.

"Careful!" Vincent called out loudly.

He motioned for Edward to take care with Jerry's body. He knew full well what Edward would find within Jerry's dead open maw.

Edward removed the small figure of an artist and held it up to Vincent. Black was its hair, complete with a paint brush and painting pallet in either hand. The paint pallet had exactly the same arrangement of paint colours printed on it as that of Roberta's. Vincent gloved his hands and then took the figure from Edward to examine it further.

This final figure linked back to the Figure Killer's very first victim, Roberta the artist, all those weeks ago. The Figure Killer's circle of work was now complete it seemed.

"I am sorry this happened to you kid." Vincent whispered to Jerry again.

"We finally have our artist figure." the Chief stated aloud. He too looked at the figure Vincent held precariously in his wrinkly hands.

"Jerry thought the killer was building to something. You think they're finished?" Murphy asked.

"Maybe, I certainly hope so. But at what cost?" Vincent sighed, looking to Jerry again.

"We were too late." Murphy added.

Vincent handed the figure back to Edward. He took out an evidence bag and dropped it inside, before sealing the bag shut. The Chief turned to leave the scene.

"What do we do now?" Murphy hopelessly asked.

The shock of Jerry's murder seemed to now be sinking in more.

"What do we do Vincent?" Murphy desperately asked again.

"The same thing we do with every murder scene we investigate Patrick. Process it, look for clues, get witness statements, you know the usual shit. I am sure we will not find anything new though." Vincent sighed defeatedly.

He took one final look at his young partner laying dead on the ground, before leaving the grim alleyway.

"What are you doing?" the Chief called out after Vincent passed him by.

"My job." the old man simply replied.

Stooping under the police line tape again, Vincent shoved his way through the crowd of press that had begun to form outside the precinct. Numerous microphones were shoved in Vincent's direction, eager for comment.

"Ray Sanders, Hallow City News," began one reporter. "detective is this the end of the Figure Killer? What more can you tell us?"

Vincent gave no comment, instead continuing to forge a path through the crowd, batting away more microphones that sprung out at him.

"Detective?" Ray Sanders asked again.

Experience was telling Vincent that he wasn't going to solve Jerry's murder in time. Especially not before his retirement. Over three decades of working for the HCPD had come to a sour end. The Figure Killer had won.

"You ready for this?" Murphy asked from the doorway.

Vincent sat at his desk, mentally preparing himself for the inevitable. He slowly ran his fingers and thumbs over the surface of his metal desk plaque, unintentionally leaving behind a greasy fingerprint trail. The plaque read 'DL Vincent Harrington, Hallow City Homicide'. The burnt out detective immediately saw the irony in leaving behind his own DNA evidence. If only he had had the same for the Figure Killer case.

Vincent took another anxious look at the clock on his office wall, painstakingly watching as the minute hand slowly but surely ticked away before finally settling on three o'clock.

"Here we go then," he sighed. "let us get this over with."

The tired old man gingerly replaced the plaque back down on to his desk. He pulled himself back up on to his feet and walked out to face the crowd that had been speedily gathering around outside his office. The crowd, comprised of his many colleagues, clustered around Vincent as he approached the Chief. Some had smiles on their faces, others had a hint of sadness to them. Both knew that he wasn't going to be around the precinct any longer. For today had been his final day as Detective Lieutenant Vincent Harrington, and as a member of the HCPD.

It had been months since the Figure Killer had struck again, Jerry's murder appearing to have been the very last of their work. Vincent had solved the vast majority of cases over the course of his long and illustrious career. But the case of the Figure Killer it seemed was doomed to remained unsolved, tarnishing his otherwise sturdy record and linger in the back of his mind forever. He had delayed his retirement as a result, the old man still holding out some hope in uncovering the mysterious killer's identity. But it had proven to have been all in vain, with Vincent no closer to the truth.

"Here he is, the man of the hour!" the Chief announced.

Vincent stepped out to meet the Chief's hand shake in greeting, causing a small applause to rise up from the watching audience.

"It's going to be a damn shame you not being around here anymore Vincent. You've been one hell of a detective over these past thirty years." the Chief reminded.

"Thank you Glenn." Vincent thanked.

As they continued to shake hands, mutual respect somewhat passed between the two men.

"This place isn't going to be the same without you," Murphy added into the conversation. "now hurry up and retire already you old fossil!"

A small wave of laughter rippled throughout the audience after Murphy's lighthearted jab, even raising a smirk on Vincent's grizzled face.

Vincent carefully reached into his jacket to take out his badge and unclip his gun from its holster. The badge lay in his left hand and the gun in his right. He looked down at these two simple items, reflecting on all the times he really needed them and what they represented to him. In that moment Vincent felt very reluctant in giving them up, as if he were ending a life long friendship. He then thought of Jerry's badge, laying next to his mutilated body in the alleyway, and how he would never need it again.

"Everything ok Vincent?" the Chief enquired, after Vincent's initial hesitation.

"Yeah, just a second." he replied, not looking up.

After a short pause of hesitation, Vincent sighed to himself and handed them over.

"I officially hand in my badge and my gun." he said, before giving them both to Chief Matthews.

"I graciously accept these two tokens from you Vincent and I wish you a long happy retirement." the Chief replied aloud for all to hear.

To which note the surrounding spectators erupted into thunderous applause and whistling. One by one the crowd of his colleagues took their turn in saying farewell to Detective Harrington. After minutes of hand shaking and awkward hugs, a large cake was soon divided up amongst everyone. It was a vanilla coconut sponge, Vincent's least favourite. He had purchased it regardless, knowing its overpowering flavour would satisfy most precinct tastebuds.

"I shouldn't really. Wouldn't want to ruin this God-like physique of mine." Murphy quipped.

He looked down at his slowly widening waistline.

"A moment on the lips, a lifetime on the hips Patrick!" Clark cautioned him from close by.

Clark and Reed had both joined the low key farewell gathering, each enjoying their own slice of cake alongside Murphy and Edward. Before long adjacent waste bins were jammed full with paper plates and plastic forks soiled by icing. Soon afterwards everyone had returned to their desks to carry on with the rest of their normal working day.

"So that is that then. Over thirty years of my life and everyone just carries on as normal." Vincent uttered to himself.

"You know how it is here Vincent." Murphy reminded him.

"Goodbye Vincent." the Chief said again.

With one more handshake he bid Vincent a final farewell, before the day's work called him back to his own office.

"And what about you huh? Back to work also?" Vincent motioned to Murphy.

"Well no actually. I'm going to put in for a transfer to another precinct with the Chief, either Cove or Garden Ridge City. I've just about had enough of Hallow now." Murphy responded.

He ran a sweaty hand through his thick auburn hair.

"Jerry was the final blow for me." he sighed.

"I do not blame you one bit." Vincent sympathised, hearing some familiar truth in Murphy's words.

"I guess I'll see you again in another life huh? This place really isn't going to be the same without you." Murphy remarked, shaking Vincent's hand also.

Murphy moved to place a comforting hand on Vincent's broad yet heavily burdened shoulder.

"Goodbye Patrick. Take care of yourself." Vincent said, bidding his colleague and good friend farewell.

"You too Vince." Murphy prodded, knowing this nickname irked the old man so.

Murphy coyly smiled back at him as he left the speak with the Chief. Now alone, Vincent took one final walk back over to his own office.

Into the empty vacant room he again entered, it stripped bare of his personal belongings and his investigation into the Figure Killer. The white board in the corner of the room was wiped clean. All the notes and photographs on the Figure Killer case were now stored away in boxes and files, doomed to become a cold case. At the empty desks sat no detectives, with no piles of paperwork and no stale cups of coffee on either of them. One final stubborn coffee stain from the base of a mug was all that remained on Jerry's old desk.

"So long kid." Vincent whispered, imagining Jerry once again sitting at his desk.

"Hey, you're still here?" Clark noticed, appearing from behind Vincent.

"Just saying one final goodbye to the place." Vincent responded.

"How was the service?" asked Reed as she came over to join them.

"Sorry we couldn't make it Vincent." Clark added.

"It was a small service but pleasant enough. Jerry and Grace had hardly any family, apart from Grace's parents. All they really had was each other, right up until the end." Vincent recounted.

"Sorry again for not being there pal. We've just been too busy on this new case." Clark apologised again.

"Getting anywhere with it yet? Any evidence or potential leads?" Vincent asked.

"Nothing concrete yet. Someone has been abducting construction workers and young athletic men from several gyms all across the city." Clark began.

"All we've found so far at each abduction site are faint traces of cement powder. Fewer homeless people have been reported across the city also, as if they're disappearing as well." Reed added.

"You shouldn't concern yourself with this Vincent. Go and be free of this life and this city." Clark advised.

"Sorry, I guess old habits die hard." Vincent chuckled to himself.

"Once a cop, always a cop right?" Clark rhetorically asked.

"How are you getting to the Coral Isles then? By air or by sea?" Reed asked.

"By sea," Vincent answered. "that will give me a day or two to enjoy the ocean views, whilst simultaneously saving on credits for my retirement."

"Sounds wonderful Vincent. I'm very jealous of you right now. I had a friend in college who came from the Coral Isles. I always wanted to go there myself." she mentioned.

Reed's memory cast back to her friend Kula, and their evenings spent together on the golden shores of Cove City. She had hoped of seeing her again one day, having lost touch several years back.

"It is never too late Natasha." Vincent reminded.

"Maybe I'll come visit you there sometime, you know when I retire also. But maybe give it a few more years though." Clark thought.

"I suppose you two would be needing a new office at some point. One with a better view. Why not take this one?" Vincent offered, looking again at the vacant room.

"That's a lovely gesture Vincent. We'd be honoured." Reed thanked.

"Yeah thanks pal." Clark added.

"I have squared it with Glenn already." Vincent reassured.

Vincent took his hat and jacket from off his coat stand. Now that the blistering heat wave was beginning to subside, they were becoming far less cumbersome. Replacing his signature fedora back atop his head and putting on his jacket, the tired old man picked up his suitcase and was finally ready to go.

"So long Vincent. I wish you well." Clark bid farewell.

"Don't forget to write us a postcard now and again." Reed suggested.

"I will be sure to remember Natasha." Vincent promised.

"Goodbye Vincent. We'll all miss you here." Reed said.

238

She firmly hugged her superior in one final embrace and kissed him goodbye on the cheek. Although she had not worked with Vincent for very long, Reed still felt a strong kinship with him.

Clark and Reed stayed behind in the vacant office, surveying their new surroundings whilst Vincent walked his way towards the exit. The familiar sounds of phones ringing off the hook and officers chasing up leads filled the air. He gently rubbed the side of his cheek where Reed had kissed him. It had been so long since he last felt the warmth of a woman's affections.

"Farewell Hallow." he uttered under his breath.

Vincent bid his life of law and order goodbye, leaving behind him so many memories. But not all of them pleasant.

Chapter Thirteen

The Figure Killer

Night had once again fallen over Hallow and with it came the notorious and ever elusive Figure Killer. They quietly snaked their way through the dilapidated buildings and crept amongst the shadows. It was early morning as the killer returned home to their old killing ground in the basement of Doyle's Toy Chest. The now derelict building, once full of smiling children, had previously served as their former residence, having lived upstairs above their father's toy shop back when they were still a mere child.

The killer made their way down the side of the building via the dingy alleyway. A feral cat caught the Figure Killer off guard, startling them enough to noisily fall back against a dented old garbage bin. They paused for a moment and anxiously held their breath, fearing they had attracted unwanted attention. As the mangey feline ran away, the only response the killer had garnered was a dog's distant barking from a few streets away. They swiftly continued onwards, soon coming to the building's back door which was no longer locked by them. It had been kicked in by a determined officer of the law only weeks earlier.

The killer stooped under the yellow police line tape spanning across the doorway to enter inside. They quickly made their way down into the basement, knowing that they were taking a huge risk in returning to their old home, fearful that the authorities might have set a trap for them. But the Figure Killer wasn't that foolish, having already staked out the area weeks before their arrival. Now safely back down in the basement, the killer produced a flashlight to illuminate their familiar surroundings. The basement was virtually empty now, having been emptied of all its contents for evidence. The problematic and interfering authorities had taken away the killer's many tools for working, but they had fortunately not recovered everything.

The Figure Killer squatted down to awkwardly pry up a single floor tile in one corner of the basement. With nervous fingertips, they fumbled it upwards before sliding it away to one side. They breathed a huge sigh of relief, now seeing that their valuable possession had not been discovered and removed by the investigating authorities. Both of the killer's gloved hands tentatively reached inside the secret dug out to retrieve the small red safe. It measured less than a foot both in length and diameter.

The killer carefully placed it down to one side before taking out a matching key to its simple locking mechanism. They quickly inserted the small key into the lock and turned it open. The Figure Killer gazed down upon the safe's contents in the glare of their own flashlight, beholding what they had risked returning home for.

"Hello old friends." they whispered.

They were the picture perfect family, a loving mother and father with two twin children. Jack Doyle's Toy Chest had been barely staying afloat with his simple wooden toy designs, but times were changing. With the rise and popularity of plastic toys looming over his business, Jack finally decided to turn his hand to plastic toy manufacture. With the help of evening courses, connections with friends in the industry, plus good old trial and error, Jack Doyle soon struck upon his idea for Plastic Heroes.

He cast the moulds for his prototypes, impressing even himself with his new found skills. Ideas for his tiny plastic characters would be endless, already making them a big hit with his own children. Jack soon afterwards designed the logo he would brand upon his product. Only managing to mould it onto a few of his later figures, he was on the verge of debuting his little creations to larger companies for mass production. But the peaceful existence he and his family held would soon be shattered forever.

One fateful night a group of crazed drug addicts from the nearby Easy Street broke into Doyle's Toy Chest in hopes of acquiring some quick cash. Jack and his wife Gillian both awoke to the commotion downstairs, with Jack calling the police before investigating the disturbance himself, armed only with a baseball bat. But the desperate youths overpowered him and took his whole family hostage, forcing them down into the basement so their neighbours wouldn't hear their cries for help. They had come for more than just the money it seemed.

One by one the depraved junkies took turns in having their way with Gillian, while Jack and his two children could only look on helplessly. So violent was their treatment of this poor woman that one of them even bit off her nipples. The continuous barrage of assaults was only ended by the leader of the gang taking a nearby wood knife from Jack's work bench and slitting Gillian's throat, knowing her death would leave one loose end tied up.

Jack had tried to fight back but it had been futile. His wife now lay prostrated before him and his children, quickly suffocating on the blood now flooding her airway. The murderous youths then turned their attention to Jack's young daughter. The heroic man fought back harder this time, managing to connect his fists several times with the leader's smug face. The children cried out for their father's bravery, only to be gagged by having the nearby Plastic Heroes shoved into their screaming mouths. As both men fell to the floor, the gang leader sadly fought back even harder. The sharpened carving knife used to kill his wife now repeatedly found its way into Jack's abdomen, almost completely eviscerating him.

The children's severely injured father collapsed to the floor, blood seeping out of his many knife wounds. The gang leader, infuriated by the attack, stood over him and plunged the blade deep into Jack's temple. One less witness to their barbaric crimes. Before the young Figure Killer and their sister now lay the bodies of both their parents. The children's young lives had been horrifically altered forever in a matter of minutes.

The gang leader took hold of the Figure Killer's sister again, their lustful desires now taking a far more twisted and perverted approach. He decided to do her with his own blade, taking it out from a hidden ankle holster. Using its razor sharp edge, he carved a line down her face and across the surface of her eye, causing the young girl to scream out in unimaginable pain.

Something snapped inside the young Figure Killer as the gang leader continued his brutal assault on their sister. An opportunity of mere seconds arose as the Figure Killer's captors dropped their guard to watch the evil spectacle unfold. The bloodied knife used to murder their parents lay on the ground only a few feet away from their reach. The child spat out their choking figures and lunged for it. Taking hold of it in an angry, bloodied clenched fist the child violently plunged it deep into the gang leader's back.

The young Figure Killer, now possessed with utter hatred, struck the knife down hard into his back again. The gang leader immediately stopped their assault on the young girl, collapsing to the basement floor and coughing up blood from a punctured lung. Stunned by the sudden onslaught, by a mere child no less, the rest of the gang were quickly incapacitated by the vengeful youngster, who hacked and slashed their way through two more of their family's attackers. After slicing through tendons and fracturing knee caps, they quickly fell before the child.

The last remaining junkie left standing panicked and quickly turned tail to flee the scene. They scrambled up the staircase and were never to be seen again. The Hallow City authorities eventually arrived, only to be met by the sight of three badly wounded drug addicts and the children's dead parents. The young Figure Killer and their sister sat huddled together in a stunned catatonic silence, the knife still at their feet, denying any involvement.

A large pool of blood, from both their parents and their attackers, had encircled the children on the basement floor. The young killer's stomach turned upon the sight of their dead parents again. The two officers led them away to the safety of a paramedic's ambulance. Their sister sat clutching her injured

243

face, tears tainted red with blood beginning to stream down from her blinded eye. The children had nothing now but each other, embracing one another over the loss of their parents. The officers had arrived too late to stop the savage attack and save their small family.

After the court case, for which they were cleared of all charges against their attackers, the children returned home again to gather up some personal belongings. The young Figure Killer secretly made sure to collect all their father's plastic figures in an attempt to preserve his memory. The child only hoped to somehow carry on his work and legacy one day. They were then sent North of Hallow to stay at Garden Ridge City Orphanage. The siblings had only each other for company over the years to follow, with no other family members to take custardy of them.

They were never to be adopted, due to their inseparable, cold and distant nature towards others. The young girl hated it there, the other orphans repeatedly making fun of her scarred and brutalised face on a daily basis. She soon learned not to be afraid, but to be feared instead. The other children quickly realised not to mock her disfiguring scar or else they would suffer the consequences. Along with her sibling, the only other friends she had were the many spiders that crawled throughout the orphanage and spun webs over her bed at night.

She would come to despise law and order, distrustful of the promises made by others, particularly the authorities. She would one day vow revenge for the murders of both her mother and father, blaming the two officers and the HCPD for not responding soon enough. She grew vengeful, fantasies of retribution becoming obsessive and filling her daily life.

Years past and the children would come to leave the orphanage as young adults. The siblings stayed together for a few more years but eventually split from one another to pursue their own endeavours and ideals. The future Figure Killer returned home to Hallow City in hopes of laying old ghosts to rest and start anew.

But dark inner desires, the result of their past trauma, would come to manifest themselves in a most horrific way. They soon came to learn that their parents' killers were back on the streets of Hallow walking free again, released early due to a technicality.

The blossoming Figure Killer hunted them down one by one, taking them back to the basement where it all began. They made sure the gang members knew exactly who they were and what they had done to them, before violently hacking away their tools for rape and cutting up their bodies to dispose of later. Only then during the begging and pleading for forgiveness did the Figure Killer learn of a child, a single child born from the loins of the man who killed their parents. They vowed to find them and make them pay for what their own father had done to their family. The killer would delight in ending his bloodline, only then would they have total vengeance on the men who destroyed everything they held dear.

In this grim carnage the Figure Killer came to revel in the pain they delved out, wanting others to feel the same agony they felt rotting away deep inside of them. Their father's precious figures were never too far away, silently watching the unfolding chaos taking place before them. As the killer's sanity began to slowly fracture, murderous instructions from their father started to whisper in their head, to kill again and again, making sure he and his wife were never forgotten by Hallow. In order to conceal their true self, the killer changed their identity to help avoid suspicion, allowing them to plan their next move more carefully and keep their new enemies close.

Inside the Figure Killer's secret little safe were their father's remaining figures. They included, among others, a fireman, a nurse, a waitress, a mailman, a dancer and a surfer, complete with their own miniature accessories. As the Figure Killer looked upon their remaining diminutive treasures, they fondly remembered the ones they had parted with over the last few weeks.

The killer thought back to the beauty of their first figure kill, Roberta the artist. Watching her in secret at the college, admiring her from a distance over several days was how it began for them. Each day they got that little bit closer to her. By the time the killer was close enough that they could smell her perfume, their heart raced with nervous anticipation and desire for what was to come. They even snatched a hair from her redheaded friend as a secondary keep sake. They soon followed her home one evening and waited for nightfall, knowing her parents were already away. Breaking silently into her house whilst she slept, the Figure Killer delighted in how Roberta had squealed when they smothered her with the chloroform. They soon shoved the Brazilian beauty into the trunk of their car before quickly driving off.

Sitting behind the wheel, the killer calmed themselves down as they drove her back to their prepared and awaiting killing lair, excited by what was to come. The sight of profuse blood had come to unnerve the Figure Killer, reminding them of its stain on painful memories from their past. They made sure Roberta's had all but drained away before they proceeded to take her body apart one limb at a time. She still looked beautiful, even after the killer had severed her pretty head from her shoulders. But it hadn't felt as perfect as they had hoped. It hadn't been all that they had dreamed it would be. Perhaps it would feel better for them next time.

The killer remembered Peter the butcher, their second figure kill. They had so easily blended in with the faces of his other customers, hiding in plain sight when entering the butcher's shop one day to purchase a link of sausages. Due to the warm summer weather outside the butcher had guessed that they were to be used in a barbecue, completely unaware of what the killer was really planning to do with them. The killer looked to the empty space where their band saw once rested. They remembered how heavy Peter's body was when they had dragged him down the stairs and thrown him on to the work table. Severing his rotund torso from his portly waist was more exhaustive than Roberta's nubile and limber frame.

The killer's third figure kill, Becky the snake charmer, had been most fun to play with indeed. They remembered visiting her place of purveyance and watching this curvaceous girl cavorting around a bright red pole. The killer had taken out a large note of money to entice the girl closer to them, like a monstrous deep sea anglerfish luring in its unsuspecting prey. Her severed parts were delightful to handle, giving the killer plenty of time to admire her surgically enhanced chest and detailed snake tattoo, before proceeding to cut her serpent-like body in half. They removed the arms that tied her to the Fox Glove's main stage with relative ease. As seductive as the snake charmer was to them, the Figure Killer had never pursued their own sexual gratification. The way of human flesh only reminded them of its usage in the most depraved of ways.

The killer thought back to their fourth figure kill, Joshua the surgeon. They had gone to see the doctor for a consultation about having some work done on their own face. It was all a clever rouse though, allowing them to get much closer to the surgeon. The killer already had their suspicions about Joshua even before their meeting, back when they were busy combing Hallow for plastic surgeons. It was this shared predatory instinct that helped them identify a fellow sinister individual. The killer had been initially apprehensive in shaking the doctor's skilled hands upon their first meeting, masquerading that they had the flu. The hands of Dr Langland had not only saved so many patients from their own internal hate but had also inflicted pain on others in a far more misshapen way.

Of all the processes the killer used to complete each work, they had enjoyed cutting off the hands of the surgeon the most. After the surgeon's disposal, the Figure Killer still wanted their evil deeds to be known. A quick search of his apartment uncovered the evidence they needed, leaving it beside Joshua's body for the very same detectives hunting them to find. The killer had hoped to slow their pursuit with the bait of another fellow monster.

Harold the merman was the killer's fifth figure victim and took them in a different direction from their usual style of working. To Cove City's fish market they went, in order to seek out a large fish of some kind to complete their work. Finding an old three pronged trident had proved even more problematic for the killer than finding a big enough fish. In the end it was a chance find in an old antique shop down a secluded Cove City street. The killer looked to the now vacant spot in their basement where the melting pot of plastic once stood. Sealing the merman's freshly cut body with melted plastic was easy enough, but the headless fish had to remain behind in Cove City. It was hidden in secret, for later completion on the merman's luxurious yacht.

The killer's next figure kill, Eliza the zoo keeper, was another risky abduction. Hallow City Zoo held monthly evening talks on endangered species and conservation programmes, one of which was conducted by Eliza. It was to be her last. The Figure Killer went along to this presentation, blending in with the faces of the large crowd in hopes of finding their zoo keeper. After speaking briefly with Eliza at the end of her presentation, the killer knew immediately that they had found their next victim. They waited until everyone else had gone home and that Eliza was the last person to leave the zoo on lock up, only to ambush her in the parking lot. Before the evening's presentation had gotten under way, the killer had made sure to purchase a soft toy tiger from the adjacent gift shop, to complete their work later in the tropical house.

Alexi the photographer, the Figure Killer's seventh figure kill, could have been the end of their work. They had gone to see Alexi about having some family photos taken. This had all been a lie, allowing the killer to study their next victim, hoping to uncover any opportune moments for attack. It turned out that Alexi worked late some evenings, his newer clientele from Easy

Street only being able to visit him during these night hours. The killer returned to him one evening, arousing suspicion in Alexi. He wondered why this family person would be there at such a late hour to see him.

Unlike their other prey, Alexi had fought back harder against the killer, almost managing to escape. But by now the killer was too well rehearsed in their methods for subduing their victims. They had expected it to feel different somehow, when they stuck their blade deep into Alexi's throat. But the photographer bled out exactly the same as the others. They remembered taking Alexi's camera. The Figure Killer had arrogantly taunted the investigating detectives by snapping the photographer's own picture in their studio, ironically turning the photographer's camera around on himself.

Kristen the bride, with her bouquet of yellow flowers, had been so hopelessly wrapped up in her own selfish little world. So caught up in planning her wedding ceremony, the bride didn't even realise that Hallow's own Figure Killer was standing right behind her. She had so rudely barged past them whilst talking on her phone, unwittingly divulging information about her location the very next day. The Figure Killer had listened on intently, quickly formulating their plan of attack. As the killer sealed her child bearing temple they remembered the tired old phrase '*Until death do you part*', amused by the thought of Kristen's husband never seeing her alive again. But the bride had surprisingly made the killer deeply reflect on their own personal life and how they would never be able to feel true romantic love like so many others.

The killer's ninth figure victim, the graduate, could have been one of so many at that time of year. Instead the killer chose one from many years earlier, throwing the investigating detectives off their trail with the help of some DNA evidence from another keepsake. The killer remembered going to the graduate's apartment, who was completely unaware of what they had really come for. She was so beautiful to them, even as her good looks gave way to sheer panic when she awoke in their new killing lair. The Figure Killer almost felt sorry for the poor woman, having barely survived the barbaric assault from another. They apologised to her, saying it was something they had to do. Bleeding the graduate's body and severing her into the five crucial pieces was now almost as easy as breathing to them. Her death would also secure added heartache upon their final target, the one whom all their work had been building towards.

The Figure Killer came to the memory of their final target, the policeman that had been hunting them all those weeks. The policeman had been so naive, so full of life and yet so adulterous and flawed. He had come so close to uncovering their true identify. Little did the policeman know that the killer's work had all been for him, slowly building towards their final meeting and revelation. Only when the policeman learned of his true parentage did the killer take their ultimate revenge.

The policeman couldn't bear to hear the truth about his own birth father, anger and sorrow simultaneously intertwining. The killer would never forget the look of absolute horror on the young policeman's face, after learning their true identity and the knowledge of his fiancee's final moments. The killer couldn't decide what they had enjoyed more. Waiting eagerly for the policemen to return home that evening or the moment they thrust the knife deep into his neck. As the blood poured down over his face, the terror in his eyes was washed away and replaced with emptiness. His adulterous manhood would never cause such pain and heartache for another woman ever again. The killer knew their sister would approve of this last kill, striking back at the law and order that had failed them both decades ago.

The night was waining fast and the Figure Killer needed to be on the move again. They took one final look around their old killing basement, knowing they would never be able to return. Their parents' murder had impacted on them more than they ever thought possible. With every figure the killer parted with, they could only hope that the murderous whispers inside their mind

250

would slowly leave them, allowing old ghosts to finally rest in peace. But they still echoed back at them. It seemed their work had not ended with the policeman as they had hoped. They were doomed to continue their work one day, a set of new victims to leave throughout Hallow.

The Figure Killer closed the lid of the safe and stuffed it deep into their backpack. They swiftly climbed the basement staircase again and exited the abandoned building, venturing back out into the warm night air of Hallow City. The killer made sure to bid farewell to their surviving family tree, standing tall outside their old home. Slipping silently through the shadows again, they made their way out of the city and away from the legacy they had left upon so many poor souls.

They missed their sister terribly, having lost her to the depths of a dark underworld of organised crime and narcotics back in Garden Ridge City. But they knew she was safe, happy in the knowledge that their sister was where she wanted to be. In her exile she had grown powerful and had become feared like no other. Upon her return to Hallow, she would bring all her furious might and influence down upon the authorities there. The Figure Killer looked forward to their reunion with considerable anticipation.

"So, who wants to be next?" they wondered, silently reflecting on their remaining Killing Figures.

Printed in Great Britain
by Amazon

81361469R00142